Scruffs

By: John E. Andes

Scruffs: Those parts of fruits and vegetables that are inedible and therefore of no value i.e. apple cores, carrot leaves, pineapple fronds. In common parlance, scruffs refers to members of society that are of little or no value.

I

Why is Missus Treadway's class soooo boring? English Literature, not Lit, right before lunch. You know it's boring when the swill they serve at "The Trough" is more appealing than the swill she serves. I mean these guys are dead. Their style is dead. Their stories are dead. I hope no one can hear my stomach over her droning. Is Dorothy looking back at me? She's slowly opening and closing her knees and flashing me a sign. Her khaki skirt rides toward her buttocks. She has no panties. Goshdarnit! I knew there was a reason I liked this class. All the desks are drawn in a circle to allow us to focus on Missus Treadway or, in my case, the girl across from me. Dorothy is licking her lips, and I can't do anything about it. She stretches, leans back, and reveals chilly nipples under her denim shirt. The shirt's top three pearl buttons are open, and the form of each breast invites more than a passing glance. What a tease. Please, don't call on me, 'cause I am not paying attention to the dead heads.

The bell arrested Mike's development. Clamor replaced reverie. Motion supplanted inertia. Twenty seniors of Big Horn High School in Carter, Wyoming gathered their wits and books. They shuffled to the door. So many bodies, so little space. The students were loudly reminded of Missus Treadway's English Literature homework assignment, as noted by the neat calligraphy on the blackboard. "There would be no excuse for not completing the work," she threatened. The bodies swarmed into the hallway like a school of fish. Each guppy heading to a specific locker to dump a load of educational hardware, before spewing into the cafeteria, a.k.a., "The Trough".

Dorothy found Mike and clasped his hand. Part ownership, part affection. They headed for their side by side lockers in hallway N-2, the senior's hall. The cowgirl and the cowboy were in love. He was dressed in real work jeans with a large silver belt buckle he'd won at the last fair paired with a red and green checked shirt, cut full for the 42-inch shoulders and narrow for the 30-inch waist. The intimacy of their whispering and touching was interrupted by screaming in the main hall. They rushed to see what the matter was.

The screaming was in response to the loud firecracker pops. Boys and girls were frantically trying to get away from something or trying to go somewhere. Then a series of loud, yet muffled, booms rattled sealed windows. Smoke roiled from the side halls and the front door. The lights went out. The freshly waxed tiled floor offered the same amount of traction as leather soled boots on ice. The metal lockers were jagged obstacles. When someone fell into a locker, flesh was torn. More screaming, more pushing, and pandemonium. The students were being moved by an unseen force. They had to go into the cafeteria, couldn't go right or left into the darkened halls. The mass oozed away from the front door where three silhouetted Clanton-Wannabes emerged. Encased in smoke, the cowboys were backlit by the sun outside the entrance.

Broad-brimmed hats. Long rider coats. Collars turned up in the back and pointed down on the sides. Skinny legged denim pants. Boots with spurs. Six jingling spurs sparkling in the smoke filtered rays of the sun. Huge silver and gold buckles like the ones given as rodeo prizes. On the belts were rows of cartridges that began at the coat openings and disappeared around each side of the three bodies. The three unmasked invaders seemed to glide inexorably toward the throng. Now three faces. Kids' faces. A few pimples. No facial hair. One wore glasses. No smiles as they spun their thirty thirties to their hips, simultaneously cocking the guns to the ready.

The slaughter commenced. Slug after slug was discharged from the rifles. Cock the lever. Pull the trigger. Repeat. The action of the rifles seemed to set the rhythm for the carnage. Tragically, children killed children. Bullets ricocheted off the walls, lockers, and floors. Those not hit by fusillades stumbled over the bodies of those who had been hit. Some of the fallen wounded had the good sense to stay down and feign death. The three cowboys casually discarded their rifles and drew the formerly holstered Colts. It all appeared choreographed: The steps; the pacing; the tossing aside of the long guns. Every action planned to the minutest detail and in the proper sequence.

The handguns rapidly and independently disgorged projectiles for more death and destruction. The Three Horsemen of the Apocalypse pressed on. The distance from the front door to the students had been one hundred feet. Now the distance between killers and death was less than ten paces. The crowd was becoming crammed in the cafeteria entrance. Backs were turned to the butchers. The retreat slowed. If the kids got to the cafeteria and blockaded the doors, they might find a haven. Girls were crying out names and pleas for help. The older boys were yelling, cajoling, and shoving the girls and underclassmen down the hall to safety. Stepping over dead and wounded classmates, blood and flesh were treacherous surface additions to waxed linoleum. In the cramped hallway, slipping and slithering slowed progress.

The smallest of the shooters screamed, "Let's waste all the little shits!"

There was time for the killers to reload while stepping over the bleeding and dying. By not stopping, the menace was intensified. The three had faces of youth, not of innocence. They showed anger held until the boiling point ... and this was it. The doors of the cafeteria were forced open over the protestations of those hiding within. After all were inside, the doors were closed, and the top and bottom bolts inserted into the female receptacles. Tables, folded flat, were then stacked three deep against the doors. Braced by chairs, the doors formed a shield. To the rear entrance, serving carts were wheeled to cover the delivery doors. Stacked on top of each other, the carts created an oddly shaped metal barricade.

Above the noise and commotion of things being moved, cries from the outside were audible. Like lambs bleating before slaughter, when the sources of the cries were discovered, they were silenced by the handguns. Numerous shots were also fired into the cafeteria's entrance. Some pierced the doors, but none got through the wall of tables. No one had a cell phone. They were regularly confiscated by school administration. Someone found the cafeteria landline telephone and called 911. From under one tangled twitching heap of dying, the hands of two teenage lovers clasped in the grip of love and death could be seen. Blood had pooled beneath a denim blouse and khaki skirt with suede trim. The raised skirt revealed the wearer wore no panties. The male body lay on top. Did he fall last or was he trying to protect his lover? Two oozing holes in the back of his red and green checked shirt and a large cavity in the back of his head epitomized the human destruction.

A cacophony of staccato reports from semi-automatic guns stopped all the shooting. It seemed like for the next ten minutes the only noise was the complaining of the wounded. Those in the cafeteria milled in stunned silence.

A firm deep voice called for calm. Local cops? SWAT? The hallway dissonance had masked the arrival at the back door. Identification led to entry, cries of relief, sobbing, some catatonic looks. There was no more gun fire. From the hall, another deep voice asked the students to remove any obstruction from the door to the cafeteria and open the door. Men in black raid suits entered. No gunfire. No one to shoot or who would shoot back. The slaughter was over. Now began the gruesome mop up of aid to the fallen still alive and the identification of others.

****

Gene Benton's cell phone vibrated repeatedly. His tranquility of a mental health day by the pool was interrupted by his sister's tortured scream, "Dorothy's dead. She's been shot at school. Some crazies came in before lunch and blew the fucking place apart. Killed twelve kids then the cowards self-destructed. Cops and SWAT all over the place. I need you here now. Please, I'm falling to pieces."

The words were stuttered between the sobs. The volume of the screaming made the facts almost unintelligible. Gene got the gist of what happened and what had to be done, "Mary, calm down. I'll go to the airport and get to Carter immediately. Once I know my flight schedule and timetable, I'll call you. Keep your cell phone open and with you. Use the landline for calls to and from your friends and Dorothy's friends. Do you have any tranqs? Take two now."

"No need. Already done. How else would I have the strength to call you? Hurry, Gene I really, really need you."

"Love you, Mary, I'll be there."

Gene called the taxi and packed while the van plied its way to his house. He was at the airport in less than one hour from Mary's call. Checked American, after having impressed them with the urgency of the need. The fastest way to get to Carter was through Dallas, change and board a plane to Denver, then catch a commuter flight to Boise and rent a car for the two-hour drive to Mary's home in the hills. The entire process would take two-time zones and four hours, if all the connections were made. *The desk attendant promised me that all connections would be held for my arrival. It's the least they can do. I had fifteen minutes to call Mary. She's groggy. I suspect she washed down the pills with at least two single malts. She's anxiously awaiting my arrival.*

The flights and drive were uneventful. All connections were made on time with a minimum of grumbling from other passengers. All the while thoughts of Dorothy and her death: *There had be time between life and non-life when there's no sensation except dull awareness. No fear. No pain. The moment could seem to last an hour or two if the mind died after the body, but really might last for only a millisecond when the mind brought death to the body. The absence of closure was not an event. The senses didn't kick in or out until the Nano-second of closure. Physical death versus mental death. The time lag or gap could be substantial. One fast and one slow. Which was which? Sometimes one and sometimes the other.* The net of all this psycho-ramble was that he knew Dorothy was dead. Her state irreversible. He now had to deal with the grieving living, her mother, his sister. His ass was draggin;' his body told him it's somewhere between later and earlier than his watch told him.

****

Mary's directions were terrific. Obviously written with the adult mind in mind, much like the directions on toys to be assembled on Christmas Eve. From the Interstate to her door took twenty minutes. The lights marking the driveway and a few floods kicked on as he arrived. The driveway was extra wide, as was the walk to the front door. Designed and built with the wheelchair in mind. Mary had not escaped the scourge of Polio. Jonas Salk's magic bullet missed her. Mary contracted the crippler after Dorothy was born. An infant and the disease were too much for Harry. He drove off to work one morning, never came home for dinner. He was killed in a drug deal that went bad, somewhere in Arizona. Three years after she was abandoned, Mary was a widow. The front door ... extra wide, and the doorbell ... extra loud. Mary used a video and voice system for security and because it's a pain in her ass to get from wherever she is to the front door quickly.

Button pressed; lights immediately activated around the front door. The front porch was bathed in the brilliance of three spots. In a minute or two he was buzzed in.

"OK, Mary, where are you?"

Gene listened intently in the foyer. All was dark except for the lights outside.

"I'm here on the porch. Join me for a drink."

He negotiated through the living room and den with furniture pieces far apart for ease of negotiation, so he didn't stub toes, bang shins, or trip (parts of his normal routine in most dark rooms). *There's Mary's chariot.* Her constant reminder of her half-life. In the shadows, the wan smile and sad eyes. Delph blue eyes and coal black hair were the visible bond between siblings. Hers had become salt and pepper. His mostly salt. The canvas bag settled on the floor.

She raised her arms for a hug to absorb and reduce her hurt. If he could take one percent of the pain from her by hugging, he would hug her for one hundred days until her life became bearable. It's expected of friends. Beyond the fact that they were siblings, they were dear friends, always straight with each other. Always telling the truth, teasing and goading to do better, sympathy in times of duress. But no coddling. No bullshit.

"Oh, Gene, it's terrible. My baby was murdered. Dorothy and her boyfriend, Mike. Slaughtered by some crazies. They killed at least a dozen. In school, for Christ's sake. School is supposed to be a safe place.

Teachers, administrators, even the euphemistic, Resource Officer. If cops can't protect the kids, who the fuck can?

"Where did the bastards get the idea? It was too well planned. The little fucks must have spent days dreaming up all the details. How did they get all the guns and ammo? Where were their parents? Why did no one notice? Did the other kids know anything about the three?"

The questions were rapid fire. She was beginning to repeat them. Gene had no answers. Hysteria commenced. Her voice was louder and shriller with each question. Now the sobs were interfering with communication clarity. Many words were missed, but not the message. She was pissed, really, really pissed. She demanded the truth.

"Mary, have you eaten anything today?"

"Fuck food. I want another drink, then I want to sleep and wake up with this whole thing behind me like the nightmare it is. Fix me a big one, please."

As she turned on the lights, her tears erupted and cascaded down her cheeks, following paths created by omnipresent pain. *She looked like hell.* That's a dumb thought. The loss of a loved one was enormous. The sadness of a parent losing a child—incomprehensible. It's just not supposed to be that way. The child is supposed to outlive the parent. But, when the child dies first, the parent is left empty: Extreme anguish. The physical torment visible on the parent, even to strangers.

The bar was incredibly well stocked with two bottles of Balvenie and one each of Talisker, Craggenmore, Dalwhinnie and Glenkinchie. The "waters of life" in a house with one less life. He found two tall glasses, poured and added twice the scotch volume in fresh spring water. No ice. Ever. From the corner of his eye, he saw Mary wiping her face with the tissues she kept in the large undercarriage box, her mobile purse. It even locked for safety when she was out of the house. *She weren't gonna be purty, jes clean.* The flicker of his smile emerged, release after the eruption.

She lit more table lamps using her remote-control system. With the black wand of power, Mary could light her world, open her doors, and enter her car. There was also a connection to the police, fire, and medical emergency. She's wired for life. The house is wired to her. Mary's extraordinarily gifted in the areas of electronics and technology, a hacker par excellence. Gene was glad someone got Dad's gift. He could barely replace a fuse and used his computer for word processing. Mary always said he got the beauty, and she got the brains. She got both. With the lights on and some faint level of normal returning to her, Mary assumed the role of big sister.

"You can sleep on the couch or in Dorothy's room. It's your choice. Either way, you will want fresh linen. Her room will be quieter. The dogs and I sometimes roam at night. For me, it's the best time in space. I can talk to all the 'nutsos' and practice my exploration techniques; that's hacking to you. When I roam, I turn on a few lights, go to the kitchen for food and listen to my short-wave radio. It can get a bit busy and might be disturbing. But it's your choice."

"Thanks for no choice. I'll throw my bag in the other bedroom. I'd like to shower so that I smell less like the cattle on the hills and more like a twentieth century human. OK?"

"Suit yourself. There are fresh towels and bed linen in the hall closet. All dirty ones can be tossed in the hamper in the closet. I'll be here or in my ComRoom when you're all clean and sparkly."

The closet revealed queen sized sheets and four pillowcases in a set. Somewhat feminine pattern of small flowers, but, under the circumstances, more than satisfactory. Gene was not used to the thermal protection necessary for sleeping in the cold mountain air. Welcoming the blanket, he headed for the bath.

Really strange. While he had hardly taken notice of Dorothy's nest decoration, he's slammed by the fact that this was a woman's bathroom. The female stuff on the counter, the sink, under the sink, on shower windowsill, and in the medicine cabinet. Many colors of eye shadow, six shades of lipstick, skin cleansers and gloss, curlers, three shampoos, crème rinses, lots of cotton balls, astringent, skin lotions, perfumes and other fragrances, two deodorants, nail files, tweezers, nail polish and polish remover, a cuticle stick, clippers, two toothbrushes, toothpaste, floss, mouth wash, phony eyelashes, eyebrow pencils in four different shades, ribbons, clips, scrunchies, mousse, extra, extra hold gel, body wash and bar soap, disposable shavers in various colors, shaving cream, styptic pencil, feminine pads, tampons, aspirin, decongestant, antihistamine, feminine wipes and an opened twelve pack of condoms. Just by looking, he learned so much about his sixteen-year-old niece but knew so little. Never talked to her. Why was this atrocious thing done to her? What did she do to warrant this? Whom did she offend?

In Florida, he turned on the water and stepped into the shower, not in Wyoming. Here the cold water was cold. Adjusting the water temperature to be user friendly took time, patience, and precision.

He washed and cried. Purging the grime began to purge the pain. As he toweled off, he realized all of Dorothy's stuff would have to be boxed and tossed. How easily we discarded the everyday necessities of the dead from when they lived.

The little things that meant a lot then now meant nothing. Who wanted a used or partially depleted supply of a personal item? We shunned this, while total strangers grabbed it in a heartbeat during a garage sale. Did we shun the item because of inferiority? Too personal? Because we couldn't deal with its memory? Did it matter?

"Well, baby brother looks almost presentable. Clean body and clothes. How is your soul? Look at this. These are the amateur and news videos of the police as they gathered and then entered. I needed to search the record of the event, so I pulled some strings, sort of like looking at a car wreck or the ovens at Buchenwald: disturbing yet hypnotic. There are the first uniforms. And there are our local SWAT members. Then the state paramilitary arrives. Who got there first? Who was in command? I copied all the footage and I'm going to edit it to get a timeline on the events. Occasionally, I'll break for a Chat room and the short wave. So, pull up a chair and spend the night. Or as long as you can last." Mary was in work mode.

"I've never been able to refuse a beautiful woman, so how can I refuse the secret love of my life."

"Don't go there, smart ass. Come here and give me another hug. Boy, it's good to see you again. Even, if you look much older than I do. It must be the hot fetid air of that nether region called Florida versus my pure, fresh mountain air that keeps me young looking."

Her sarcasm and her smile were back, if only a half-smile. Her eyes were no longer dull. The attitude had returned: I can do anything. It's genetic. The DNA of the clans, who dwell in the moors and glens. Someone had fucked with her baby and she was going to find out why. Then she would see to it that a very painful, ugly and slow vengeance was heaped upon the evil doers. The smoke and blood circus were a start.

"Make yourself really useful and make us dinner. The kitchen has always been your domain, whatever is there is yours to use. If you truly need anything, Jack's Market is open all night. I can give you directions if need be. Now scoot. I'm hungry. God, I feel like I'm on a quest. But I don't know what I'm looking for. If you know, tell me. Otherwise, get thee to the scullery."

He was hungry, too. Something not realized until she raised the issue. Certainly, the thought of Mary in a kitchen would crush any craving for food. If it came in a can or could be nuked from the freezer, she was up to the task. If it required ten minutes' prep and an oven, she couldn't handle it. He spoiled her by rattling pots and pans, heating the plates and using more spices than salt and pepper. He uncovered things that looked like pork chops. The preprinted label confirmed the first guess and the date of purchase was four days ago, safe to eat. All was ready in twenty-five minutes.

"Madam, dinnah is served. May I assist you to the dining room?"

"Be a dear, put the meal on a tray and bring it into my ComRoom. I'm in the middle of some real fascinating stuff. Come. Look at this. See that big van? The dark one to the right beneath the trees? Why is it just parked there? And notice no markings? Can't see a license plate. Now watch the activity of the bodies being disgorged. They rush into the school. Black outfits with no logos or markings. Not locals or state guys. Now they return to this van as if it were a base. Are they reporting or getting something? That's one area we need to note for further digging. Here. Look. After they come from the van, they give commands to the locals. These van guys seem to have taken control and are directing the show. Who the fuck are they?"

"Enough for now. Take a break. I was in your antediluvian kitchen sweating up a storm to create this monster meal for us. If you don't eat it while it's hot, I'll be very pissed. So there. Let's have quiet time about the events of today ... er yesterday."

Mary went west to find a life. With Dorothy and no husband, she found her economic calling in the world of technology. She fervently dove into the lake of cyber knowledge and taught herself how to be a great swimmer. In a few years, she became tantamount to an Olympic Gold Medalist. Teaching at Carter Community College, she was recognized as the go-to instructor in the statewide system. If there were a question about computer systems, Mary was the source for the answer to the problem. She lectured around the country. Sat on a few advisory boards. She was offered an important position at the federal government, but she turned them down. She doesn't deal well with large political organizations and she enjoyed a tremendous amount of autonomy here in Carter. In this case the mountain came to Mohammed because she was not going to it. Her home reflected her technological, non--familial love. I don't think there was anyone long term after Harry. They talked about Wyoming and Florida, respective business paths.

She wondered how long he would stay, as long as she wanted. He had taken vacation time. Accumulated forty-six days of Earned Time Off. This could be one of the true plusses of working at Intx. The big, Dutch insurance conglomerate believed in earned time off. They did not pay as much as their competitors but offered more time off. He had seasoned people who could cover during a short absence, but not a long time. Some knights-errant, who have pledged corporate allegiance, would love to put dirks in his back. Sometimes he thought Mary was right about structural politics: It wasn't the work that will kill you; it's your fellow workers.

"That meal was fit for a queen, me, little brother. God, if men only knew their places were the kitchen and the bedroom and that they should be summoned to either at a woman's wishing, what a wonderful world it would be."

"Don't get me started on genders. From birth, the fairer sex makes up the rules. Women seek domination. Little girls giggle, big girls wiggle, and women smile and rub. The same as in the animal kingdom. Poor helpless 'schlubs' like me are dead meat. First our hearts go, then our loins are purloined, our pockets picked, and souls crushed. We are seduced and abandoned. All we have left is the camaraderie of the jailed."

Her gales of laughter were wonderful. Hyperbolic brother-sister sparring was good for the soul. Their bond was strengthened. He cleaned up the kitchen because that was his function tonight in her world. Besides, she should continue her digging. It's now two am. Soon he would retire, and she should also. With the morning, more video to analyze, maybe some more amateur video from the locals. When he returned to the ComRoom, Mary was sound asleep in the chair. Some videos were on hold, some on continual loop, and some screens blank. He struggled to maneuver her chariot to her bedroom and hoisted her onto the bed. Even at one hundred forty-five pounds, she's heavy. A momentary stir, some mumbling, and a small kiss on the cheek. He covered her with a quilt and exited, leaving the door ajar for the dogs.

The dogs, Hither and Yon, both mixed beasts. One of them, he was not sure which one, was a Shepherd and Rottweiler mix. He would guard the house and kill intruders. The other dog a mix of Puli and Coyote. He would herd the intruders into the garage and butcher them, one at a time, for food. Both were devoted to Mary and Dorothy. After a proper introduction, they treated Gene with the disdain of an acceptable interloper. The introduction required that he lay on the floor and let them smell him from pate to penny loafers, all the time Mary talked to them in soothing tones. After they were done with this primeval form of metal detection, they backed up and went to Mary's side. She praised them. Gene rose and was permitted to pet them. If Mary liked him, he must be OK.

The ComRoom, Mary's phrase for the room with all the electronic equipment, resembled a decent TV studio of the aughts. A bit more sophisticated. She could receive, manipulate, and send images, data, and sound from this room. When in this room, she was normal, which, for a crippled "technowhiz" is an important perception. People knew her words, thoughts, and voice, all of which seemed as if they came from a normal person. Gene pulled up an office chair to study the console and the various monitors and switches. *It's interesting that a "technodolt", like me, could ascertain her work patterns by scanning the buttons and switches.* Those with the color cleaned off or surrounded by the dirt and oil from innumerable finger hits were the buttons critical to every activity. The gradation or intensity of the color on the buttons and the amount of finger dirt around it let me know the frequency of hits.

He stopped a loop and restarted it. Unfroze a frame, then refroze it, went back to the loop and slowed it down. Studied the action, the setting, the background, the interaction and studied the activity other than that of the focused players, what was he looking for? The cars, people, and a school. He saw the van near the trees, the smoke resulting from the explosions, the police arrive, men in uniforms leaving the van and going to the police, the pointing and orders followed. This was all so painful. His eyes began closing as he stared. *To bed sleepy head.*

****

The sun was bright and the air quite cold for a Floridian. Daylight happened without him taking off his shirt and pants. No noise other than nature outside the house. It took a few moments to realize this was his niece's bedroom. Easing from the bed and padding to the door, he listened for the dogs. Silence. Opened the door and smelled coffee. Peeked in the ComRoom: No Mary. Her bedroom: No Mary. No bathroom water noises. No dogs. My God, he had been deserted. The note on one of those yellow half page pads advised him that she had gone to town to secure any new footage from the local TV station and asked around if anyone else had taken a private record of the events. She hoped to return by noon. Gene called Mary.

"Hello, sleepy head. I thought you had been drugged by your own cooking.

Yes, I have caller ID on my system. I've been to the local station. Not much new. There may be another personal video at the college. I know the student who would have it. I can go to her house if need be. News conference at eleven am. Are you OK? You should not eat before your run. Take the west trail. It's easier for out-of-staters. Now, you called?"

"Good morning, Mary. It's so nice to be talked to by you. What can I do here while you're bouncing around Carter like you're on speed? Why don't I tape the network feeds of the conference and any supporting footage they use? OK?"

"Gene, I can't be bogged down by remorse. I must learn as much as I can as quickly as I can, so I can put this damned thing to rest. You know, closure, that over used psycho-babble term. Can you work the console? After you're fully awake, give me a call and I'll walk through a checklist with you. Now get to your run or you'll be late for class. Oops, sorry. That sounded like mom."

The run was good. The air a little rarer than he was used to and much cooler. Loved it. Showered. Went back to ComRoom for his assignment. Four monitors. One on the local Fox station, one on CNN, and one on NBC. Ten forty-five am. He was ready. Called the teacher.

"Let's do it by the numbers, Grasshopper. All monitors on?"

"Check."

"Cassettes inserted?"

"Check."

"Ready to press record?"

"Check."

"When I get home, I'll convert all the tapes to CDs, so we can play with them tonight. Thanks, for being my friend despite the blood."

The sheriff related the events of the past twenty-four hours. His face, expression, and words were bland. Talked of safety and security. Isolated incident. Numerous leads. Blah, blah, blah. Nothing concrete. The alleged perps killed themselves. *I thought I saw something strange about some of the faces in the crowd.* A few were Government issue. They avoided direct camera contact, by moving out of range or turning away. Strange behavior. Normally, they just stood there. Questions dumber than answers. Would not release all the names. Some families away for the opening of small game season. Tell more at a news conference set for three this afternoon. The entire event took five minutes.

A reporter for CNN relayed, from an unidentified source, the gist for the notes left by the shooters. They wanted someone to pay attention. Someone to listen to their pain. They were tired of being ignored and hurt. Death rules.

II

The stress of the six-day trip, the intensity of the stay, and the numerous time zone changes took their toll. Gene needed a vacation to regroup from his time off. Sunday, the day of rest. The New York Times, the local birdcage liner, and the Sunday TV news shows were the perfect remedy.

"This is Newsmakers, where you learn what will happen."

Somewhere after the item in the newspaper about two twelve-year-old boys who fell into a sinkhole and were rescued by their neighbors and before the story of a police chase gone awry wherein an innocent driver was run off the road to her death, came the deep tones of the senior Senator from Pennsylvania, Baldwin Miller. The voice started calm and measured, and gradually increased in intensity and volume. The pleasant melody of a professional speaker became the fervent tone of a confrontational salesman. Senator Miller was decrying the plethora of violence, he and his followers saw, in the high schools around the nation. All the statistics, dates, and names were his litany. His marching orders: The fallen shall be held high, the criminals dealt with. His recital became ranting, "You are either part of the problem or part of the solution."

The rallying cry of the extreme right and the extreme left; each will broker no middle ground, no compromise. They held to strong black and white areas. They ignored the huge gray area known to all as the real world. Senator Miller bewailed the issue, "How could the murderous event of last week occurred? How could children kill children? Who's to blame? Who is accountable?"

Then he itemized the list of much battered culprits: "The NRA and the loose gun laws make it too easy for anybody to have guns. The champions of unrestricted personal freedom without commensurate individual responsibility foolishly believe we all have the right to carry weapons from revolvers to automatic rifles. The Second Amendment to the Constitution allows people to carry guns if they belong to a well-regulated militia. Said militia, by definition, owes allegiance to a government. To what government do the Aryan Brotherhood and the Voodoo Kings have allegiance?

"The entertainment industry, which foists death and destruction on all of us. They target the young and impressionable. Bigger and more powerful guns. Explosives in all shapes and intensities. Car chases, plane crashes and dismemberments by the dozen. Continual savagery and brutality now come is all shapes and sizes. All for the sake of money or ratings.

"Pornographers. Make no mistake about it, pornography is violence. Pornographers are the purveyors of hatred. Hatred of women. This is a travesty of humanity. And, how about the sellers of booze and the dealers in drugs. Wherever the emotionally insecure want to be, other than where they are, the drinks and drugs will get them. These malignancies take money away from children and families. Take resources away from our economy and destroy the workforce.

"The schools don't care for children. They have forgotten: Spare the rod and spoil the child. The school people won't discipline. They adjust. They're afraid of lawsuits from parents. Afraid of gangs in the schools. But most of all, they are afraid of failing to be perfect. So, they do nothing and promote platitudes that are Politically Correct. Do you know that the first use of the term, Politically Correct, was by Chairman Mao? So, to be Politically

Correct is to follow a Communist Doctrine.

"Professional athletes and their sports associations are the worst. The partially educated pro athletes, the ones who barely got out of high school and never graduated from college, want everyone to love them for their athletic antics. And they insist on being paid an obscene amount. But these same highly visible miscreants claim not to be role models. And the leagues say it's OK to do drugs, just don't take steroids or kill anybody. If you do these two heinous things, we will have to suspend you for two games and fine you a dollar.

"And our government leadership is a sad, an unbelievably bad joke. The present administration and the party that has run the country for the past sixteen years have allowed the moral fiber of the country to degenerate. Their tactics of power and re-election have been to favor and promote the various personal agenda of pleasure and money.

"We the People are the solution to the problem. We must take back our lives, take back our communities, take back our nation, take back our government and take back our rightful place as the moral leader of the free world. And we must do it now.

"We must establish a new life free from depravity. Our children must be safe. Today, my team is introducing an inclusive, simple, and effective six-point platform for the American people. A platform to help us take back America. Help us ensure a Secure American For Everyone... S.A.F.E. Here are the six points of S.A.F.E.:

"Number One: Talk and listen to your children and neighbors.

"Number Two: Participate in government, in schools, and in your community.

"Number Three: Demand security and safety from government local, state and federal.

"Number Four: Demand control of weapons and dangerous substances.

"Number Five: Demand the highest moral standards from leaders in all aspects of your life. Use extensive background checks.

"Number Six: Have faith in your higher power, but guard against the liars.

"Thank you. Now, I'll answer questions."

The guy started off like the voice of reason and ended his spiel with morsels of truth slathered by the hysteria of innuendo. God, the Senator's timing was impeccable. As Newsmakers returned, Bob Trumet had a nervous smile.

"Welcome back to Newsmakers, I'm Bob Trumet, your host. And today we are talking to Senator Baldwin Miller of Pennsylvania. Senator Miller just introduced a six-point plan, which he calls Secure America For Everyone, or S.A.F.E. Our switchboard is completely lit up. But, Senator Miller, before we go to the first caller, let me ask you two questions. First, what do you expect to get from S.A.F.E.? Second, how can the people learn more about S.A.F.E.?"

The Senator smiled a marginally genuine looking, but incredibly transparent expression: straight-from-the-heart, I'm-here-to-listen-and-serve, see-my-blue-eyes-pearly-white-teeth smile. He leaned into the camera ever so slightly. He did not stare, but looked intensely as if he really, really cared. The façade says trust, but there was something untrustworthy lurking beneath. His dark blue suit, white shirt, and red and light blue striped tie flag his belief system. Dark hair, solid facial features and subtle gesturing communicate the image of a strong father figure. Then something disconcerting happened: The eagle at the top of the six-point program, the same as the lapel pin worn by the

Senator, is depicted in flight, wings spread, and beak and talons open. Is it in a raptor mode?

"Bob, first, S.A.F.E. is for the people, by the people. I am just bringing the issues to the attention of all good and true Americans. It's the people who can solve the problems and be safe and secure. They have the power. They have the right. We want to hear from the people. S.A.F.E. will be an expression of the will of farmers, factory workers, clerical workers, teachers, retailers, all the hard-working Americans who pay their taxes and who make this country great. America can be great again, because of them and for their children.

"Second, if the people want to learn more about S.A.F.E., they can go to our web site, www.S.A.F.E.com, search their souls and talk to each other. Then tell us what they want. Do they want security and safety? Do they want to leave their children and their grandchildren a nation that isn't secure?"

"Thank you, Senator Miller. Now let's hear from our first caller."

"Bob, this is Eli Nachtvogel from Mechanicsburg, Pennsylvania. Me and my wife just want to say, thank you and God bless you to Senator Miller. It's about time somebody recognized what the working man and his family want. We want to be safe. And we want our kids to be safe. I just want to say we want to help the Senator in any way we can. Let us know how, and we'll do it. We're in the telephone book, Senator. Thanks for looking after us."

"Mister Nachtvogel, thank you for volunteering. It's volunteers that made this country great in the seventeen seventies and can make it safe again. Please go to our website, www.S.A.F.E.com and register. We will get in touch with you."

"Caller two, Senator."

"Good morning, Bob. Senator Miller. You are right, Senator, so right. Where can I get copies of your six-point platform? I want to give them out in my neighborhood, at little Jenny's school, and at the plant where James, that's my husband of twenty-two years, and I work. I'd like to get the church involved, too. Do you have a mailing address? Oh, yes, this is Jenny Creighton from Moline, Illinois."

"Thank you so much Missus Creighton. If you go to our website. www.S.A.F.E.com and complete the information form, we will send you as many copies as you ask for. Then, will you do something for all America? Write and tell us how we can help you feel safe and secure. We will post your inspirational words on our site."

"Next caller, you're on the air with Senator Baldwin Miller."

"Good morning, Senator. This is Bill Lincoln from Biloxi, Mississippi. Let me ask you, how did we get in this state of moral decay to begin with? If we can learn how the problem started, we can learn how to correct it."

"Your question deals with the root of the pervasive moral decay. We believe the root of the problem can be found in not caring. Over time, we didn't take responsibility for our own actions and lives. We let the other guy do it. We let the government take care of us. We let big business take care of us. Our lives became filled with too much comfortable stuff like cars, vacations, and self-gratification.

"All of this did not happen overnight. It happened almost imperceptibly over the last fifty years of prosperity. Like sand shifting invisibly in the desert wind. Soon the sand has moved completely, so that the dune that was on the right is now on the left. No one noticed the change, it just happened. Prosperity blinded us or made us look the other way. We let it happen to us. And, we had many willing accomplices. For everything we gave up, there was someone who would take it. But Americans can take back their lives if they want to. Americans can take back their freedom, rights, and responsibilities."

Bob Trumet subtly wrests control of his program from the senator, "Well, that's all the time we have for this spirited discussion. I'm sure we all appreciate Senator Baldwin Miller for sharing his views with us today. And, while we must go off the air, we will keep our lines open for further dialogue between our viewers and the Senator. So, don't hang up. Until next week, this is Bob Trumet of Newsmakers, where you learn what will happen."

Well, that was disturbing. Gene checked his computer. Mail. Gene's first son wanted to know about his aunt. *How she was holding up? Terri was expecting their third, convinced it was another boy, because he's so brutally active. They wanted to know if they could name him after my father. The new one child would be William David Benton II.* That pleased Gene and he knew his dad would be honored. The second son wanted to know what was going on. *Work bit the big one. The time demands were nearly intolerable. He met a wonderful woman in Edinburgh. They were together once a month increasing to every three weeks as she traveled for the Ministry of Commerce.*

Gene's boss wanted to know if he'd be in to work tomorrow. *Talk about the projects that were started before Gene left. There was some pressure building to complete the projects and get them into the field. Some company restructuring, which would impact his troops.* The department admin wanted to know when she'd see him. Not sure he had an answer. Well, back in the saddle of complacency. Nothing new had happened in Gene's absence. The light on the phone tells about messages since the system was swept on Friday morning. Some bill collector threatening to ruin his credit. Shit. The credit rating went down the tube years ago when Miss Fit walked out the door with Mister Wonderful after cleaning out most of the joint assets. She took about one hundred grand in cash and convertibles and he got about half that in debt, excluding the mortgage. Was he stupid, or maybe just wanted the entire mess to come to an end. The end is never in sight. That's how Sisyphus felt.

****

At six am, the home away from home was barely visible. Parking spot still there. A good sign. Not having your name painted over on the weekend meant you had employment for at least another week. The office was clean, and the worktable desk had three stacks of publications, brochures, and correspondence. The stacks had been labeled: *Must Read Today - Action Required, Must Read This Week - Direction Required, and Must Read Over the Weekend - Knowledge to be Gained.* The critical mess gets resorted in three sub-stacks: *Let's Talk, What Can We Do?* and *What Is this?* More of the same boring crap that filled the days was on the books. He was grateful that, at least, that had remained the same. Nothing else had.

****

The lead story on the evening news concerned a Presidential ad hoc commission formed to study the problem of citizen safety. The commission comprised of the highest profile luminaries the President could find on such short notice. Senator Miller's shot across the bow got the desired reaction from the reigning party. All the President's men scrambled to create this Committee. And now their credentials were displayed for all the world to see.

John Wenger, PhD, professor of Social Anthropology at Brown University, published six books dealing with twentieth century mores and social actions of international population sub-sets. He was one of the vocal proponents of the theory that attempted to establish similarities in domestic and international social ebbs and flows. Not population shifts, but dress, food, living and other manifestations of each culture. The theory was based upon the tenet that historical imperatives are no longer the strong influences they were in the nineteenth century due to advancements in communication, transportation, and information. Doctor Wenger, big on the lecture circuit, was always promoting a one-world foreign policy. Rumors had it, he's been a big contributor to the President's campaigns and might be in line for an ambassadorship.

Leslie Tremaine, a political activist for the downtrodden blacks, received her undergraduate, masters, and doctorate degrees in Political Science from Cal Berkeley. She led non-violent (mostly) and successful (always) protests against the university three times during her tenure. Miss

Tremaine fought for better public housing, day care for working mothers, and clinics that care for the substance abusers, who seem to populate her nether world. Miss Tremaine, mother of two, chose not to marry. In fact, she urged single mothers not to feel shame, but to strive and grow. She did. She showed the way. They could do it. Miss Tremaine, a community leader often where there was no community.

Brett Tucker had been nominated for three Academy Awards. One for her portrayal of a teen prostitute, one for a crusading newspaper reporter, and the most recent nomination for her role as a young widow who fought the system of economic discrimination. In real life, no husband, no children, no public love affairs. She established schools for young men and women who dropped out of high school but who wished to get a degree. U Graduate Now! Schools existed due to private donations. Several tons of Hollywood money. All given with great fanfare. No public assistance. Admission, classes, and books are free. Attendance and participation in class mandatory. Graduates were required to contribute to the schools with time and energy.

Huang Tsai, Genghis terrible of Silicon Valley, moved to Dallas where he and his followers developed the programs and games known to kids in video arcades and dens throughout the country. Tsai's Troops were not on the cutting edge, they were beyond the edge. Clothes, language, hairstyles and attitude. The Troops are Chinese, Japanese, Vietnamese, Blacks, Mexicans, and a mix of white brats. All with a penchant for the fantasy world of cyber life: Their drug, their booze. And they loved to shove their world in the faces of their parents, teachers and all in authority. Companies, which cater to the eleven to seventeen-year-old consumers spending the billions acquired from their yuppie parents needed Tsai's Troops to be competitive.

Elizabeth Pendleton, Chairwoman of the National Parent Teachers Association, had an alphabet behind her name and a pedigree of experience from years of teaching and school administration, as well as raising four children. The widow had been a face in the media, advocating stricter parental control of the schools. The poster child for zero tolerance against gangs, gang dress, and violence. Under her leadership, the PTA secured better salaries, more media centers, and many more Resource Officers. Elizabeth had the ear of the President and three years ago did not deny her interest in a Cabinet position.

Roberta Ramirez, President of the League of Woman Voters. Robbi is Puerto Rican, Yale educated, and an attorney. Walked the lines. Sat in after sit-ins were no longer fashionable. Waved the power of a huge block of votes like a beautiful banner when she needed to or wielded it like a truncheon if the opposition was recalcitrant. On more than one occasion, she said that the terrible, high birth rate among Black and Hispanic women was the strongest factor limiting their ascension to economic equality. The fact that men refused to take responsibility is a huge burr in her saddle blanket. Robbi advocated legally forced responsibility and sharing of the father's revenue. Even went as far as to promote the concept of work farms with wage garnishment. Although well educated, Robbi continued to speak with a heavy Spanish accent and lapsed into Puerto Rican Spanglish to spice up her speeches. Her husband was always there. Supportive, but in the background.

Chakka Uhuru, inner city National Merit Scholar from Lancaster, Pennsylvania. The wheelchair a result of a drive-by shooting. Just in the wrong place and the wrong time. Caca pasa. Chakka rose above poverty, no mother, a second-rate school and a near crushing disability. Perfect SAT score and perfect GPA. Valedictorian. Interned with Doctor Wenger. Mother left home to chase the pipe. Father a bus driver. Chakka, or Ka, never frowned. Sometimes came across as militant. Loved and admired by all. Sympathy is a strong underpinning for admiration.

These are The Magnificent Seven of President Paul Sessler.

III

A shotgun, a great hunting gun, or a vicious weapon up close and personal, depending on what was hunted and the particulars of the gun. The normal barrel could be sawed off. This allowed the shot or pellets to spread into a wider and unpredictable pattern quicker than possible with a regular length barrel. But it limited the effectiveness at distances over twenty-five yards. Pump action permitted the shooter to get off five or six shots rapidly. Shotgun loads, or explosive charges, ranged from dainty to bison killer. The shot inside a cartridge from BB to aggie. A shooter with a sawed-off pump action shotgun shooting heavy loads could make a wasteland of a living room and the people at the cocktail party. Or a school bus filled with children and a driver.

****

The thirty-one-inch monitor in Gene's office was set to the Financial News Network. Rarely noticed the details except during lunch at his desk: "We interrupt the regularly scheduled program to bring you this breaking news from Menthen, New Hampshire. Live from Menthen Area High School is Phil Howart. Phil, can you tell us what is happening?"

"Ralph, it is utter chaos. Here is what we know: Two boys here at Menthen Area High School in Menthen, New Hampshire entered a bus that was waiting to take students home after the day's classes. The two, we believe they were students, closed the doors of the bus and began blasting away with what have been described as pump action shot guns. They just began shooting without any apparent provocation. The boys were dressed in black long rider coats, black broad brimmed cowboy hats and boots with spurs. No names yet. Not for the boys and not for the children on the bus. We think there were sixteen. The bus driver was also slaughtered. His name was Elwood Suggins. He had been a driver and custodian with the school district for over twenty years. The brutality is staggering. Windows blown out. Chunks of the bus side panels missing. Gaping maws seemingly cry out in agony. The back door is open because it was ripped from its hinges. Looks like it took three or four shots.

"We have no footage and what I am about to describe may not be suitable for the young and squeamish. So, some viewers may want to turn down the volume. There were body parts everywhere. Arms, legs, and heads had been separated from torsos. I don't think the officials will ever be able to put the children back together. Chunks of flesh and mounds of what looked like hamburger. Entire backs of seats torn away. Gashes in the roof and craters in the floor. The blood was dripping through openings in the bus. Smoke from the burning seats had settled like fog over the dismembered corpses.

"There were two headless horsemen seated upright on the last bench in the bus. Shotguns in two laps. I assume that these were the culprits. The guns and all the children on the bus were silent. No noise. Screaming surrounded the outside of the bus. Friends crying out for fallen comrades. Ralph, it looks like a damned war zone. The police and SWAT members are here now. They responded in about ten minutes. Eleven minutes too late. As I learn more, I will relay it. That's all for now."

Gene was stunned. Wiped out. Sat in the Eames desk chair and stared at the screen. Cut the volume to five. Kids killing kids. This was a bad case of *Déjà vu* all over again. The description of the abattoir and the mystery people were painfully familiar. From their hats to their boots, these copycats just upped the ante to get in the game. Slaughter was a game no one can win. What else was familiar? What did he see? What did he not see? Was there a pattern emerging? Did the killers kill themselves? Did they leave notes? Where would they be? Did anybody see this coming? Was his niece somehow connected to this event? How? Who was responsible for this and the Carter butchery? Are they linked? Was he unduly paranoid? Are these two isolated events: one real, one a carbon copy?

****

Home again. By the pool, but no drink. Alone. Serenity. Eyes closed ever so briefly. Two hours passed and Gene awoke, and his stomach confirmed it was time for dinner. As he scrounged in the fridge for salad elements and some remnant of meat, out of the comer of his eye, he caught the twenty-four-hour news channel broadcasting scenes from Menthen. Repeat footage of the slaughter forced him to stop and stare. A panoramic view of the school parking lot, school, and athletic fields in the background. At the center of the video, the bus looked like it had been parked in the Syria as a target for the allied bombing raids. Couldn't determine if there were pools of blood or just many small dark shadows caused by the setting sun. Then he noticed something in the far background, near the trees to the left of the school. A dark colored or black van. No visible markings, windows had been heavily tinted. No activity around it. Suddenly, a body and face approached and entered the side door. Another and another. Five in total. The van crept away from its space. Now the news conference. Gene turned up the volume because every word counts: "Ladies and gentlemen. Thank you."

The news conference was led by the sheriff, who related the events of the past eight hours. His face, expression and words, were emotionless. He talked of safety and security. Isolated incident. Numerous leads. Blah, blah, blah. Nothing concrete. The alleged perps killed themselves. A few of the faces in the crowd seemed out of place. They avoided direct camera contact by moving out of range or turning away. Strange behavior. Could not release all the names until all the families had been notified. A stringer from Boston asked if it was true the boys left suicide notes. Did they just want someone to pay attention? Someone to listen to their pain. No answer. Was there a connection to the school shooting in Wyoming? No answer. The entire event took twenty minutes. The crowd of reporters and authorities dispersed. The similarity to the Carter news briefing was eerie.

The questions were coming faster than Gene's brain could log them. They spun into absurdities, doubled back on themselves, and were reinvented as something totally unintelligible. School kids, the brutality, the van, the faces, the evasive answers, suicide notes, news conferences. It's too much now. He needed release from the tribulation of intellectual recrimination.

He had to stop thinking or cross the razor's edge between sanity and insanity. Light into darkness. His episodic depression was frightful. It disabled him twice. The episode could always repeat, had to be on guard to avoid this. He recalled the days of single rooms, sunrooms, and soothing music. Casual clothes with no belts. Nights of lights out at ten, bed checks at eleven. Chaperoned as if we were hormone driven teens rather than disoriented adults. He was sure there was some bed hopping during the one month stay at the restful ranch. The young kid in room three forty-five seemed to be very friendly with his next-door neighbor, the topless dancer with the crack habit and pimp for a boyfriend. Mediocre food and great meds. Rest and relaxation. Counseling. Individual and groups. Exercise was permitted after one week. Twice daily for Gene.

After four weeks, it was time to reenter the world of the multiple agendas, work pressures, con men, and governmental deceit. The people at the ranch were slightly unhinged, but mostly honest. The people on the outside were dishonest and crazy about the benefits of their errant behavior. Gene was stacked, packed, and jacked. Mind was clear. That was fifteen years ago. His mind was clearer than ever. And emotions finally well grounded. Sometimes, when under pressure, his cognitive capacity expanded exponentially, but in a very haphazard way. *The light saber pierced the darkness only to become engulfed by it. His fear was that having pierced the darkness, the darkness let loose and could flood his mind forever. No more light. Ever. Insanity was a large package of C-4 he carried all the time.* He was making no sense, so he stopped.

****

The telephone saved Gene from darker emotional contortions. The caller ID told him it was Mary.

"Hello, Mary. How are you?"

"Hello, Gene. Listen, there are two things you need to know. First, Dorothy was into some weird websites and chatrooms. She was known as GirlFromOz. Yes, she went to the usual info rooms and some very adult rooms. But she also went to a few rooms that are beyond reality. These are places where the lunatic fringe rambles and rants, places that, I'm sure, are monitored by authorities. The feds are there to listen, just listen. I heard through the cyber grapevine that one time the feds knew about a major bombing, and that is why it never happened. So, Dorothy was into a chatroom of various militia: One for a radical third world group, and a few, which featured discussions about the rights of all Americans. Strange and frightening. If she goes to the rooms, she must learn something. And when does curiosity become acceptance and acceptance become belief? Also, when she goes there, she leaves a trail, which can be followed by anyone with a deep working knowledge of the net. What does this have to do with the school slaughter, I don't know? But I think there must be some connection. Waddaya think?"

"I think you need to slow down and take a breath. As a matter of good health, take five deep breaths then tell me about the second item."

"Really great news. I sold my place and quit my job. I got a great deal on the building and the land from some developer who is looking to build mountain condos for the bored rich. I had been in negotiations for about a year. He just met my price. The university paid me through the end of next year. Officially, I am on sabbatical. I'll retire and become a consultant. So, I have a big wad of cash little brother, enough for about ten years of living large. And here is the best part: I'm now crossing the Tennessee border on my way to you. I know you have room and will enjoy my company. Oh, yes, the dogs are with me. As is all my equipment. So, we can set up a ComRoom and continue our investigation. Well, what do you think? I mean I spent a small fortune on my home on wheels. The RV dealership made it road ready for the trip. God, I had no idea tires were so expensive. And mechanics get thirty dollars an hour in Nowhereville, Wyoming. The dealership could have closed for a week after I paid my bill. But they made my van safe for me to drive the distance from where I was to where I want to be."

"Mary, it'll be wonderful to see you again. Will you be able to find my cave? It's intentionally obscure from the eyes and ears of the world. I, like my much older sister, love privacy. You know, back roads and a hidden driveway? Even the mailbox carries only the road number. I'll clean up the room I reserve for guests. The dogs? A ComRoom? Jesus, Mary, thanks for the advanced notice. I'm sorry, if that sounded snotty. It's just that this all comes as a huge surprise. Of course, you're welcome to stay as long as you wish. I look forward to seeing you. What's your ETA?"

"About dinner time tomorrow. How will I find you? God, do you mistake me for a dullard or a dolt? I fed my complete address and your complete address into the Maps App and I got a detailed map of roads, turns, miles, and time. Plus, I have GPS. You are not invisible, you know. The dogs can stay anywhere you want. By the way, I assume that I'll have no difficulty parking near the house. My toy is thirty feet long."

"I'll meet you at the door. Drink in hand. We'll worry about the house on wheels later when you are relaxed."

****

Gene was reminded of the schoolboy in England who was asked to use the word 'marvelous' twice in the same sentence. He spoke to the teacher: "My sixteen-year-old sister got pregnant and my father said that was marvelous, bloody fucking marvelous." Well, she's not pregnant, but Mary was coming to stay and that was 'marvelous, bloody fucking marvelous.' His mind bounced with consternation. Real schizoid consternation. The push-me pull-you. He would have to work hard to avoid the pit of the passive aggressive.

How would she fit into his life and he into hers? What about the hounds from hell? What about her stuff? She got her own room and his home office, albeit meager, would become her ComRoom. Did he need another telephone line? How about surge protectors in the lightning capital of the Western world? Didn't want her equipment to fry. He felt put upon but didn't want to put her out. She has been through the ultimate rejection: Death of a loved one. He wanted to protect his life yet open his heart. His world with all its patterns, sameness, and security was about to be turned topsy-turvy. Could he handle the change easily? No! But he looked forward to the challenge. Hell, if Mary handled the loss of her daughter, he could handle Mary. Maybe, he was meant to help Mary in her struggle.

****

She was exceptionally prompt. At 6:05 PM she arrived in a boat. One story tall, longer than Gene had thought, and wider than he had feared. The door opened, the driver's seat turned, and a lift plate appeared. The seat was the wheelchair, which she glided onto the plate. The plate lowered via the hand controls. A ramp flipped over and permitted exit onto the ground. Brother rushed to greet sister. All smiles and hugs. Entered the house, the double front doors eased the awkwardness. Her room with the bath attached. The house's internal doors were a squeeze. This had to be remedied as soon as possible. Retrieve four bags. That's it? All her personal needs. Four bags. Dad used to say that a true Scot could pack and disappear from the English in ten minutes. It may have taken Mary twenty, but she was a lot faster than either of his wives. Hither and Yon seemed content to stay in the mobile hotel. They had their beds, food, and water. The dogs will run three times a day. Gene's backyard seemed big enough for the two, not as big as they were used to. Maybe they could stay with Mary, in the house, when he is gone. God, Gene was resizing doors, building dog runs and making a new nest. Maybe the intrusion was not an intrusion, but rather a massive revision. Onward, ever onward.

****

"Well, that meal was terrific, little brother. Do you cook all the time or just for visiting dignitaries? Seriously, I know this is awkward, to say the least. And I deeply appreciate your welcoming me with outstretched arms. I needed to get away from the scene of my angst and devote myself to uncovering the issues, both criminal and familial of this situation. I have a plethora of DVDs and discs. I need to sort through all of them: Align them chronologically, analyze the visuals and re-listen to the words. It will take me only a day to unload all my stuff. It may take another day to hook up my equipment and get everything in running order. Next, I'll have the boat emptied except for my babies no later than Saturday. I hope you don't mind. But I desperately need this time and space. I won't interfere with your comings and goings. Where you go and what you do are your business."

"Mary, understand it will take me a while to get used to all of this, but I love the idea that you thought of here and me. I am just a little disconcerted, that and any cramped feeling will melt away, my soul will become warm again, and we will learn to coexist. God, that sounded so sappy, didn't it? I, too, want to get some answers. Dorothy may be the key or simply an innocent bystander. We won't know until we dig deeply. Now here is a brave step: Let's get the dogs into the house for a brief visit to smell the space and me. I've never had pets. So, this will be more difficult for me than for them."

They exited and retrieved her children and protectors. They remembered Gene. Thank God. He got to keep his hands, feet, and throat. Now he learned that Hither was the mix of Shepherd and Rottweiler. Yon, the Puli and Coyote blend. Hither weighed about ninety-five or one hundred pounds, depending on the size of the mailman's leg he just ate. Yon weighed a skimpy seventy pounds. Hither plodded at a gait. Yon walked, then sprinted. He could cover forty yards in three point two seconds. If he only had hands and could run the curl pattern, Mary could retire on his contract with the Tampa Bay Bucs. Yon could leap over or crawl under any fence. Yon had been known to walk along roofs and the top rung of a split rail fence. The Puli trait. Hither would run through the fence rather than jump it, feared nothing, because everyone, except Yon, feared him.

The two never slept at the same time. They were devoted to the protection of Mary. They ate once a day, in the morning. They expected water all day. This would be particularly important in this new heated environment. They get a snack in the afternoon. They liked to gnaw bones. Some of their favorites looked like femurs from a T-Rex. For all their physical prowess, what was most uncanny was their way of always keeping an eye on Mary. This was why they must come into the house as soon as possible when she's home. When she's away, they paced. No barking. Just pacing like the Bengal tiger caged in the zoo. The tension was palpable. A spring about to be sprung. Humans don't own dogs like these. The dogs let a few select humans into their world and nurture them to animalhood. Glad they are with Mary. He hoped they were glad to be with him.

IV

"We are honored to be with you people in Big Pass. We want to hear what you have to say about the safety and security of your families. What do you want? How can we help?" Senator Miller begins his grassroots campaign. At this first town hall forum, the original six points are on display. The poster is huge, about 30 feet by 40 feet, and the dark colored eagle is a powerful, almost threatening symbol. Miller is cheerleading input from a new constituency in a small town. Every small town represents a part of constituency much broader than his own in Pennsylvania. He is apparently running for some office higher in the food chain than that of Senator. "Before we start the discussion, I'd like Pastor Carl Waters of the Main Street Methodist Church to lead us in prayer. Pastor Waters."

"Heavenly and gracious Father, protector of your faithful children, keep us safe from harm, and grant us the courage and clarity to open out hearts and minds to hear your word and to do such things that please you. We ask that your guidance be with us tonight as we strive to return to the basic tenants of human decency and Godly love."

"Thank you, Pastor Waters. Now, the combined choirs of East High School, Big Pass High School, Central Vocational School, and York County High School will lead us in the National Anthem. Boys and girls."

As the anthem dies down, the applause and whistling swell to a deafening level. National pride runs deep in the heartland. As the audience shuffles and sits, there is a great deal of waving, handshaking, and general greeting. The noise and commotion are exhilarating, a real pep rally (just no football game). There is a commonality to the look of the townsfolk. For the men, flannel, denim, or khaki work shirts are the norm. There are a few T-shirts underneath, each with a logo or a message. The hats are blue, green, or red depending on the farm equipment of choice. The hats are not removed. Black lace up Stride Rites are to this set what Gucci or Bally loafers are to their distant cousins in Chicago. The women have on their size sixteen/eighteen checked or striped dresses and sensible shoes. They carry handbags, not purses. The hairstyles reflect the owners' desire for simplicity and neatness, cut short, but not butch or dyke like.

The faces of both the men and women are right out of a Rockwell or a Homer. Ruddy complexions, enough lines to make them interesting. Blue eyes abound. Light hair. The women have bigger hips than the men, reflecting that they are breeding stock. The men look like terriers: wiry, piercing eyes, and quick darting actions. Very few fat men. When you work on a farm twelve hours a day, six days a week, you burn up all the food calories. There are numerous teens in the assembled throng, but no small children. Many young folks. This is their future.

"Welcome, ladies and gentlemen. May I say how gratified I am to see such a huge turn out? Maybe we should have up-linked this event to all the high schools in the state. I hope that by now all of you know the original six points of the platform. We have taken the liberty to provide leaflets with the six points, our mission, and our telephone numbers. Also, so that I don't forget our purpose, my team has given us this reminder poster behind me.

"Before we take our first question or comment, let's remember to relax, have fun, and treat your neighbor with the respect and dignity you would like from him or her. There are no network TV cameras here. Obviously, the big city power mongers, or is that mongrels, have stayed in the city."

This draws the desired hoots and whistles, so he continues, "Maybe those fine folks don't think much of what you want. The microphones are so that we can hear each other. OK, who's first?"

A man stands: "Senator Miller, my name is Jack Williamson. My wife, Luanne, and I have three children and we are scared stiff. We see stuff on the television news. We call them the three Gees: guns, gangs, and godlessness. My family wants to be safe and secure. But how do we get there without more violence?"

"Mr. Williamson, thanks for being the lead-off batter, going first takes courage. I don't think this great nation of yours needs another revolution. I say, get involved in local government. This is the entry port to the sea of political change. If you can influence local government and the state government representatives who live in your town, they will influence the national government. The problem, as we see it, is that in the past fifty years, politics and political power have shifted away from the local law-abiding citizenry to those who live in an ivory tower called Washington. And new rules have been handed down to you good citizens.

"To wrest power from those in power is not easy, because those in power will not go quietly into the night, but you good people know everything worth having is worth the effort. Plants don't grow without fighting the soil, elements, and vermin. It takes a lot of effort. It's the same with reclaiming your country. It's worth reclaiming, so it's worth the effort."

Next a woman: "Senator Miller, Marva Locker. I would first like to thank you for coming to Big Pass. You're the first national politician we've seen in three years. Our own Senator, Old What's-His-Name, never seems to have the time to stop by for coffee and pie, even during the County Fair." The applause and cheering are thunderous. "Anyway, what I'd like to ask is once we've begun the process, how do we know that the people in Washington won't just shut us out like they've done in the past? And second, do we need new laws?"

"Thank you, Miss Locker. I'd be honored to be invited back to Big Pass anytime. Just one question: What kind of pie will I get? I'm partial to apple or peach."

The laughter reverberates throughout the auditorium, even a few cheers. He has won their hearts. Their minds and votes will follow. He resumes, "Seriously, it will take a lot of work. But quitting is not an option for you. You will probably have to elect new leaders. Men and women, who believe as you do.

"Now to your second point: No new laws are needed. What is needed is firm enforcement of the laws already on the books. There are state and federal laws which regulate and control dangerous things like guns and drugs. There are state and federal laws which establish prosecutorial guidelines and punishments for abusers of the gun and drug laws. Let me ask you to think a minute about guns, because that's the thornier of the two subjects. The Second Amendment to the Constitution clearly states that gun ownership is based upon the need for a militia.

"Let me quote: 'A well-regulated Militia, being necessary to the security of a free State, the right of the people to keep and bear arms, shall not be infringed.' The militia would, in turn, act at the orders of and owe their allegiance to the government. In the period of international revolution, this was the government's way of maintaining individual freedom and controlling any widespread abuse of weapons at the same time.

"Today, there is not a right-thinking American among you who would call for the removal of hunting guns. Rifles and shotguns are for sport and self-protection. Do we need automatic weapons? Do we really think it's a good idea to make automatic weapons available to children and the emotionally unstable? What's wrong with licensing these weapons like we do cars and doing background checks on the people who want to own them? These two steps would go a long way to ensure the Safety and security of the decent, honest citizens? We do not need the Posse Comitatus and myriad of paramilitary, neo-Nazi, white supremacists, which feel they and they alone can protect us. Who will protect us against them?

"And we surely don't need the rampaging drugs that are threatening future of our youth. We have strict laws outlawing cocaine, crack, crank, meth, smack, and every other imported or hometown destroyer. But our police have their hands tied by the judicial system that coddles the criminal. The police can't do this, and the police can't do that. The rights and freedoms of the criminal are held above the safety and security of society. Use the laws that are on the books. Encourage the courts to act without fear. If they will not, get new responsible judges who will. Remember the judges are elected or appointment by elected officials. They all owe their bench to someone and that someone ultimately is you. The future is in your hands. This is what we believe. What do you believe?"

The admirers were on their feet. The applause lasted well over two minutes.

"Thank you, my friends. I hope I'm not being too presumptuous to call you my friends. I am excited. I feel the energy of goodness. I feel the strength of conviction. I feel the concern. I know there is a better way and you are the answer."

Another speaker stands after the cacophony has died down, "Senator Miller, God bless you. You and your wake-up call. How do we protect ourselves against the liars, deceivers, and charlatans? Oh, sorry, my name is Ida Hess. This is Thomas, my husband of twenty-nine years. These are my children, Tom Junior, Grace, Richard, Sarah, and Mark. And, I have six grandchildren. We didn't bring them along tonight, 'cause they're all full of spit and vinegar. And this is a grown-up night."

"Ida, thank you, and God bless you and your clan. Well, protection against liars? This country is blessed with the highest degree of technological expertise in the world. And, because of a free market system, the cost of this technology is reasonable and even inexpensive when the benefits are weighed against both the actual costs and savings generated by use of the technology. There is a wealth of information about places, companies, and people in files throughout the world. Let us use the information for safety and security. You can do it. And, the sooner, the better.

"It is possible to establish a national clearinghouse of information, of personal files, to be checked by the proper and duly elected authorities. We have a system already in place. This single source would have more useable, important information than the Internal Revenue Service or the credit companies and it would be substantially more accessible. If we can establish this data bank, we can control our destiny.

"OK. That pretty much covers the basics. Can we take a half hour break for restroom and refreshment? Then we'll reconvene for further discussion. Those of you, who must tend to little ones at home. We understand if you leave now. The children must come first. This evening is for the children. We thank you for coming. If you would be so kind to leave your names and addresses in the books by the doors. We'd like to send you literature about what we are learning and doing. Also, please take a few of the pamphlets in the baskets. Give them to your friends. Let them read the material at their convenience. If something strikes a favorable chord. Tell them to let us know. Write to us or call us on the eight hundred number. Those of you who can stay, please be back in the auditorium in thirty minutes. It's now eight forty-five. We'll restart our discussion at nine fifteen."

With that, Senator Miller takes a big drink of water, smiles, and waves to his enthusiastic supporters. Then, he turns to the dozen men and women behind him. They form a small discussion circle. All of this while the rafters are shaking from the applause, shouting, and stomping. The place is going wild. He is on his way.

The morning's work has exhausted Gene. He thinks, *I'll avail myself of the executive health spa. Pump a little. Steam a little. Nap a little. Eat late and light at my desk.*

****

His nap lasted a little longer than he had planned. Finished eating by three. Mary emailed and asked that he pick up a few things at Electronic Land. She is putting her equipment together and needs items listed by description, number, and manufacturer name. What is on the electronic news and in the national financial newspaper? Nothing and nothing. The usual plethora of dearth. Stare at the work. Double and triple check the overall impression. Look for flaws. The spinach between the teeth of the naked woman, looking for any inconsistencies is mesmerizing. When he gazes intently, he drifts into a trance-like state, time and place mean nothing: Two seconds become an hour, an hour is a millisecond. Gene is in his office. *I am on the beach. The telephone comes to my aid. Like the light that pierces the darkness. This time the darkness is shattered.*

"Gene, have you seen the local paper today?"

"Mary, I don't get a second copy at the office. What is so important?"

"Senator Miller had his inaugural townhall meeting last night, somewhere in Kansas. There was a picture and small UPI article on page six of the National section. The text is banal. But it's the picture. There is the good Senator waving to the crowd. Behind him, I think I see a face or two that seem familiar. They may have been in Carter. I can't wait for you to see the shot. We'll need to get a blow-up of it and dig into the details. I can do some cross matching with lifts from the videos of the other tragedies. Hurry home."

V

Gene's used-to-be home office looked as if it had been redesigned by Rube Goldberg. Boxes were stacked three high and seemingly held together by bailing wire and duct tape. Cables ran all over the place: Under, over, in front of and behind the boxes, the desk, the worktable, and the control panel. The small room had become visibly much smaller. The walls had been moved inward eighteen inches to two feet by the equipment. Like a Poe short story this shrinking of space was disconcerting. Multiple screens were on, off, and flickering. Broadcast and cable stations were visible in the comer. Floor lights on low so as not to interfere with viewing the screens. In front of a large monitor, displaying the internet was Mary's keyboard. The wheelchair couldn't be driven freely throughout the small space because of the intertwined clumps of chord on the floor. Mary devised paths. The cables were tagged so she knew the workings of the intricate system. This, Gene assumed, would facilitate repair. The floor looked like an old English garden maze. There was a visible entrance and exit...one and the same. Gene's office had become Mary's electronic womb. The dogs somehow wormed their way into the small space and stretched out protectively near their queen. She was in hog heaven.

"I was trying to fire up this puppy but couldn't. So, I'm fixin' to standby to get ready. The stuff you bought at the store will complete my project. Please put the bag on the table somewhere. But don't move anything."

"How will anything new fit into this space?"

"It's not so much that this is additional, rather faster and stronger replacements. I'll be able to eliminate about half the cables. The ones you bought can carry more. They do more. And they take up less space. You'll see. By the by, take a gander at page four of the National section of today's newspaper. Upper right-hand corner. There he is in miniature. Looming in my soul larger than life. Senator Baldwin Miller, waving. His face is a study in fatherly authority. His family is behind him. I'm not sure that anyone looks familiar. Faces are too small and out of focus."

"OK, so what? Now what?"

"How do we get the original or the negative of that picture? If we can get it, I can play with the images and we can learn who is standing in support of the good Senator. It's wire photo. Can you contact them? I have no pull with the news media. You do, don't you?"

"I can call a guy in New York and find out how to get the shot."

"Could you do that now?"

"I can call Jim Larson at United Press International. Jim will find out who took the shot and how to get the neg. He will get back to me."

"Do it now."

"After the call, I'm going for a swim. I need to cleanse."

"Yes, baby brother, you may swim now. Be careful and don't drown. Maybe I'll send the dogs to watch over you. You know, protect you from yourself."

****

Gene commenced his laps. Nothing purges completely like a long swim. Swimming is a solitary activity. He had the pool built for exactly that purpose. The birdcage covering extended from the house, down the far side of the backyard. Still enough lawn space for his flower garden. Over one hundred blooming plants and flowers.

The colors, textures and aromas were calming and seductive. When he's not swimming laps, the pool will accommodate two floating chaise lounges complete with headrests, arm rests, cup holders, and the fixture for an umbrella. His aquatic LayZeeDads: Gawd, the single life encourages self-indulgence.

The pool had no diving board and no deep end. Just a constant four feet deep, sixteen feet wide, and sixty feet long. Forty yards to a lap and twenty-two laps to a half mile. Good enervating relaxation. A great way for him to maintain some semblance of a shape other than pear. Somewhere between lap eight and eleven, Gene breaks the wall and gets his second wind. There was a reasonable cadence to his strokes, breathing, and kicking. It may not be the fastest combination, but it's comfortable. His lungs no longer feel as if they were about to implode. The desired warmth seeps into his muscles: This meant the effort was working. He heard the hounds and caught a glimpse of their antics at the next turn.

Were they dancing? Mimicking his struggle, they were running back and forth. They're bounding poolside barking uproariously. Sprinting, ducking, and lunging as if they were herding animals or small children. Were they concerned that he was in some sort of trouble? Did this mean that they cared or that they are worried that if he drowned, they wouldn't be fed? Through all the barking and scrambling, they never took their eyes off him. Finally, he completed his workout, stopped, and called them. They saw that Gene was not in danger of drowning and that they would be fed. The ruckus stopped. They cautiously approached the water by the narrow side steps. First, Hither put a paw in the green blue medium. Then another. Part in and part out. Yon backed up and sprang into the pool. The resultant waves cascaded over the canine partner.

Hither lunged ahead. They both swam toward Gene, the target of their anxiety. They did not attack, although the clawing and clamoring pushed him under. To be killed by the saviors would be sadly ironic. They began to push Gene toward the stairs leading to dry land and safety. Their noses were prods, strong with soft tips. And they really did doggie paddle. Their bodies wet appeared to be much smaller than when they were dry. Their fur matted by the water caused them to gain weight. This new weight would pull them under if they weren't so powerful. Their paws were like canoe paddles. Their faces and eyes were not menacing, but rather showed concern for his state. They were convinced Gene was in trouble. Once on land, they shook dry. Gene towel dried and they went their separate ways. The dogs ran around the yard, out to the hedges and back. Gene plopped into a chair.

****

"Well, did all my boys have fun in the pool?"

"Mary, these dogs are amazing. I think they actually care for me...a little bit. Either that or they see me as a great toy not to be lost, broken, or drowned. What would you like for dinner? Given the fact that I am wiped. Let's make it simple to prep and clean. You know your kind of meal."

"How about a big bowl of everything in the fridge?"

"You got it. And we'll dine poolside."

****

After dinner Gene stretched out on the couch to read some trade journals. The tedium of their text had a narcotic effect, particularly powerful after exercise, at the end of the day, and on a full stomach. He drifted off with the last magazine opened and resting on his chest.

Hiking is a phenomenal way to go outside to get inside. The Appalachian Trail is one of the great gifts Americans share. I've walked the Georgia section several times. Each time I experience something new about nature. The topography, the trees, rocks, path, and the sky are different every time. Then there are the people. Similar goals from dissimilar lives. All the time I walk, I think. Wherever my mind leads me: I have settled family disputes, understood the inner workings of the primitive computers, contemplated love in its many and diverse forms, argued with myself, prayed a lot, stared at the stars and comprehended my insignificance. All these things are possible when I am alone on the trail.

As I reach a crest, I survey where I've been and where I must go before I make camp. The clouds are darkening. Wind is picking up from breeze to abrupt puffs. The roiling clouds sporadically obliterate the horizon. Everything happens quickly out here. Or at least it seems so because I am distracted by inner thoughts and outer beauty. No time to rest. Down the other side of my conquest. Down is just as difficult as up because the climber uses different muscles. The slope is slippery. Switchbacks are severe. Switchbacks can double or triple the distance traveled. I must pick up my pace. One of the great things about hiking alone is the aloneness, which is also the not so great aspect of the hiking. I miss another's presence, but I don't miss the required interaction. I've been out here alone, in a small group, and with seven others. Alone is best. The weight of the pack is no different. But my schedule is my own. Four miles on day one. Eight the next. Three nights out. One week alone.

It's almost dark. The combination of no sun, the heavy clouds, and the overhanging trees has created a forest primeval for my trip down the other side of the mountain. The branches bow. The trees bend. Bark and twigs from the forest floor are kicked up against my legs. Vision beyond twenty feet is impaired. The rustling of the leaves, the cracking of thunder, and creaking of the trunks and branches are a threatening cacophony. Footing is precarious. The rain has increased the moisture on every surface. Damn! Falling to one knee causes the pack weight to shift nearly over my head. Pushes me precipitously downward. I am now rolling. Well, more like flopping. Arms and legs going every which way. I try to grab anything to slow the inevitable process. The pack weight, my weight, and momentum rule out any possibility of stopping. Just tuck and roll. Prevent breaking an arm or leg. Cover my head to limit damage. Stumps and fallen branches dig into my torso. They really hurt. Suddenly there is nothing between the earth and me. I have fallen over some edge.

Crash. It was a hole. I landed feet first but am jammed into the crevasse, stuffed like a hand in a glove. Wind has been knocked out of me, so I gasp for breath. Rain is beginning to cascade over me. Can't unhook pack. Arms pinned against my body. Must wriggle and squeeze my arms over my head. Great effort for extraordinarily little result. Struggle to right of my body and to pull myself up using the vines. Pack jammed to the walls, will not move easily. It's about eight feet from the top of my head to the outside. Test *the vines. Slippery, but they appear to hold me even with the jammed pack. I better be quick about it. Get out before the water loosens the vines' grips on the cave walls.*

The pack is imbedded in the walls and creates an extreme impediment to upward movement. Slowly I begin my ascent. One inch at a time. At this rate, I'll be out of the tomb in an hour and a half. Or I will have drowned. Dig toes of boots into earth walls. Pull on base of vines. Very gradually I rise like Lazarus. As vines break or pull away, I pause and rest on my toes. I can't lean back, or I'll drive the pack deeper into the muddy wall. I must press my body forward. Face flat against the muck. If I rush and pull too hard, the vines will come out from the sides. If I wait, the rainwater will weaken the vines' hold in the walls. Damned if I do and damned if I don't. Gradually, I hoist my body. Pausing only to seek a stronger vine or a deeper toehold. The rain is gushing over the opening's rim.

The thunderclaps are deafening. So close that I can't even think the word, one, between the flash and the crash. The storm must be right on top of me. Maybe inside my personal hell. If I look up, muddy water with leaves and sticks blinds me. If I look down, I can't see my next step. Or next vine. The rain. The noise. The position. I'm scared and about to be done in by Mother Nature. The vines are barely holding. The toeholds are crumbling. I freeze. The rainwater is building in the bottom of my cavern. If I wait much longer to escape, the water will overtake me. I'll drown. Can't go upward. Won't go back. Muscles are beginning to burn and ache. I hear voices through the storm's rage. They're almost laughing. Males seem to be calling. I call back. "Help. Help me. I'm down here. Stuck. Can't get up or out. Help." Two shapes appear at the mouth of my earthen coffin...my boys. They call, "Dad. We're here. Reach out your hand, we'll help you out. Dad. Dad." "Gene. Gene. Can you get up? Get up. Gene, get up." My eyes slit open. It's Mary holding my hand gently.

****

"Gene, wake up. You've been having a frantic dream. You're OK. Here, wipe your face. You're sweating up a storm. What was it all about? You were reaching out and up as if for someone or something. Like the moment before death. Reaching out to God. Calling out to be saved. From what or whom?"

"Mary, it's a dream I've had many times before. Except this ending was different and much more rewarding. I think I understand it now. Many thanks for being here. At this time. Right now. I think I'd like to get out of these clothes. Change the linens. Have a weak drink and go back to sleep."

"Not before you see what I've found. I hate to one up your psychic revelation, but I think I just tapped the motherlode. Get showered and changed. Then come to the ComRoom. Yes, it's important."

Gene did as he was told. He, the dutiful bro. The entire changing and cleansing took fifteen minutes.

"Now what is so important?"

"Chatroom heaven...or hell. Here are a few of the places Dorothy went late at night. She was GirlFromOz. Check this out. Here is the first: HouseAfire. Scrutinize the message board and you'll get an idea about the purpose of the room and the personalities of the Chatty Kathies and Kens."

Gene sat and stared at the screen. Mary played scroll and click to speed the process. HouseAfire seemed to promote anarchy. She would do away with all governmental restriction and repression. Protests and violence were directly below the surface of her writing. RichBitch wanted to know if guns would be made available to all or just the leaders. What will happen to the good parents and the benevolent leaders? WarEagle told her to either play on this team or the enemy's. He would make war when he was ready and at the site of his own designation. Destruction will rule. FarmerJohn praised WarEagle for his courage but warned him against the foolhardiness of the ego. FarmerJohn philosophized that from the many planted seeds, only a specific crop would spring. If they worked with natural forces, they would be stronger because they shared the strength of ancestors and allies. They would overthrow the powers that regulate their lives into slavery. To rush ahead unaware of fate, friends and foes would ultimately bring about the crushing of the cause. Look to the East. The land of their elders. Look to the farmers. Farmers nurture. They must rise up and recapture our heritage of freedom.

"Shit, that's nothing but sophomoric drivel. Noisy tin drums.

They barely talk the talk much less walk the walk. Just weirdos who love the sound of their own printed word. And, incidentally, don't any of them use spellcheck? They are not telling anybody anything."

"Open your eyes and ears. These people are trying to tell anyone who will listen: They are filled with angst. They may have information they want to share but do not want to be caught sharing. Take this room as a place that could contain one piece of an excessively big and strange puzzle. Here is another: BoldWorld. He says...

'The future of man is in his hands. He must take control of his techno-faculties. The space around men and women is theirs to rule. Those who deny this are the enemy of the future and the enemy of the people. SeeingEye pines for the time when governments and big business serve the people. The time when we are connected with the other planets and other life forms, which have been kept from us and we from them. Our PCs will be the connecting points. This will require a liberation and international distribution of resources. Governments will have to work together, or they will be abolished by the People's Committee.

The planets are aligned for an event, which will bring recognition to our struggle."

FaithBlinded wanted to provide food for the millions who are starving because of governments' lack of interest.

"No money, just foodstuffs and basic ingredients which were rotting in the granaries and warehouses all over the world. Storm the silos. Feed the people. Before we venture into space, we must feed the children. Weapons of power have been stashed throughout the world. Look and listen. Read the signs and follow the map."

"Just more claptrap. Little voices in the night sounding bolder than they are. Verbal testosterone. Silhouettes on the shade. Smaller than life. This is so much bullshit. Mary, your information gathering conspiracy theory is like the adage that if you put ten thousand monkeys at ten thousand typewriters, they would produce Shakespeare's entire body of work. This may be true given two or three millennia. But, within the time constraints of life and reality, the monkeys would produce gibberish. It's the same with the interpretation of these *volk-sprachers*. If they say enough over a long enough period of time, some morsel of whatever they say will very likely occur. We used to have street crazies, who would pace all around and mutter nonsense. The crazies are now accessible via the Internet. Look, Mary, I'm exhausted from my dream. I need my rest. See you in a few hours if you are awake when I arise. It's not that I don't care. I just can't see the handwriting on the walls, as of now it's just graffiti. Take this kiss."

****

The workday was eleven hours long before noon. The afternoon was longer. By the time Gene got home, all he wanted to do was go to bed. He was not required to exchange niceties with his sister, and she is not required to do so with him. They cohabitate. The Early Network News was mumbling softly about tonight's American Forum from the studios in New York City. The President's Commission on Citizen Safety had been convened to hear the outcries of America. The Magnificent Seven would take telephone calls from anywhere in the country. For ninety minutes, including limited commercial interruptions, the politically correct celebrating diversity group of over-promised intellectuals would tell the factory workers, laborers, and members of other service sectors how to behave and what to think. All within the confines of a safe and sterile television studio. Jesus H. Christ, what's wrong with that picture. Limited reality, maximum governmental control, and no humanity. Other than these shortcomings, the program was hugely beneficial for the American public. *I will watch the event, nonetheless. I also watch car wrecks.*

"Good evening, ladies and gentlemen. Tonight, you will be a participant in a breakthrough public forum. A revolutionary format of national proportions. Tonight, the federal government's Commission on Citizen Safety wants to hear from you, the citizens of this great nation. You see around the table seven of the most distinguished people of our time. People from all venues, men and women selected by your government as those best able to give the administration advice in the area of citizen safety. Advice from you, through them, to the President. Let me introduce them: From my left: Doctor John Wenger, noted teacher and lecturer in the field of Sociology and

Anthropology. Leslie Tremaine, social activist and leader. Brett Tucker, founder of the Graduate Now! High School. Huang Tsai', software and program pioneer. Doctor Elizabeth Pendleton, Chairwoman of the National Parent Teacher Association. Roberta Ramirez, President of the League of Woman Voters. Chakka Uhuru, National Merit Scholarship winner.

"To speak to this panel, call the eight hundred number presently on your screen. Operators are waiting. The panel members will provide their own interpretation of each subject. Each panel member will be allotted ninety seconds to answer each viewer's question. We urge you to gather your entire family into the television room for this, the first of four open forums. So, without further ado, let's take our first question."

"Hello, my name is Raymond Smalley. From Littletown, New York. My question is this: Because humans are, by their very nature, violent animals, is it reasonable to anticipate that a free society can mitigate or eliminate violence?"

"Thank you, Mister Smalley, first up will be Miss Leslie Tremaine."

"Sir, I disagree entirely with your basic premise. Humans are not violent by nature, rather they have within them the capacity for violence when they feel threatened or when they are hurt. Fear begets or triggers violence. All animals have this defensive reaction to harm. Humans have, throughout history, subverted the defensive capacity into an offensive action, such as a preemptive strike or an attack long after they perceived they have been injured or wronged. So, to avoid violence, humankind's imperative must ensure that no segments or subsegments of the population are hurt or wronged. No more fear equals no more violence."

"Thank you, Miss Tremaine. Now on to Huang Tsai. Mister Tsai."

"We must cleanly separate violence from action. Violence is rooted in evil because it causes injury, harm, or destruction. Action has no moral value. It can be good or evil depending on its roots and consequences. Situational ethics apply to action. Man acts, but man is not violent. Most people, particularly the older unenlightened ones will take the time or exert the energy to be active, but not violent."

"Elizabeth Pendleton?"

"Yes, humans are and can be violent. We, who are leaders, must set the example of restraint and control. This example in our daily lives clearly communicates to our peers and our children how one should live. To sustain control and thereby provide a safe and secure environment for our children, we must elicit the involvement of governing bodies. The governing bodies must institute a system of protective measures, which will not adversely impact the law abiding, but will protect us all from the violent members of society. Violence has been and will always be a part of the psyche in certain segments of humankind. But we can control it with appropriate measures and constraints."

"Miss Tucker."

"Education is the key. Pure and simple. Humankind, uneducated, is savage. The broader the education base, the better. A thoroughly educated society can take humankind beyond the jungle to understand that violence serves no short-term or long-term good or benefit to society. Opening of education to all people is critical. This will require greater private and governmental involvement in the education process, from pre-school to college. By investing in education, we can be sure to ultimately eliminate violence engendered by ignorance."

"Mister Uhuru."

"Well, education is fine up to a point. But, sooner or later, and most often sooner, all the education in the world falls flat if the educated are not held responsible for their actions. Therein lies the core of violence. I can be loving, neutral, or violent. But, in all cases, I must be responsible. If responsibility is truly enriched in each and every one of us, there will be no violence."

"Miss Ramirez."

"It's amazing. Some of us are skirting the issue of the root of violence. We cannot just usher in a police state and slap control on everyone until they listen like good boys and girls. I, like my learned younger colleague, passionately believe in the concept of responsibility. I look to the male of the species to lead the way as he has over the centuries, and all of it starts with accountability. Men have sustained a pattern of domination without accountability. Today it's manifested in illegitimate births and the abandonment of children. These are violent actions because they harm the psyche of children and women. But, if men are required to be responsible, their actions would lead to the elimination of violence."

"Doctor Wenger, your next and our last contributor to this question."

"Mister Smalley, it is reasonable to hope that we can eliminate violence from our society. I believe that if we look at the trends in this country and throughout the world, we can see this day coming. What brought about these favorable indicators? Education. Solid and very thorough education for all. State supervised curriculum which have led to a fuller realization of one's place vis a vis others and society in general. It's that simple. It is easier to be angry or violent with a stranger than with ourselves. Education will eliminate violence."

"We take this moment for a commercial break. We'll take a second call after the break."

Gene could see each panel member bristling at the others. All the while keeping an ingenuously concerned face to the camera. A mask. There were more moral high grounds in that studio than during a papal election. And tons of ego agitation: The shuffling of papers, the tapping of pens, arms folded and unfolded, seat shifting, knuckle cracking, all the signs of unrest. Unrest caused by panel members having to listen to the canned responses of their associates. God, these intellectual sphincters were out of kilter with each other. Each is so sure he or she is the right voice, that each was dismissed by the others as totally wrong. Dialogue among the crazies. Gibberish and gobbledigook.

To bed before nausea sets in.

VI

Recess. Playtime. Fresh airtime. No teacher staring down from the blackboard time. At one o'clock in early May, it's pleasantly warm in Lutztown, Pennsylvania. The sun bright because it was spring. A bright sun was integral to the planting season. It's been this way for centuries. First the Indians, then the political refugees flocking to Penn's Woods, then the Amish and Mennonites, the religious refugees. They were married to the land. The old ways don't really die; they're just modified ever so slightly every century. They never quite fit with the mode du jour, but the old ways didn't clash that much either. The Amish and Mennonites tried to keep to themselves, as much as possible, to avoid confrontation with the "outlanders." Farming was the primary way to isolate, their own school was another. However, with each generation a few more of the young ones went out among the English, tasted the fruits, both bitter and sweet, of the foreign world, and never came back. Some people hoped for change and some people hoped for no change. Today and here, the children hoped to be first to the slide or the swing. A game of kickball could be started on a Monday and completed during Friday's last recess of the week. This day was no different. So far.

****

The first shot kicked up the soil near the big slide. The second ripped an arm off Leslie Taylor. For a brief moment, the schoolyard was deathly silent: No voices, no yelling, not even Leslie. She was stunned to stone. The kids frozen in time and space. Paralyzed. Not panicky, yet. The crack of the foreshadowed event was so great that even the teachers sitting on the benches sipping coffee were stunned still. Then the outburst. The rain of death from one hundred yards. In the time it took Missus Fellenbaum to put her mug of decaf on the bench, there was a shower of bullets, all concentrated on the four swings and two teeter-totters. Six little bodies were simply heaped onto the ground. Blood gushed from little torsos like grain from punctured burlap sacks. No movement. No sound. As she stood to rush to the fallen, Missus Fellenbaum, mother of one, teacher of twelve years, loses her right leg from the knee down, then her face was removed by the impact of a huge slug. She fell before she screamed in personal pain or distress for her children. Another lump of former human was on the ground.

The cloud of doom showered on the kickball game about fifty feet to the left of the swings. Because the players were dispersed on the unused baseball diamond, the carnage was not intensive. Still, Jimmy Leonard playing second base, Henry Brubaker at one shortstop, and Gwen Wenrich at the other short stop bounced as they fell. Gwen tried to crawl or slide to second. It's impossible to crawl with only one arm and one shoulder as the functional parts of a body that had been traumatized by pain and impact. Her white barrettes, flung from her hair by the impact of the slug, floated in small pools of blood where she fell. Facedown and still, Henry appears to have the kickball resting on his back, but the big red blob was nothing more than the contents of his internal cavity oozing through the hole made by the bullet that entered below his sternum and exited above the base of his spine. His once yellow shirt was now the same crimson as his jeans. Jimmy was seated with eyes open. No motion from the battered life-sized doll on the base. A dime sized hole replaced the polo player monogram on his shirt. A through and through, as the New York City cops would say. Death was instantaneous. Missus Mikler screamed in panic and dove under the concrete and oak bench, spilling her coffee on route.

The cloud of death continued its rush to the building. The teachers and children couldn't see or hear the familiar pelting of big raindrops from the nourishing early spring rains. They could hear the windows and their frames being shattered. Splinters and shards flew twenty feet into the bright sky. The brick walls of the forty-year-old structure lost chunks and chips to the hot metal shower. There was no one inside except the administration staff and the janitor, Les Rutt. At the instant of the downpour, Les was entering Missus Mikler's classroom to empty the wastebasket, check the paper towel dispenser, and touch her chair. This latter was his reason for his duty and the first two were required by his job. He adored Ruth, but she was married, and he was just a school janitor.

His entrance was his exit. His body unceremoniously accepted three slugs and was thrown against the blackboard. The impact of the unplanned meeting of body and slate cracked the slate at the letter G, written in cursive Italics, capital and lowercase. Ruth had written the letter three times on one panel. Three children at a time were required to come to the board and copy her work. Then they would return to their seats to repeat the process from afar. This method would be repeated until everyone could properly, without coaching or example, write the alphabet. This week was G-H-I. The lesson stopped before recess. Les's body and blood erased a great deal of hard work by Bobby Slotkin, Jack Messersmith, and Georgianna Kunzler.

The children outside were now in true panic modality. Most of them were running aimlessly, screaming at the top of their lungs. A few of them were standing stalk-still and staring, nowhere in particular. Billy Stow tripped over Mary Ruth Martin's body. He fell and scraped his knees and hands. He whined in pain. Mary Ruth's body did not move. She said nothing because she had no jaw.

Assistant Principal, Gerald Dance leapt into action, a rare activity for a life-long bureaucrat. He ran on the outer rim of the gaggle of panic. Herded the children by waving his arms in a constant upward and outward motion directing the little ducks to the side of the school away from the frenzy. He called their names, imploring, demanding, and pleading for them to run to the safe place. This activity is both good and bad. Most of the children respond as required and flock to the comer. Some stand immobilized by panic and pandemonium. The standers present obstacles to the others seeking safety around the comer. Small jumbles of small bodies cropped up, then dissipated as the on-rushers rush on. As the herd clumped, each clump became a target for renewed onslaught. The herd was being culled because they were there. Not genetics. Not race, creed, or color. Just presence in the yard.

Mister Dance presented a substantial target, and although he was active, his motion was not rapid enough to reduce his vulnerability. One slug twisted him completely around. He staggered backward, turned, and pushed forward, ever herding. He moved around the circle of innocent humanity. The second slug drove his face to the earth. He pushed himself up to his knees, screamed to the children to run and hide. He turned to see if the other teachers were following his lead. The he took the third and final round about one half an inch above the bridge of his nose. His dandruff encrusted scalp was lifted from front to back, the mental machinery spewed into the air, and Mister Dance flopped on his back. Gerald Dance, too young for one war and too old for the next, died on the playground. The last of the students and three teachers scurried around the building to safety. All was well except for the eleven third graders, two teachers, a janitor, and an Assistant Principal. In less time than it took to write the three letters of the week, fifteen universes were obliterated. There was no life on or in them.

****

"How come reloading takes so damned much time? You'd think the companies that make these guns would have figured a way to shorten the time it takes to remove the spent clip, insert a fresh one, and get a load into the breach. Shit, somebody could get hurt or killed just getting ready to re-fire."

Georgie Greiner always complained about something. Nothing was ever good enough for him. His ego and his father told him he deserved perfection in people and things around him. His father felt he deserved perfection and beat this into George Junior. George Senior was always getting the short end or the filthy end of the stick. People and businesses tried to cheat him or take advantage of his good and giving nature. He was Number One on the union grievance list in both quantity and complexity of complaints against Lutztown Machinery. Somehow the union covered for George. Took his grievances to the company and covered his frequent post payday absences with alibis. George Junior learned from the master. Now, the gun didn't work to his ideal.

"Shut up, you pussy. You're always bitching about something. Now you have a chance to make everything right, for people to take you seriously. Make your mark. And what do you do but piss and moan? Ya' know a little less bitchin' and a little more finger twitchin' would do you a world of good."

Freddie Douts was a bully. George needed this father figure, but Freddie was extreme. He had a tattoo on his back that read, 'Take no prisoners and rip the watches off the dead.' Freddie loved to hunt. The gentler the game, the better he liked to kill it. Rabbits were perfect. There were over twenty guns in his household on Duke Road. His formal education stopped at the tenth grade, state minimum. He went to work with his dad and two older brothers fixin' stuff around other people's houses, mowin' lawns, plowin' driveways in the winter. General handyman activities. The quality of their work was satisfactory. Never exemplary. Their living was modest, but the family needs were more. Or so they were convinced. And, while there was never enough for better basics, there was always money for personal indulgences, such as many rifles and handguns, regular visits to the local saloons, and several partially repaired tractors and trucks. Viewed from a normal plateau, the Douts clan lived just above the poverty line in a junkyard.

Freddie was the baby and spoiled rotten by his dim-witted mother, who was also his father's cousin. Therein lies the root of the problem: He got what he demanded. Stomped his feet. Screamed. Pushed. Even hit. Mom took it. Dad looked the other way because Freddie was just following a fine family tradition. Freddie even beat up his older brothers. All he was good at was bullying, and he was damned good. He was a regular on the county sheriff's sign-in sheet. Four times he had been charged with breaking and entering and vandalism. Four times he had been excused, and four times his family covered the cost of the damages by doing odd jobs around the property. Freddie always promised to be good. He lied.

"Yah, Georgie, you're nothin' but a big pussy. Cryin' because you've been fucked by everybody. Well, now it's your turn to do the fuckin' and you're still bawling. Maybe we shoulda' brought along your titty bottle to make you feel good. You don't hear me bein' a baby."

"Shit, Al, all you ever say is what Freddie says. Can't that pea brain of yours come up with its own thoughts?

You're nothin' but Freddie's echo shadow."

Alvin Slaughter was dumber than a box of rocks. On top of that, he was fat and ugly. A great three-way combination that endeared him to his chronological peers. If someone can be the butt of jokes, Al was the prime, fat bun tightly puckered aperture. His folks even picked on Al. They thought it was just cute teasing. He was hurt by it all. His sister rarely acknowledged their relationship and never wanted to be seen with Al in public. He was good at and for nothing. Barely read. Loved cartoons with the big pictures and those on TV. Could write his name and little else. No hygiene habits. Same clothes every day. A fucking mess that didn't care. But Al was a great follower who harbored as much hatred for the outside world as trust in Freddie. He made Mortimer Snerd look like an independent thinker. He was a parrot to all the venom Freddie could spew. All the cruel words that made Freddie feel bigger and better made Al feel alive. Someone cared. His idol cared.

The three warriors against life had embarked upon a path of social and personal destruction, driven by anger and their desire to do better than the punks in Carter and Menthen. If those assholes could kill, George, Freddie, and Al could destroy. Quality was more important than quantity. Sure, anybody could shoot fifteen little weenies in a hall or school bus, where they couldn't run, but these three had sworn to shoot in an open area. More motion. The targets could duck and cover. More difficult for the hunters. More credit for the shooters. Plus, they wanted to take out some pigs. Those rotten motherfucker cops who had chased and harassed the three over the recent years. Shooting the kids was bait in the trap. It was now payback time. They were secure in their keep.

The bunker from which they shot had a rock wall, eight feet high at the rear. On the other side of the wall was a straight drop of thirty feet. So, attack from the rear was out of the question. The earthen front had three slits carved into it. The slits were nine inches high and two feet across. Between the bunker's front wall and the rock wall was a trench ten feet long, three feet wide, and seven feet deep. There were little steps at each slit, so the boys could fire then step down into the safety of the trench and reload or get a new gun. The trench was a good replica of those in World War One. They each had two automatic rifles and a handgun. The rifles' clips, barrel and banana, held from twenty-five to forty-five rounds. The handguns were matched. Blue black forty-four caliber Ravens. Fourteen in the clip and one in the chamber. Boxes of ammunition appropriate to each boy's weaponry sat in three small wooden boxes at the right side of the appropriate slit. There were cooler chests of food and water. The food was of surprisingly high nutritional value. No junk. Fruit. Bread. Meats. Eight gallons of water. A large pee hole at the south end of the trench and plastic bags for the collection of feces. The bags would then be lobbed over the rock wall. Like defenders of a castle. This operation had been planned and prepped scrupulously for weeks.

Freddie and Georgie had never been inside the downtown library before, but this time was special, and the old ladies even showed them how to use the computers. Got on the Internet for books and pamphlets that they could take home and study, helped them with the details. They stole the material with the diagrams from the local Army and Navy store on

Prince Street. They had thought of everything and were proud of their efforts. They knew people would talk about them for years to come. They would be immortal while all the smart-ass turd balls, who had made their lives miserable, would die and be forgotten.

The police bullhorn noise came from the side of the school: "Put down your weapons and show yourself."

The response was immediate.

"How stupid do the cops think we are? 'Show yourselves.' Yah, show yourself and be shot. Hey, assholes, why don't you come up here and make us show ourselves? We can pull down our pants and show you the big ones we got."

The bullhorn stolen from The Big Store had proven its worth in one use. For the moment, the three teenage gladiators could taunt the authorities. The thugs were truly above the rest.

"Al ... George. It's time to show them how serious we are. Take your weapon with scope sight and cause some real damage to the badge bandits."

The three carefully slid their versions of sniper rifles through the openings and targeted three different policemen. In rapid succession, twelve shots exploded from the face of the hill. Two cops went down and the third dove under the squad car.

"Hey, dummies, why don't you put down your weapons and show yourselves? How big are your balls? We'll waste you just like the little kids." The taunting chief bully was feeling powerful.

Al was so excited he peed himself and George's face was twitching as if he had some form of palsy. Freddie was in complete control and the hormones rushing through him were giving him an erection. Power was an aphrodisiac and killing was the ultimate power. He wanted to masturbate, to mark the moment, but he knew these two fools would not understand his action. So, he gave each one a big hug and small kiss on the cheek. They were his army. They knew, but didn't want to know, they were going to die. Just like the innocent children at the school. It's what he wanted and what he had planned: Die in a blaze of glory. Defending the keep against the evil authorities. The oppressors. Three righteous avengers. Dying for their honor.

"Waste the little bitches and the blue bastards."

Before the bullies could fire, the first return shot from near the school tore into the center slit and made it a little wider. The second and third shots hit around the opening. No damage. Then there was silence. The boys remounted the steps and returned fire. Spray and pray. They extracted their weapons and sat on the floor of the trench. Four more thumps around each cleft. Once more a return of fire. Withdraw. Ten minutes went by. Suddenly there was a tremendous fusillade around the firing portals and the top of the trench. As the two boys were about to mount the steps to return fire, Freddie waved them off.

"The fucks are just sighting us. If we fire back now, they will rain holy hell at the slits. So, we wait, because we can wait. We have ammunition and supplies. We can wait until they offer us the respect we deserve. Remember, we're better than all of them. We're on top." Freddie had the situation under control.

"But what if they just wait forever?"

"George, you're bellyachin' again. Shut the fuck up."

"Al, pass out water and an apple for each of us."

Dutifully, Al did as he was ordered.

Twenty minutes passed. Freddie crept up the center step and peered out the slit, "Holy fuckin' shit. You guys gotta see this. There must be ten squad cars, four firetrucks, half a dozen ambulances and three SWAT vans. They know we're for real. I guess the first priority for them is to remove our kill. Then settle in for the siege. Don't both of you jump up here at once. But you gotta see this."

First Al, then George was impressed by the reactions to their actions. Hell, they even knew some of the firemen and two ambulance drivers. Certainly, they were on speaking terms with the local cops, not the state troopers or the SWAT members. They counted the vehicles the way a hunter counts the points on a buck's antlers. They were smug with their accomplishments but failed to notice the black van parked beneath the elms about two hundred yards away from the rear of the redoubt. The boys couldn't see the man to the side of the black van giving orders and the men taking them. Blissfully unaware, euphoria set in. Big grins and laughter. No one really knows when the end is coming.

"Well, men, let's let them know we are still here. Fire at will. Empty your clip. Drop back and rest. At the count of three. One. Two. Three."

Three boys, three slits, three scoped rifles. Three shots from behind them. Al died instantly. Georgie lost his right ear and was screaming in pain. Freddie couldn't see because the bullet from somewhere kicked dirt into his face.

"Fuck, man I'm hit. Help me."

Then the explosions. Grenades that stun and tear gas that blinds. The trench filled with confusion. Freddie and Georgie are twisting and scrambling in a daze seeking fresh air and comfort from the pain in their heads. "George, shoot at the top of the trench. Above the slits. That's where they're coming. Shoot anywhere and you'll get a few, like this."

Freddie knew the end was near. Somehow the police had gotten up the hill. Maybe because the boys couldn't see down the slope, only outward from the slits. Freddie emptied his clip and started to pull his Raven. Four slugs slammed him and drove him to the bottom of the trench. Four slugs from behind. George never got off a shot as one well directed magnum stilled his complaining forever. The impenetrable had been penetrated and justice was meted out. Two men dressed in camouflage had come over the back wall and ended the skirmish. The two shadow shooters disappeared faster than the smoke cleared. Back over the wall. Down the drop. Into the waiting van. Exit stage left. The play is over. Draw the curtain. No audience applause.

****

The school would never be the same. The town was forever changed. But the Amish and Mennonites will plow, plant, grow, harvest, sell, and consume. This permanent cycle would not be altered by a little bump in the road.

The shock quasi-news media mavens were all over this horrific episode like paint on a house. Not real time on the scene coverage, because it all happened so fast. From start to finish in less than thirty minutes. Enough time for the police to set up roadblocks designed to both keep out and keep in. Before the TV trucks and their crews could figure a way around the circled wagons, the slaughter was over. The bad dudes are dead. The black van was on the road again. There were no in-progress pictures, motion or still. And the police had removed the dead and wounded. Everywhere was proof, the result of the carnage: pools of blood, glass and brick shards and body fragments. Hysterical children and adults were receiving treatment in ambulances and then escorted to their homes. So, it was up to the aggrandizing imaginations of the missed targets, three passersby and the reporters to create a complete story. The who, why, when, where, what, and how differed slightly by TV network. Some facts were constant, but the overall thrusts and underlying factors were so unknown that speculation served as truth.

The county sheriff and a major in the state police fielded all questions. Some of them as badly as Marv Thronberry of the original Mets. One reporter dared to ask, how this could all happen so rapidly. How could the police arrive so quickly after the start of the shooting? How could a command center be established? How could it be drawn to a conclusion without the usual standoff and siege? How did the police know to scale the escarpment behind the salient? Who was in charge? All the unanswered questions were referred to a later news conference in the Lutztown High School Auditorium. Tomorrow at eight am. Thank you. Exit stage right.

Television shows were interrupted all night to bring the audience of bloodsuckers all the latest non-news. A loop repetition of the day's events. Profiles of the killers, the school, and the families of the slain. Fluff with just a smidgen of reality to justify the intrusion into the safety and security of dens and living rooms. Mary was in the ComRoom. Gene was reading some incredibly bad magazines and drifting off to sleep.

VII

Jim Larson of United Press International returned Gene's call and was very pleasant once Gene's connection to a mutual friend was introduced. Jim gave Gene the name of Mike Duncan, a freelance photographer, who was responsible for the shots at the Big Pass Rally. Mike was homebased in San Diego but was wired to the world. Jim felt sure Mike would be willing to part with a dupe neg or a blowup of the original. UPI could not put any pressure on him. The shooter owned what he shot and just leased the shot to the wire service. Mike was a 1099...there was never an employment agreement. Gene thanked Jim and called Mike.

"Mister Duncan, this is Gene Benton. I was referred to you by Jim Larson at UPI. He thought you could be of help to me..."

"Hi, Mister Benton. How do you know Jim Larson?"

"Jim is a friend of a friend. He thought you might be able to help me. Actually, my sister and me. You see, we understand you took some photos at Senator Baldwin Miller's S.A.F.E. rally in Big Pass, Kansas the other week. The photo made our local fish wrap along with the obligatory caption, which said nothing. We're interested in getting either a copy of the negative or a blow-up of the original shot. Is that possible?"

"Really? Well, I have a number of great shots from the rally. I took a couple of rolls. How do you plan to use my work?"

"We don't want to use it, just review it. Explore it."

"Why?"

"That's personal but I will send you a notarized affidavit that the photos or any parts thereof will not be used in any way commercially. And, of course, we'll pay you for your time, material, and pain and suffering for letting loose your babies."

"Payment is a given. What I must know before I agree to anything is why."

"The why should be of no concern to you Mister Duncan."

"Please, call me Mike. And the why is of paramount concern to me."

"OK, Mike, the why is personal and somewhat convoluted. Here goes: My niece was one of the children killed in Carter, Wyoming. My sister is a computer whiz. She captured all the footage of the incident and analyzed the pee out of it. To her, there are a few faces that are unexplained. Faces that were there for some unknown reason. People in the background and the shadows. I realize this sounds paranoid. You know, just another grand conspiracy theory like who really killed JFK? She now claims that she recognized some of the same faces at the Big Pass rally. So, she is making a quantum leap in her thinking process. She just needs to confirm or refute her suspicions. I understand this all sounds crazy, but I owe it to her to help find answers. Put to rest much of the angst that rages in her soul at the loss of her daughter. Does this make sense?"

"Somewhat. Or it may be the best damned smokescreen I've ever heard. On the surface, it seems harmless enough; if you'll fax me the signed document you mentioned and agree to pay one hundred dollars for each negative and shot I send you. All at my discretion."

"That's steep, considering we just want to look at them. And how do we know we will be getting negs of everything you shot at the rally and not just the ones you want to send us or the supposed good ones."

"I'll gladly send you dupes of all the shots. As I said, there are about fifty. So, you can see every dark corner, shadowy profile, and out of focus countenance. But first I'll need the letter and the money. Cash. No checks."

"What assurance do we get that what we're getting is everything we ask for."

"My word."

"And your understanding that if you are less than truthful, you'll have a tough time selling another photo to the wires services. Notice I used the plural."

"I don't take kindly to threats, Mister Benton."

"That was not a threat. It was a promise. A threat involves the potential for violence. I am not a violent man, but I have friends in high places. I'll discuss this with my sister and, if she agrees, I will draft the letter for both our signatures. Hopefully, I can fax the letter to you by tomorrow for your notarized signature. Then I'll overnight the money to you. And you can overnight the negatives back to us. Is that fair?"

"Sounds fair. I'd like to get this deal wrapped up very quickly."

"Do I sense a cash bind, Mike?"

"That's none of your concern."

"I need your fax number and a physical address. FedEx will not deliver to a post office box, and FedEx is all I use." *Not really true, but I am a negotiator and I want control.*

"Only one number. Just press the pound key during the message. It automatically kicks over and I receive. And the address is 1221 Hunsicker Avenue, San Diego, California, 80045. By tomorrow then, OK?'

"OK. One way or the other, you'll hear from me."

****

Mary said yes before Gene told her all the details. The amount was chump change relative to her pain and anxiety. Besides, she was convinced the photos would unlock the riddle or, at least, shine a light on the path of knowledge. Gene drafted the letter, emailed it to her in the ComRoom. She made a few revisions. Emailed it back to Gene with her signature already on it. Attached was a copy of her driver's license confirming her name and signature to be notarized. Not quite kosher, but close enough for my bosom buddy (bad choice of words) in payroll. The letter was notarized and faxed a day early. Hell, within two hours of the conversation with Mike Duncan. It came back signed, but not notarized in thirty minutes. Gene resent the original and demanded notarization. The second response was dutifully executed by someone named Rahjid at The Mail Bin. Mary had wired the necessary funds to Gene's bank account. With a series of clicks and he was instantly, but temporarily, richer.

Gene left work for an hour, got the five thousand dollars in hundreds, and took the bundle to FedEx. Never use the office FedEx account. No need for anyone else to know. He felt a little paranoid. The complete package, including the appropriate return envelope, was sent to his new BFF. Then, the wait. Will he return the negs? All the negs? Just how trustworthy was this unknown, but recommended individual? What leverage did Gene have if he got fucked over? Truly little. Mike must not know that. Gene waited and stewed. His time limit before he took corrective action was seventy-two hours. After that, the first step will be to call. Second step will be to get Jim Larson to call. The third and final assertive action would be to fax letter outlining the points in Gene's lawsuit. We are a litigious society.

****

Before lunch of the second day, the mail boy delivered a FedEx package addressed in Gene's hand. The sucker was thick. Gene couldn't wait. He was like a kid who got a toy with his hamburger and fries. He was told to not open the package until the family got home. Fat chance. Gene scattered the photos and negs over the office table. He could easily put the negs in sequence by roll, but he didn't know which roll was shot first. Then there was the hand scrawled note:

This is everything. More than I had thought. Sixty-five is sufficient. I won't ask for more money, 'cause a deal is a deal. I would like to know what you find. I plan to cover Senator Miller's campaign for my pictorial of grassroots politics. If I know what you want, I will be sure to get it for us.

Somehow the math didn't compute. Three rolls of twenty-four would be seventy-two. Two rolls of thirty-six would be seventy-two. No matter what combination Gene tried, he couldn't get sixty-five. Mike said fifty. But he sent sixty-five. He should have sent seventy-two. Was he holding something back? Was he just a bad shooter and seven shots were wasted? Should Gene call Jim Larson and dig deeper into Mike's talents? The prick held some back. As many as seven. Were these critical? For now, this would be a secret. Back in the envelope. Home to Mary.

***

"The mother lode. You done good, boy. Now I need to scan all of these in sequence. Which roll was shot first?"

"Tried to figure that out, but failed, Mary. Does that really matter?"

"When you're performing an autopsy, you must eliminate all extraneous factors. It will take me hours to scan and format the photos and even longer to get the material ready for enlargement and fact extraction. What's for dinner? By the way, I invited a dear friend to stop by this evening. I promise she won't hit you.

"Her name is Karen Leach. I met her through my internet network a bunch of years ago. Then, numerous times at conventions for the teaching nerds, like me. She was a vendor then. I had forgotten that she lived up the road in Lake Wetton. I think you'll like her. She is smart as hell and takes no shit from kids or men. Quiet divorce about three years ago. You may have even read about what caused the divorce, but at the time you didn't know the players or the result of the activity. Karen discovered, just in time, that hubby dearest was using their finances to amass a snow mass big enough for skiers. His plan was to move the Peruvian nose candy to the Northeast and unload it. Feds and state narcs short-circuited his plans by about two days. She was in hot water for a while. He tried to implicate her to lighten his hit. Fortunately, the narcs saw through his lie, used him to get the sellers and distributors in New York, Baltimore, and Boston. The entire operation netted about forty missing links in the coke chain. Mark, that's the husband, is in the Witness Protection Program somewhere. Karen lives an almost protected life. The feds just keep a casual eye on her to make sure that she is safe. That's probably more than you needed or wanted to know. She can be assertively hostile. So be kind and somewhat invisible."

****

"Thrown out of my own house. The last time that happened was that Labor Day party at home when the folks were up in New England. You remember the party that started on Thursday before Labor Day and ran straight until noon on Tuesday after the Holiday. Thirteen fifty-five-gallon drums of empty bottles and beer cans. Food to feed Ethiopia for a week. Hundreds of people at the house. Many of whom I never knew. Well, two Yalies, who were there as guests of Artie Mann, thought I was too drunk and obnoxious and threw me out of the house. My return and introduction caused the little snotbags to turn red. I ushered them out the backdoor. Now, ions later, some dolly I've never met is forcing me into the back bedroom with the door closed just because she had a bad marriage. She is probably a dyke anyway. And yes, I'm pissed."

"I spy her car lights. Be a pleasant dear and get the door. Be nice, or I'll deal with you later."

These were the words and tones of my mother. The small knot from years ago appeared in my stomach, just below and behind the actual gut.

I must do right. If I just did as I am told, no more and no less, I'd be safe. Must try not to speak too much. Because of the tension, I'd stutter for sure. Fuck, I hated old emotional recordings. It took three twists of the lock and a hard turn of the handle to open a door that Gene opened quickly and easily about ten thousand times before. His hands were clammy. *I'm sure I am sweating and look pale.* As the door swings inward, Gene turns on the porch light.

There she was. *The object of my historical neurosis. The raison d'etre for all my nervousness. A vision. A nightmare. I stood and stared for roughly six hundred hours. She is my sister's friend.* Initially, perceived as intrusive, she was transformed into desirable in about four tremendous heart thumps. Gene flashed back to the high school sophomores who were geekettes when he was a senior, but who were incredibly desirable by the time he finished Brown. Did they really get better looking or did he just become more discerning? Karen reminded him of the neighbor who is not gorgeous, but who gets better and better looking with each Fourth of July picnic and Christmas party. She was dressed nicely yet looked comfortable, but not sloppy. Low maintenance.

Self-reliant. Beautiful in a long-term way. The impact of her presence quickened his pulse to well above 80.

"Hello, my name is Karen Leach. I've come to see Mary Benton. Is she at home?"

She extended her right hand. Gene's corresponding appendage obediently rose from his side. The limp fish was in the firm grasp of a warm, non-threatening soft hand. Gene barely moved his arm. She had to do the greeting shake. Their hands were directly over the doorframe. Gene was safely inside the house and this attractive, but threatening psychic force was on the outside.

"May I come in?"

Gene snapped back to real time and space, "I'm t-t-terribly sorry. Forgive m-my rudeness. Of course, Mary is here. P-p-p-p-please come in, won't you."

Gene thought he had achieved perfection...as in perfect asshole. He had retro-morphed and become a teenager. The only two things missing were acne and a cracking voice. The stutter, the perspiration marks, and hand clamminess signaled that this quivering mess of a male standing before Karen was totally out of control. This hadn't happened in years. Not since he met the daughter of the Chairman of Intx. And all she wanted to do was coke and screw. How can he break this trance? If he spoke loudly and quickly, she wouldn't notice his state of discombobulation. *Yeah, right.*

"Mary, Karen is here. Let me show you to her ComRoom, an ever-decreasing space she shares with two large dogs and more electronic stuff than my mind can deal with. Would you like a drink? Beer? Hard liquor? Coffee? Tea? Soda? Water? Can I get you anything to eat?"

As he walked her down the hall, he continued to yammer never giving her a chance to answer. Finally, they completed the odyssey to the open door, "Watch out for the cables and wires. These are the dogs, Hither and Yon. And Mary."

"Karen. So nice to see you. Come on into my lair. I'm just scanning some photos and negatives. A mindless process. What have you been up to? How's the job? We have so much to catch up. Where to start? Where to start?"

That was Gene's cue to exit: "Excuse me, will you? I have some work to review. We're looking to add to our staff. I'll be in the den if you need anything. It's nice to have you in my house, Karen. Please make yourself at home."

****

Gene turns on the TV after he pours a tall strong one. He hopes the trembling will stop after a few sips. This was the second installment of President's Commission on Citizen Safety bestowing rhetoric on the unwashed. Broadcast once again in a safe hideout away from the contamination of truth and humanity. Tonight, was also the second of Baldwin Miller's town meetings. He'd really taken it to the streets. This time Bricklersville, Tennessee. It seemed that the stations from Nashville and Atlanta sent crews. Nothing would be broadcast live. Just filmed reports with highlights and post-tirade interviews. Was he becoming The Mouse That Roared?

"Mary, Senator Miller is conducting a tent revival somewhere in Tennessee. Should we get the footage?"

"What the hell do you think?"

"I'll call Tony Seton at Channel Ten and see if he can scrounge the footage, used and unused, from his counterparts who are covering the event."

The phone call took thirty seconds. He'll be glad to oblige. The tapes would be sent in a few days. Can't reveal urgency. Just strong curiosity. Now Gene owed Tony...six hours of handling the incoming calls during the County Wide Charity Telethon in September. Quid pro quo.

Listening to the blathering of all the President's men and women, Gene realized, this was no more fact finding or pulse taking than a college professor's lecture. People asked and were told what to think. With Sessler's stooges there were various versions of reality or truth. Gene wondered if there were some sort of immediate electronic poll conducted with each query. Who in the television audience believed which of the panel the most? Which one of the responses touched the greatest number of hot buttons? This being the assumption, the extension was that this data would be reviewed and analyzed by others. The final report, most likely, would become a white paper for the President, who could then urge Congress to pass laws. These laws, being the voice of the people, would be designed to provide new or strengthened safeguards for all. The assumption seemed reasonable and the extension logical. But, then again, Gene had been married twice and bet on the Saint Louis Cardinals to win the National League Pennant each year. He surfed to CNN to see if any of Senator Miller's barnstorming was being aired or analyzed. Financial news greeted him. He left the security of his den and ventured into the witch's lair.

****

"I'm fixing some cheese and fruit. Would you two like some or a drink of any kind?"

"That would be nice. A plate of whatever you're having and some iced tea for me. Karen?"

"That sounds perfect. No sugar. Just lemon in the tea."

Now that he promised, he'd better deliver. Gouda, Brie and Caraway Swiss. Water crackers. Green grapes, orange slices and strawberries. Two large glasses of cold tea with lemon in one and lemon and sugar in the other. A small carafe for refills. God, it looks like a feast for Caesar. Delivered.

"If you need anything else, let me know."

Well, he didn't stutter. But he must have acted like a little boy with a terrible crush on one of his older sister's friend. So? Back to the den just in time to see them go live to Bricklersville, Tennessee.

****

"This is Mary Fulton, from Bricklersville, Tennessee, the scene of the second in Senator Baldwin Miller's stops on his nationwide tour. The purpose of the tour is to promote S.A.F.E., Secure America For Everyone. Senator Miller plans to travel to small towns throughout the country, asking people what can be done to, and these are his words, keep them safe from the rampant violence that is threatening the very essence of the country. We've talked to a few of the people who attended the rally and here are their comments:

"The man makes sense to me. He asked us for our views. You can tell he listens. He's got people on the stage taking notes and he promises to incorporate our wishes in his program."

"It's about time the Washington bigwigs came to us and asked what we wanted. Maybe we ought to get the ideas on the ballot and tell Congress and the President what to do. I mean, that's what they're in Washington to do anyway."

"I think S.A.F.E. is a good idea. I just don't believe our elected officials can agree on anything but higher taxes. Not all the people are going to agree on everything. But this is really important. It's worth a try, because we have nothing else. This country is going to hell in a handbasket and we are the only ones who can stop the destruction."

"These are just a few of the comments. It does seem that the Senator from Pennsylvania is stirring up a lot of interest in his program. It also seems the Senator is running for a higher political office. This is Mary Fulton, CNN, Bricklersville, Tennessee."

****

"Ladies, may I clear?"

"Yes, Jeeves, I mean, Gene."

"Sister you're so kind. Then I am to bed. See you tomorrow, Mary. It was nice to meet you, Karen. I hope to see you again soon."

"OK, how about tomorrow evening? I'll bring the dinner and the three of us can get to know each other better. No separate rooms. Agreeable?"

Her smile was genuine and inviting. Gene had to refocus, so as to not stutter or make an ass out of himself, again.

"That sounds terrific. About six?"

"I look forward to the evening very much. See you then. Good night."

Gene was enticed, promised, and dismissed in thirteen words. His emotions were aflame. His mind spun like a waterspout; he went to bed.

VIII

There was an edge in Mary's voice Gene had never heard. She seemed to be talking in circles. And she was using the home landline, not her cell phone.

"Gene, this is no longer weird. It's frightening. A few of my suppositions and suspicions are closer to the truth than I had thought possible: The faces, the people, the process. It's more than we want to know, and way much more than I can deal with."

"Hey, you're talking in crypto-ese. Slow down and give me details."

"I can't over the phone. When can you come home? It's really important we talk, and you see what I've found."

"This afternoon is slow. Whatever I have, I can push to tomorrow. Let me clean up some stuff, and I'll be home in about ninety minutes. OK?"

"See you then. And thanks for indulging me. You won't be disappointed. Fearful, yes. Disappointed, no."

A few odds and ends to clear up. The drive home was mindless except for the stop at Food-A-Rama. About to pick up something for dinner when Gene realized that was Karen's duty. So, he got two bottles of a '92 California Merlot.

****

"OK now, sis, what is so damned important that it was necessary to pry me away from the fun factory?"

"Sit and just listen. After you went to bed last night, I stayed up and went back into the nether world of chatrooms. I was GirlFromOz again. I went to three new ones, BloodNourishment, JonnyGetYourGun, and HandsHeldHigh. They were similar to the two we entered the other evening. Somewhat more violent, as you would expect from their names, but all seem substantially similar. Well, I went from room to room, and chatted with the occupants. One sweep. Then I went back to HouseAfire and BoldWorld. I uncovered something strange. Immediately after my Dorothy's posting in HouseAfire came a posting from TruthSeeker and immediately after the posting in BoldWorld there was a post from BrokenArrow."

"Yes, and what does that have to do with anything?"

"Please listen, then we'll talk. I found TruthSeeker and BrokenArrow had posted immediately after I had posted in all three rooms. This is too much for coincidence. I posted a second time, then I went back to HouseAfire and BoldWorld for Dorothy's third visit and found my new best friends had come in after my second posting. I have not posted anything inflammatory or confrontational, yet these two have spotted me, or Dorothy, and they are now tracing my every step. If they can trace me, I have to believe they might have the technology to back track my entry and locate my system and physical situation. Said another way, I'm willing to bet they, whoever they are, know where I, we, live. If they know where we live, they can monitor our lives. Our computer activity. Our telephone conversations. Fuck, even our garbage if they are so inclined. These chatters, I am convinced, are not amateurs. They are professional hackers of some sort. Most likely feds. I'm not sure what that does for them, but it scares the hell out of me. "

"Whoa, big girl. Take it easy. You have taken an increasingly slippery trip down the anxiety trail. What you have discovered, may or may not have any basis in reality. From this, you make a set of assumptions which are just that, assumptions without irrefutable confirmation. From these assumptions, you have made several SWAGs, that's Scientific Wild Ass Guesses. So, at the end of the process, you are in a Twilight Zone. Now, you call us to act and react as if the ubiquitous and ever evil are right outside our windows about to unleash a death ray. I love you, but you stayed up all night and are suffering from sleep deprivation, which fuels your natural grief caused by the loss of your daughter. So, before we go off sealing the house in an electronic cocoon and fashioning tinfoil hats for both of us, you need to get some sleep, and we need to review all the information in the cool light of a well-rested morning."

"I realize this must sound bonkers to you, the unschooled in cyber technology. Like I was finding evil behind each and every door. But I'm not through revealing my discoveries. This has way more substance than the Kennedy Murder

Conspiracy Theories. So, just be quiet and listen to this."

There was a razor-sharp edge to her voice and demeanor. She was tired, afraid, angry, and frustrated. So, Gene listened.

"Remember all the photos from that guy in San Diego? Well, we hit the mother lode of no such thing as coincidence. I scanned them, got them in some fashion of sequence, and examined them. Look what I found."

She wheeled to the keyboard and began to work her magic.

"I'll pull up shots of Senator Miller's rally at Big Pass. Shots of his entourage on stage, then two shots of the audience. What do you see? You see three male faces in both places. On stage and in the audience. Obviously not at the same time. Blonde. Ruggedly handsome. Immensely powerful looking. They look more like bodyguards than political advisors. Now, I'll move the pictures of the three to screen left and pull up some stills we got from my friends in Carter. See those guys near the black van? They are the same three. Partial faces, body shapes and sizes, and clothes. It's a match."

"Mary, slow down. You are running so fast in circles all you can see is your own backside. I see the blurred outlines of what may or may not be men's faces. Blurred faces in Mike Duncan's photos and really blurred face profiles in the stills taken from videos in Carter. These pictures are so many generations removed from the original they don't even know their great, great, great grandparents' names. You're asking for a connective leap of faith I cannot make. And here is the big question: If we assume that the faces are somehow the same, what the hell does that have to do with the chatroom retracing? Jesus, Mary, you've gone over the line. This is like an episode of some drug induced parlor game. Except it's no game to you or me."

"Christ, Gene, stop being so fucking dense. The retracing is real. Retracing is done with cookies implanted in any form of communication by people who want to know who is in their chatroom. Once the cookie is inserted, the inserter can follow it wherever it goes. Imagine a transponder placed on a shark. The elasmobranchologist can follow the shark wherever he goes, that way the shark's migration and other important information can be learned and understood. The shark never knows he has been tagged, just like someone visiting the chatroom never knows his message has been tagged. That's the how. It's the why that's unknown. The men in the pictures are the same. They are stormtroopers for someone. We just don't know for whom. I'm on to something. And, if you don't believe me or won't help me, go away, and I'll get help elsewhere. I'll call Karen."

Her voice was now at shrill intensity. Her eyes were welling up with tears: Tears of frustration and fatigue. Her hands were trembling when they were not vise gripped on the arms of her chair.

"Look, let's agree to put all this aside for a few hours. You get some sleep, and we'll review all the material this evening when Karen is here. OK?"

"You're stalling me, you luddite. But you'll see the folly of your ways tonight. I'll show the material to Karen. She'll see my wisdom. Plus, she is objective. Then you won't be able to refute the truth of an objective third party. Now I need a rest before company."

Yes, Gene was stalling. Why did Mary have to set up a 'him versus them' battle zone? That shit went back to when they were children. He didn't like it then, and he really doesn't like it now. Particularly in his house and including an uninvited houseguest. Maybe he should go around to each of the corners in every room and mark his territory with pee. No sister allowed. Whoa. This was not good. They're fighting about something unknown, which was like the argument dealing with thirteen or twenty angels on the head of the Friar's sewing needle. What did all this mean? Could somebody really retrace the entry to a chatroom? Could somebody learn where they lived? And, therefore, who they were? Once they found them, what's next? Did they just keep them under surveillance like lab rats? Beat them up? Kill them? Did they tap their phones? How could they find out? Gene had seen an ad for a device that could show if a telephone was bugged. One of those anti-theft systems for international travelers or guys who thought everybody wanted to know what they were thinking and talking about. There's profit in paranoia. How come Gene and Mary were so important that somebody would want to spend time and money keeping them under watch?

And those photos. What a crock. The distance of the subject from the lens made details impossible. Just hauntingly vague similarities. No face shots. Only profiles and three-quarter looks. Second, there was a limited number of big, blond guys in this country. But did they travel in sets of three or four. And just happened to be in the land of the outdoor blondes, Wyoming and Kansas.

There was no apparent logical connection between the images. One set was at a shooting, the other at a political rally. The same could be said about the male subjects. One set functioned in the capacity of crime scene control. The other as the entourage of a politician. However, Gene accepted the fact that if they had been at the shooting and the rally, they should be the subjects of Mary's inquiry. But were they? Aye, there's the rub.

There was absolutely no connection whatsoever between the blurry pictures and the Internet chatrooms. Gene saw that as clear as day, and it should be so to Mary. But she was grasping at straws in a desperate drive to understand what happened to her daughter and why. Gene helped her to her bedroom. She slid out of the chariot, he covered her with a blanket, and she was asleep in two minutes.

The damned doorbell. Good God Almighty, it was Karen because it's six.

****

"Welcome, Karen. It's nice to know the Avon Lady has been replaced by the Dinner Lady. Let me show you what's where in the kitchen. I'll awaken Mary in about an hour. She threw an all-nighter last night. Now she is napping. OK. Here are the pots, pans, and lids. The mixing bowls. Utensils. Spices. What else do you need for now?"

"This all looks fine. Let me get started. Then, join me."

"When she awakens, Mary will be groggy. She'll want to bathe and change from her stealth rags to company dinner clothes. She'll be up and about by eight. Hope that helps your planning."

Karen was smooth in the kitchen. Black beans, yellow rice, and pork. These were her grandmother's recipes. She's very proud of her Cuban heritage. Her maiden name was Rocha. No children from the failed marriage. Not sure she wanted kids.

She worked as an associate in the trust department of a very upscale local bank. Karen lived north of Gulf Beach on a lake. A forty-five-minute commute. When she was away from the pressure of work, she was far away. She's about five feet four inches high. Maybe weighed one hundred and five pounds. Khaki shorts and a blue man's shirt tied at the waist and sleeves rolled up. Sandals. She must have changed at the office. Maybe she kept a change of clothes in her car. Auburn hair, slight olive complexion, and gray eyes. Skin so smooth it was almost luminescent. Legs were flawless. Her hands thin and fingers long. The puffiness of the shirt concealed her breast size, but she had a small waist and an apricot butt. She glided from counter to stove to sink to trash. Next to Karen, Salome must have been a stumbling, pigeon toed, knock-kneed clodhopper. Gene had become mired in a schoolboy crush. If Karen asked him to help, he would probably do bodily harm to himself.

"Karen, let me ask you to help Mary. I am afraid she seems to have gone off the deep end. She is talking about her entry to chatrooms being retraced by some sinister force using cookies. But she and I don't know why. And she is convinced she has found a connection between some faces in Carter and Big Pass. Remember the photos I brought home last night? Well, she scanned them and claims to have found the faces of men who were at the Carter, Wyoming slaughter and at Senator Baldwin Miller's rally in Big Pass, Kansas. Now, here is the triple crazy part: She firmly believes these two factoids, the retracing and the faces, are related. Joined at the hip. She could use the help of a cyber-expert friend, not a brother, to help her come to her senses. Maybe she should see a grief therapist for a while until she no longer considers these connections real. Would you listen to her? Then tell me what you think. I'd appreciate it. And I know she would."

"I'd be glad to spend some time with her after dinner and try to find out what is troubling her. I know she must be going through hell. First Dorothy, her best friend and daughter, dies. Then she sells her home of twenty years. She quits her job of twelve years. She moves to a place that is geographically different and where she has only two friends. All of this in less than two months. She hasn't had time to grieve or to get her life in order.

Her soul must be bouncing around inside her like a single pea in an empty mayonnaise jar. Mary was an acquaintance a few years ago and our friendship grew long distance, occasionally at tradeshows, but in a somewhat removed mode. I'm not so sure I am the right one to analyze her discomfort. Why don't you do it? You're her brother."

"We've already fought over these issues and she needs an objective set of ears. Someone who is not blood or a mate."

"Looking around, I guess I am the only one who fits that description. How convenient." Karen shrugs.

"If you would prefer not to get embroiled in this mess, I understand. If the positions were reversed, Mary would also understand. I am only asking. Your response can be either yes or no. How and when you do the listening is up to you."

"After dinner, then. Where will you be while I am giving Mary the third degree?"

"Come on, it's not supposed to be like that. And I'll be in the den. Out of your sight and out of my mind."

"Why, Gene, how cute. You're blushing. So cute."

"OK, you two, what kind of shenanigans are going on in here?" Mary sits in the doorway smiling at the two.

"God, caught by my big sister. Don't tell mom and dad we were flirting. Nothing happened. Really nothing at all."

"Karen, so good to see you. Hell, it's good to see anyone other than this tapioca brain. Come here bro and give me a big hug. You, too, Karen. A big hug. I'm famished and the aromas emanating from this strange room are causing me to salivate. What is this room called? Ah, yes... kitchen. What's for dinner?"

"Only the scullery maid and the manservant are allowed to be here, ma'am. Black beans cooked with bay, cinnamon, clove, and garlic. Yellow rice cooked with peas, peppers and capers, and then sprinkled with fresh onions. Pork cooked in an orange and plum mélange and splashed with Cointreau. Plus, fresh Cuban bread. Washed down with Rolling Rock beer. This latter is not Cuban but my own choice. Gene, would you set the table out by the pool?"

It's amazing how much of one's personality comes out at the dinner table. Not the breakfast table or the lunch counter. Gene guessed when you see someone eat and they see you, there is not much to hide, except bathroom habits. How one cuts and chews food was basic to existence. And the manners of the table and meal consumption could range from, as the Germans would say, *fressen* to *essen*. The former was food consumption like an animal. The latter, with good manners like a human. But, even within the human species there was a significant disparity between how those of the classes handled cutlery and chewed their food. So, if everyone's place setting is the same, the only notable differences would be their conduct.

In a casual setting such as poolside with family and friends, the guard of propriety dropped. Nonetheless, Gene could tell a great deal about the woman across from him. And he liked what he saw. The conversation was day based and job related until Mary interjected her findings of the morning. Gene volunteered to clean up, as they wanted to retire to the ComRoom, so Mary could reveal her treasures of truth. Clean up was quick. Karen even brought her own refrigerator storage containers. The machine will wash the dishes and glasses. The pots and pans were scrubbed and stacked to dry overnight. They're not going anywhere. Gene poured an adult beverage and headed back to the pool. His time to contemplate the events of the day.

****

"Gene, we have to talk. Mary showed me what she found. I believe there is some measure of substance in her theories. I'm not entirely sure what is happening or why, but I firmly believe that you two and this place have been tagged. You know like a bear. Captured by the Game Commission, tagged with an electronic beeper then let loose back into the wild. The authorities track the migration, feeding, and mating patterns this way. Well, in your case they are keeping tabs on Mary and you, or just Mary. I think the latter, you're just here. Come with me back to her ComRoom and maybe she and I can do a better job of convincing you of what may be going on."

"As I was telling Karen, I believe that whoever retraced the entries made by GirlFromOz just recently learned that the person behind that verbal mask has moved from Wyoming to Florida. I cannot begin to know if they know that GirlFromOz is now a second person. So, I believe they hooked on to Dorothy and are just following the person they think is her. The only solution I can come up with for is what they do. Let me explain. I think they retrace every entry to every chatroom, which may be a potential threat to society. Hell, they probably set-up the chatrooms to attract the crazies. They started by simply monitoring activity. This is similar to those who that monitor the sex chatrooms. This monitoring can be a useful intervention tool to protect children and the unsuspecting.

"Unlike the thought police, these re-tracers don't want to control how the chatters think. But they do want to know who is thinking what. Who may be hinting at the next violence? Some chatters may already know this. So, they are bold, brazen, braggadocios. Baby bullshitters who couldn't walk the walk in my chair. Then there are some that speak the truth and are looking for converts and followers. Then there is the clear majority, I believe Dorothy was one, who are just naively fascinated by all the talk. So, unable to ascertain just who is who, the re-tracers trace everyone. At least until the real persona is revealed. I also believe the authorities are some level and form of government agency that willingly ignores free speech. Sort of like the infiltrators of the Communist Party in this country in the thirties, forties, and fifties. It's more of a cat a mouse game. You know the cat lets the mouse play until the cat is ready to pounce. All the time the mouse is under primitive surveillance, the kind that never blinks.

"Now, what are they doing to monitor me, us, here, in Florida? I'm willing to bet your next paycheck they have us under some form of surveillance. Electronic. Probative. I don't know. I do know that they have Karen under protection, which is their word for surveillance. Maybe they have not labeled us as threats to society. It gets foggy here, so I can't go on without sounding like an ass.

"We must take some action to protect ourselves from any electronic intrusion. I know how to protectively wrap the computer systems to confuse watchers. They can break the wrap, sure. But that takes more time and more money. And we may not be worth both. So, it's very likely they'll just give up and chase more desirable game. I could take care of that. Karen convinced me we are not under a telephonic watch. That was my paranoia. But the house may be bugged. I hope not. We really need to secure the primary entry port: the computer. I will still be able to safely visit chatrooms but will be followed home from new ones.

"And look what Karen was able to do with the pictures. See this left three-quarter shot from Carter. See the left three quarter shot from Big Pass. Check out the hairline, the nose angle, the ear lobe, and the strange cut of the eyebrow. This guy was at both places. We're sure of it. I am willing to bet your next paycheck that this second guy was in both places, too. See his jacket lapel. Notice the button loop at the top. Also note the strong similarity of the side cowlicks in the guy's scalp. So, what do we make of this? We're not sure but it does not sit well. Why would a gun carrier be a political advisor? Unless he, or they, are not advisors. Maybe they're bodyguards. That's heavy protection for Senator on the pre-campaign trail. Maybe they are thugs hired by his staff. Then, why the hell were they at Carter?

"So far, we know of electronic eyes and ears, and multiple personalities on TV. But we have no connection if there is one. Well, what do you think little brother?"

Gene's mind whirled...an incredulous whir. "You have made compelling arguments for the conspiracy side of the argument. I'll suspend skepticism and acid logic for the moment and agree that you may, just may, be on to something. If you are on to something, I'm just not sure what it is. I am not smart enough to understand the how's of the computer world. And I am not sure that your plan to combat it is viable. If you are correct, and I stress the word 'if,' we would be well advised to maintain contact with the original chatrooms, so that the authorities don't realize that we know about them. This will mean not masking the trail and thereby letting them follow us. We must not give them any reason to think that we know they are there. I'm not convinced the house is bugged. My guess is that we are safe from that for now. Most importantly, I believe way more digging is in order. This I cannot do. Only you can do it. Maybe you can determine who is walking the walk. See if you can discern any threats.

This sounds crazy. Maybe you can find out what's next. Christ, I'm beginning to sound like a true believer."

Mary let out a scream of delight. She had a convert. Someone who believed her. Karen smiled.

"About the faces in the crowd: This is weirder than I thought possible. I must admit there are some real similarities in the faces. It's just that their situations are so contradictory as to defy connection. We are due to get some video from Tony Seton soon. Perhaps we can find some corroborating visual evidence.

"If we can get a cleaner image, I can ask Mike Duncan to do some deeper digging. He must have access to shots of other political rallies. Maybe he knows someone, who knows someone, who knows someone, who can put names and job specs with the faces. He has expressed an interest in helping and getting rich in the process. This would be a good way to find out if he is serious about the former. Hopefully, I'll get the video from Tony tomorrow. For now, you can commence scanning for faces. Then, we can compare them with those already in your electronic file. I am not convinced this will lead anywhere except deep into the proverbial blind alley. But you have the time and equipment, and certainly the motivation."

Brother...ever the skeptic: "I still see no connection between the chatrooms and the similar faces. I believe they are simply isolated events occurring at random in a similar time frame. Sort of like a rainstorm and burning cookies on a Saturday afternoon. There is no cause and no effect. There is no link. The events just happened at the same time. But, sis, I am on your side. Each new piece of evidence will lead us. We cannot lead the evidence, OK?

"You must be exhausted. I am tired, and you did all the legwork. I am going to swim a few laps, clear my head so I can concentrate on tomorrow's work. Ladies, it's been a great evening. Let's do this again sometime soon."

"We will."

"Karen is coming back tomorrow evening when we get the tape from your friend, Tony."

"I said I hoped to get the tape tomorrow. If it's available, he will have it delivered to my office, and I'll call you at home. You can call Karen. God, this sounds like a junior high school club meeting. Now, I need my swim. Do you think the dogs would like to join me?"

"Doubtful. You swim. I'm going get ready for bed. You were right, I'm whipped."

"Does that invitation extend to me? I even brought my suit. Where can I change?"

That was sudden and smacked of planning, except many Floridians kept a spare swimming suit in the car. So, if she wanted to swim, she's welcome.

Midway into Gene's second lap, there was a splash at the other end of the pool. The partner in the kitchen was partner to Aquaman. They passed about mid-pool. Gene hadn't turned on the floodlights at night if it was just him in the pool. There was enough house light and moon glow for him to follow the lane markers. Gene made the turn and saw her stroking aggressively. Trying to catch him? Why? This was not a race. It was a form of nonalcoholic relaxation to tire him into a deep and long sleep. Karen was approaching in his lane. He moved to avoid collision. They maintained a ten-yard distance and avoided contact for the remainder of his ten laps. He pulled himself out of the pool and wrapped his body in a bath sheet, breathing deeply to stop the panting and to get his pulse rate down to the low sixties. Bath sheets were the only things he owned from Needless-Markup. They were big enough to cover his entire body and thirsty enough to create the Amazon Dessert. As she pulled herself from the pool, he couldn't help but notice her incredible body, which had been hiding in the bloused shirt and khaki shorts. The bikini top and bottom were adjusted for modesty. She swam without a cap. The entirety of her countenance was exquisite. Gene handed her a bath sheet. She enveloped herself in it.

"You swim well."

"Thank you, but what you mean to say is that I swim well for an older man."

"That is not what I said. Do us both a favor and don't ever put words in my mouth. I would never presume to do that to you. Don't you ever, ever presume to know what I am going to say. Fair enough?"

Her rebuke was tempered by something Gene had not experienced for years – a warm smile.

"I apologize. Fair enough?"

We just had a territorial fight, and no one lost. I was a little bloodied, but not bowed.

"I came out here for three reasons. First, I wanted to swim. Second, I wanted to talk to you about Mary. I don't think she is well. I think she is ill or simply becoming less well. I really have no recent standard to which I can compare her present state. The last time we were together was two years ago. Today she is much less vibrant. Everything is measured. There is much less physical spontaneity. Her mind is sharp, but she looks tired and pale. Her arms are flabby, which is not what I would expect from someone in a wheelchair. She doesn't have much strength. She dropped several things while we were together. Pens just fell out of her hands. Twice her hands shook as if she had some form of palsy. And her breathing is labored as if she has asthma. No hard coughing, just wheezing when she tries to take a deep full breath. And there is another thing. The dogs. They seem to be hovering too close to her. Close enough to give her comfort. Impart their strength to her. Have you noticed any of this?"

"I was not acutely aware of her condition. Life, in general, has been quite hectic since she and the two dogs moved in. But, since you mentioned it, I'll take a closer look at her before I go to bed. She seemed to be strong and feisty when I was with her in Wyoming. Maybe she is just very tired. Needs a good rest."

"Oh, come on. Have you been so self-absorbed as to not notice your own sister? That's myopically arrogant. I asked her if she was OK, and she dismissed the question. I even asked after the shaking and she told me she was fine, only tired. She is as arrogant as her brother when it comes to people caring about her health. I believe it's a coverup for something real and threatening. What could be wrong? Has she seen a doctor recently? Who was her doctor in Wyoming?"

Once again, the tempered verbal thrust.

"I don't know the answers to those questions. I am sure the stress of the past months has caught up to her. As she and I both told you she is most likely just tired. And she needs a vacation from stress. I will call the university tomorrow. Maybe they can help with a doctor's name or some other releasable information. When I can learn anything, I can find a doctor for her.

"I am embarrassed that I failed to notice what was obvious to you. I appreciate the fact you brought this to my attention. And I'll let you know what the next actions will be. Now is the appropriate time for each of us to separately tuck ourselves in. I'm not throwing you out. I'm tired and took this afternoon off, so tomorrow will be a day and a half, literally and figuratively. I'll retrieve your food containers and meet you at the front door."

She headed for the guest bathroom. Gene straightened up the lanai, made sure the gates were locked, and left one sliding door half-way open for Hither and Yon to roam. But, given Karen's observation, he doubted they will leave Mary's side. It must be great to have guard dogs that really guard. Three small containers from the fridge. Head for the front door. She was there. Hair wet and her shirt and shorts pulled on. Gene opened the door and walked her to her car in the moonlight. It was bright enough to see the suit in the small canvas tote next to the bra and panties. His imagination revved. Be still his teenage heart. She had her keys in her right hand.

"You never told me the third reason you came to the pool."

"This."

She dropped the tote, turned around, and slid her hands around his neck. Their lips, ever so slightly apart, caressed softly. She turned back and entered her car leaving the male agog. She drove off with his heart.

Front of the house secure: Outside lights turned on, front and side alarm systems activated. Back zone left off for the hounds. Inside lights off, except for small table lamps in den and dining room. The routine was necessary when you lived in the home invasion and burglary capital of Florida. He was comfortable that the dogs would be alarm enough. Passed by Mary's room. Saw light from the bedside table. Knocked gently. No answer. Knocked again. Same, no response. Entered delicately. The dogs raised their heads an inch off the bed. One at her feet. One at her side. Seeing me, they returned to rest position. The lamp illuminated Mary's face, shoulders and arms. A dull yellow, gray, and white flesh color. This is not the hue of health. She seemed frail and thinner than she was in Wyoming.

Then Gene heard her snore, except it was not a nasal or throat sound: A chest wheeze. Very delicate, but very disconcerting. Was he just experiencing the paranoia that Karen implanted? Confused and concerned, he exited.

****

Gene called Wyoming State University Main Campus at eight o'clock their time and was directed to the faculty administration office. There he was told to contact the local campus in Carter. There he was put on hold for five minutes while some student tried to determine if the information was available and if she could release it to him. She asked him to call back in one hour and ask for Dean Tomas. Dean Tomas would be able to help him. Sixty-two minutes later Dean Tomas was very pleasant, yet vague about what information he had and what he could give out without the permission of Professor Benton. Finally, he allowed that it would be all right to give her brother the name of her doctor in Carter. Doctor Byers was busy at the time of Gene's call. His nurse would find Mary's file and have the Doctor call

Gene. Damned runaround. Too much fucking delay. Gene implored her to pull the file and tell the doctor that he would call back in thirty minutes.

Doctor Byers was very aware of the physician/patient right to privacy: HIPPA. The last time she saw Mary was a year ago. Mary was in for her annual check-up. She was experiencing periodic chest pains. The usual tests were conducted. Doctor Byers wanted Mary to see a pulmonary specialist at the University Hospital on the main campus. Never received the results of her visit. Never saw Mary again either. Would be willing to forward her records to her new physician in Florida. Gene called Karen and related his trip through the bureaucratic maze. She volunteered to find a local doctor for Mary.

About two pm, a messenger delivered a package from Tony Seton. Gene called Mary and told her to call Karen for a continuation of the investigation. He would be responsible for dinner so the ladies could work their computer magic. He tried to sound blasé and not excited that he would be seeing Karen tonight. It was almost like a date with his sister as chaperone.

The afternoon had more than its quota of bullshit. Mary called.

"Karen is bringing the makings for a huge multi-flavored salad. Her treat. She insisted. You should be prepared to sweat and slave over running water and a cutting board. She is also bringing fresh bread which she demands must not be toasted, just warmed. The funniest thing, Gene. She asked if it was all right if she went swimming again after dinner. I got the strangest feeling I was a parent approving a date. *Tres* bizarre. Be careful old timer. Cupid may be stalking you."

"Very funny, but not likely, sister."

God, he hoped she was right. The thing he feared most was growing old alone. The thing he would miss the most was the companionship of a remarkably close and dear friend, preferably of the opposite sex. Some hippie once said that love was good friends who fuck. Gene missed love. But he was leery of being starstruck like some weak-kneed teen. Only to have his dreams dashed. He must relax and take it one day at a time. Can't make plans or promises. Karen's car was in the driveway. She had the good sense to not take his spot. Also, she was in the best possible escape position. In the door and down the drive in less than fifteen seconds.

****

"Hello, honies, I'm home."

"We're poolside. I decided to take today off and play with the dogs. I also cleaned out the last remnants of Wyoming from my wheeled house. I think it's time to sell it and get a vehicle which is more conducive to local street travel and which does not label me as a carpetbagger. Let's make that our weekend project, bro. Get the heap to a dealer and disposing of it. It has served its useful purpose anyway. I've already checked on the Net and learned its supposed value. Also, we should consider getting pontoons for the chair and some hand paddles for me. Then, I could go in with my babies and have some mobility. I am suddenly excited about life. Now, down to the serious side of why you have intruded in our world. You do have the tape, don't you? Thank you. Will you excuse us while we go to work? You are banished to the sink, cutting board, and spice rack place you call, what is that word? Oh yes, kitchen. Call us when dinner is ready if you would."

She is smiling and giggling. Acting almost childish. The day of rest and play with the hounds has worked its wonders. I knew it would. The prospects for a pleasant evening are grrrrrreat!

IX

For the native and knowledgeable, old-fashioned fresh produce roadside stands were found in every Florida county. They purveyed produce delivered daily by farmers on old flatbed trucks. It took time, energy, and a little more money to find and shop at these places. But the result was worth the effort. Karen obviously considered salad using farm fresh produce to be some form of artistic expression of her persona. So, she knew where to shop to impress the eyes, ears, nose, and palate. She brought two large brown shopping bags of numerous salad ingredients for a fresh feast. The pressure was on Gene to produce the proper produce product. If his finished creation were less than her benchmark, he would have injured her soul. But, if he could energize the senses beyond her expectations, he would win her heart.

He carefully emptied each goody bag. Content cornucopia was an inadequate description. Cherry and plum tomatoes. Bib, Romaine, and Boston lettuces. Yellow and green peppers. Watercress. Parsley. Celery with hearts, baby carrots, and radishes. Pecans. Bean sprouts. Kale and watercress. Peapods. Coconut to be shredded. Grapefruit and mandarin oranges. Red cabbage. And two loaves of fresh bread. One loaf was nine grain. The other, a rich sourdough. He had been to Calistaro's bakery before and knew how fantastic their bread was. At least he knew one place Karen shopped. Placed a tea towel in the front of his waistband. Rolled up his sleeves. Poured a drink. Turned on the old-time rock 'n roll to a blare level. The Stones, The Eagles, The Temps, and The Topps had come to his house for dinner. He called the ladies in waiting and warned them that, for the full flavor, dinner must commence by the time Mickey's big hand reached twelve and his little hand reached seven, or else all would spoil and become In-Sink-Erator fodder. A tremendous, aces up, hole in one, multi-flavored salad, Rolling Rocks, and warm bread on the lanai by the pool. What could be bad?

****

"Let me tell you what we have extracted from Tony Seton's tape. Clear and identifiable faces. Three faces. Two blondes and a coal head.

169

Three places: Carter, Big Pass, and now Bricklersville. Beyond the question of the who is the why. If we can learn who, most likely, that will lead us directly why. So, that's where we should begin. Can we call Mister Duncan tonight? There is a three-hour time difference. Let's see if he truly wants to get rich. I can email him whatever he needs to start his investigation. What do you say, bro?"

"Mary, before we go off inviting others to swim in our paranoid pool, I'd like to see the iron-clad evidence and listen to Karen's counsel. What do you think, Karen? Are we on to something other than a slippery slope?"

"I think Mary is right, and I stress 'think.' There do seem to be a few similarities in the pictures. The real problem is with the lack of fidelity in the Carter shots. There are also the various angles of the headshots. If I had to swear in court to a definite match, I couldn't. But I would be willing to bet two quarters that we are on to something. By the way, two quarters are five times my betting limit. I would like some other form of confirmation. Not just another video from another rally. It's expected that the same guys show up at the same rallies. What is unexpected is if the same guys that were at Carter would be at another shooting. It's the *if* that bothers me. I'll raise another question: What if these guys were at Menthen and Lutztown? We'll never know for sure, but it's cause for speculation."

"Jesus, Karen, I think you're on to something. How do we get tapes and photos of those events? Gene, maybe Mike Duncan can help us."

"First, let me look at your findings. Then we'll decide if action involving Mike is right. If Mary's point about the cat-and-mouse game is accurate, if someone can watch us while we search for them, we had better be damned careful and discreet. If this is true, and I'm beginning to think it is, I was smart to speak and send material to Mike Duncan from my office."

The pictures of the guys at both rallies were a match. No doubt. No big deal. The pictures from Carter could complete the triangulation, but Gene would like another expert's view. He took the disc of the pictures and headed for his office. Mary and Karen were safe with the two dogs. Out the lane. Left to the second light and right on to Ellerton drive. Six miles on Ellerton to Interstate 775. Twelve miles to exit nine. Down the ramp and left to the third light. Into the parking lot and his space. He'd traveled this route a kajillion times during the morning, rarely at night. Although it was dark in the early hours, the dark tonight seemed threatening. One nice thing about driving in the dark was the ability to see cars. There were fewer of them, and they were well lit. He couldn't see the drivers too clearly unless there was light entering the front of the car, but each car was obvious. A small, dark colored pick-up truck was behind him up to I-775. Then he spotted a sports car in the rear-view mirror behind him up to the parking lot. Was all this imagination? Was he being followed? By whom? Was this such a big deal that someone could put someone on his ass? Maybe we were on to something. Maybe he was just being paranoid. He loved Mary, but maybe she was just getting to him.

Duncan was not home, but his voicemail gave Gene his email address. He sent the disc data and explained what they were looking for. Told him to call at the office number tomorrow as early as possible in the morning. Deal done. Lights off. Guard waved at. Car entered. Head for home.

Retraced his route, like the re-tracers who Mary was convinced followed her to us. The lights in the second car behind Gene were those of a small pick-up truck. Black. The grill was vaguely familiar. The truck pulled to the left and passed Gene, only to turn into the mall beyond the Interstate. The stores were closed. *That's strange.* On to I-775.

Now it was urgent that he got home. His safety, the safety of Mary and Karen. Speedometer registered eighty. To Gene's left, and about six car lengths behind him, he noted the front end of a coupe. Or was it a sports car? He quickly slowed down to forty-five. The small gray car slowed down. But not in lockstep with his car, so it got close in the left lane. It was a sports car, and he spotted the young blond male driver before the driver had a chance to slow down and drop behind Gene's field of vision. He had been made, and he made his pursuer. The other driver knew that Gene knew he was there. The game of cat-and-mouse had taken on a new twist: Who was the cat and who was the mouse? When did they change roles? Was someone watching the game? Who had the rulebook?

****

"Gene, you're pale. What's wrong?"

"Nothing's wrong, Mary. I'm just tired, that's all. I need a brief swim and a long rest. In fact, a long night's sleep would, no doubt, do you a world of good. Why don't we all go to our respective beds and sleep? A fresh outlook on this issue would help us all."

"Jesus, you don't have to be so rude. I'm tired anyway. So, I was headed for bed. Karen is out by the pool. She was hoping to swim. Remember, I warned you."

"Fuck, I forgot. OK. Sure."

"Goodnight, crank bag."

"Yeah, goodnight."

He changed into his baggy blue and red striped suit. The boys bought it for him last Christmas. *It's a hoot. I looked and feel like the Piltdown Surfer.* Grabbed two bath sheets. Exited the master bedroom to the pool. Karen was wrapped in her own big towel dangling her feet poolside.

"Sorry, Karen, I forgot about our swim. Before we thrash about in the aqueous solution, let me ask you about Mary. How do you think she is doing? What do you think are her next steps?"

"I made an appointment for Mary with Doctor Hanan. Nine am the day after tomorrow. He is the best internist in the area, or at least that's what his peers say. His office has faxed or will fax her doctor in Wyoming for her files. So, I need to give Dr. Hanan his name. I stressed urgency. So, all will be accomplished. Consider me your native guide to the local medical professionals. I am owed some favors in the community and she is worth all of them. Yes, I think she is ill. Extremely ill. Although she put up a front of good spirits, it was a front. She had on too much makeup. Back in the ComRoom and at dinner her hands trembled, and she was sweating at the table when both of us were cool. Her mind is incredibly sharp, and her heart is strong. I just think other parts of her body are wearing out. It's this quest that gives her the drive to be aggressive. Take away the investigation and we would take away her will to fight...to live. She is more than tired. Sadly, she is near exhaustion."

"I really appreciate your help. You have gone beyond the call of friendship or duty. Knowing my sister, she will insist on getting herself to Doctor Hanan's. Her spirit is indomitable, and she is incredibly stubborn. I suspect that this is a genetic trait. I'll make a date with her for lunch after her appointment. We can start to cruise the RV lots and beat up some salesmen. That's settled until we get the results of the visit to Doctor Hanan. What about your...?"

Before she could answer, Gene held his hand over her mouth and handed her a napkin upon which he had written, 'From here on, we will need to whisper.' He continued in hushed tones.

"I emailed Duncan, told him what we wanted, and asked him to call me tomorrow. But there is something else. I have this strong feeling I was followed to and from the office. It's almost as if someone knew when I was leaving. It was not a hard-on-my-ass tail, rather it was a soft one. A few cars back. It's like they knew where I was going. But they got sloppy. I saw one of them. I think it was a young blond man. Clean cut. That's all. I am becoming very convinced they have us under surveillance. I think Mary is right. I think they have bugged the house. They are listening. We can talk about things. But we must whisper like this. Just a precaution."

"Let's dive in and fake drowning. We'll thrash around a bit to create noisy confusion."

"That's the idea. I'm so tired, maybe I won't fake it.

Diving in, the first two laps were the most difficult. The initial exuberance after the dive must be tempered by the desire to achieve appropriate rhythm. The rhythm was absofuckinglutely critical. The number of arm strokes. The depth of the dig. The power of the pull. The beat of the kick. The push of the legs. The bend of the knees. All dictate breathing and energy loss. All of these were the apparent factors, which impacted the ease at which he swam. The faster he could get all these elements to work in sync, the slower fatigue would set in. As he got increasingly fatigued, his body wiggled. He didn't turn his head properly to intake air. His shoulders shifted. His hips sank. The lack of rhythm accelerated the on-set of fatigue. His mind wanted to quit, long before his body said it was okay. So, he was constantly fighting mental fatigue. All this thinking and existential chess playing occurred in the first two laps of his swim. He would not race. He swam against the biological, emotional, and mental clocks that were within him.

Karen had a good pace. Her strokes were measured, and her breathing was every stroke. By the end of lap three they each had found their respective rhythms. Gene ratcheted down, but not much, so he swam with her. He caught a glimpse of her with each breath on the return leg and peak underwater. Swimming side by side, even if unintended, breeds competition. If he sped up, she sped up. If she picked up the pace, he followed so as not to follow. Seven laps together and they made the final turn. The pulls and kicks were just a tad quicker, deeper, and more powerful. Headed for home. Should he win? Should this be a race? Yes, absolutely. Swimming was always about winning.

No conversation for the first minute. Gasping for breath. Grasping every cubic centimeter of air to force into the lungs. Holding on to the side of the pool with head lowered does not facilitate air intake. Gene learned this years ago. So, he stood upright, face pointed to the sky and forced his lungs to work hard, sucking in salvation.

"That's great. You're good. Ever swim competitively?"

The initial sentences were short and choppy. The voices were low, almost at a whisper. Not hiding anything. Just not capable of normal volume or yelling. Questions were well spaced so that the other person could respond, thus giving the questioner a chance to breathe.

"Always been around water. Prefer pools. The gulf is for fun. How about you?"

"In a previous lifetime. Loved the water. If I could come back as anything, I would choose to be a dolphin or porpoise. Grace, speed, strength, and intelligence. Not a bad combination. Plus, they live in my medium of my choice."

She stared and motioned him to move close to her. She whispered, "Do you think they can hear us in the pool? I mean, can we talk about what's going on without being heard?"

"I believe only the house is bugged. Besides, even if the lanai were bugged, we could stand really close in the pool away from the lanai and whisper in each other's ears. Then no one could eavesdrop."

He was standing directly in front of Karen. Not touching. He moved to her right ear and began, "I appreciate all that you've done for Mary. I'm happy she has such a good friend. I'm afraid I have not been able to give her the attention and technical understanding she deserves. She is sick, and I can't fix it. Hell, you found the doctor to help."

Gene's lips are about a millimeter from her ear. He could smell the combination of pool water and her perfume. She wore Tabak, with some mid-level spices and a hint of citrus. She, most likely, chose it after great deliberation. He had luxuriated in the full-strength aroma since he met her at the front door. It's in her hair and her clothes. It was her aura...enduring and endearing. He did not touch her earlobe or the delicate ear folds that lead to her inner self. His inhaling and exhaling did. The temperature of his breath enhanced the sensation of the zephyr wafting over her skin. She sensed heat and motion. He could see the fragile, baby hairs in, on, and around her ear and on the nape of her neck stand up. They were reacting to external stimulation and internal chemistry. Bodies did not touch. The dynamic tension of physical and sexual interest restrained was a fearsome force. She moved closer. Their bodies were held together and separated by the meniscus of the water between them. He didn't have to move for her to converse.

"Thanks are not necessary. I do what I please for those who matter to me. Mary is a special person. I'm lucky to have her for a friend. On top of all that, she is brilliant. And I can learn much from her. So, we share. That's the basis of friendship. Sharing. Do you think that those who are listening are also looking?"

"No."

She was not whispering in Gene's ear, but rather talking to his neck. Her breath was hot in the cool evening air. This method of communication, at and not to, increased the tension and therefore the sensuality of the action. Her lips ever so slightly touched his throat. She skipped her partially opened mouth from side to front and around to the other side. Then her tongue retraced her path back to his right. Her mouth moved up his throat. Across cheekbone and cheek to about an inch below his eye. Her lips seemed to be driven by an internal engine. Still no hands. No holding. No grasping. Her breathing and his heartbeat were quickening, hastening toward some conclusion. Was this a race like swimming? The languorous medium of the swimming pool was perfect for the physical anxiety created by their strong and obvious feelings.

Her lips glided down to his and brushed across the dry opening of his mouth. He was quivering and panting. Still no hands. No holding. Her lips returned and stayed on his mouth. He returned the tender pressure. The contact lasted an eternity. Gene felt her hands glide from nowhere to his neck and up to his cheeks. Her fingertips were feathers. The palms never touched his electrified skin. His hands and arms responded to her advance. They sought to recapture control by gently grasping her upper arms and drawing her onto him. He felt her wet bikini bra squash against his chest as his fingernails traced small circles on her shoulder blades. Their tongues were now dancing in different mouths. Moisture, hers and his, covered the inside of his mouth. Breathing became deeper and faster. A flashback to the initial stage of the swim. She withdrew her hands from Gene's face and dropped them to her suit bottom. She lowered her body into the water as she tugged and wiggled out of the fabric encumbrance. She untied his suit, separated the Velcro fly, and removed his last vestige of modesty. Arising, she resumed her oral attack. Battle was enjoined. He was ready. He had been almost ready for minutes. Hell, like all male babies, he was born ready.

What had been gentle exploration became pressurized groping. Suddenly, she pulled hard on his shoulders and leapt up, head above his face. She wrapped her legs around his hips and lowered her body onto him. The pressure of entry was painful. She grimaced. Partial access. Withdrawal. Greater access. Slight withdrawal. Insertion completed... thrashing began. Human agitation churned the water. The bra was unsnapped. Her nipples rubbed to hardness against his chest hair. Kisses reached the frantic stage. She was pumping. He was pushing back. She leaned back, and he took a breast with his mouth. He nipped. She jolted. He nipped. She jolted. She pulled back to give him access to the other breast. He nipped again. Her whimper was barely audible. The pumping had slowed down, but the thrusts were deeper and longer. She devoured his mouth. Eyes opened a slit. Her skin glistened in the pool lights. Rhythm slowly picked up from a waltz to fox trot to jitterbug. Then she was frozen in time as she clung to him. Pulsing. Throbbing. Her thrusts were powerful. Almost painful, except this was extreme pleasure. Three. Four. Five. Six. She collapsed onto him with all the energy of a wet blanket.

Not fatigued, she was spent. The race was over. Gene had finished the race about thirty seconds before Karen did. But the greatest joy for him in the race was not the finishing, it was being with his partner as she finished. He loved women. They were beautiful. Their bodies. Faces. Eyes. Hair. Smiles. Laughs. Their process to arrive at nirvana. As they finished the race of sexual fulfillment, they were magnificent: A combination of Madonna, vixen, sister, and friend. All the pent-up emotions of years, some repressed, some exploited, spew uncontrollably. Unashamedly. Good for them. Good for Gene to be there and help them get to where they wanted to be. Years ago, he learned that woman love sex as much, or more, than men. But they had been denied that love for at least two millennia. He no longer worried about completing the race before his partner.

His goal was to help his partner get to her goal. Her kisses that covered his face and head were tender. They had conquered the race and won each other. The next step was to learn who they were. Something for tomorrow. For now, to bed. To sleep, but not to snuggle.

Breakfast was not awkward, because Mary was never awake when Gene arose for his daily grind. Karen left at the same time. She had to go home and dress for success in the financial world. He would call her later today.

****

One message on the office line. Call number one. Three forty-five am from an unknown number: "Hey, Mister Benton, Gene, I received your email opened it and examined the pictures. Who are these guys? I mean why are they important to you? Whatever. I can dig into the job, but it will cost you. I mean money and a piece of the action if this leads anywhere. I mean, I can use a big break and the attendant celebrity status. Not to mention all the jobs that this could bring in. So, why don't you call me when you get this message?

No, make that call me after eight in the morning your time. We can expand this dialogue, as you guys in the suit world like to say. As I understand it, you want me to learn who the three mugs are and what they do for a living. Is this accurate?"

Gene waited until ten-fifteen, "Good morning. We need to know what these guys do for a living, as well as their pasts. Can you help?"

"I suspect I can. They're not familiar as of now, but who knows what I can find if properly motivated. By the way, this one set of images is really washed and grainy. Are these the same guys as in my photos?"

"We think so, but that's where you come in. Can you extract clearer images from what we were sent, or do you need the original tape?"

"I will start with this but can only get so far. I'll need the tape to confirm. Why do you need this confirmation? I mean, are we looking at a major national conspiracy or what? My fee is seven hundred and fifty a day plus expenses. And I need three days upfront. I bill partial days at five hundred. Fair enough?"

"We'll send the cash and the tape by FedEx tomorrow. One more thing: We talk and correspond only at and from my office. That must be perfectly clear. There can be no deviation, OK?"

"OK. Based upon our previous work, I'll start today. I know that when you say 'the check is in the mail' you can be trusted. I'll call with results and whatever I uncover. Otherwise, you'll hear from me in about a week."

Gene called Karen. Her voicemail told him she was away from her desk. Leave message. When he was twenty, simply panting over the phone was sufficient to communicate feelings. At his present age and with the experience of two failed marriages and several affairs, expression of carnal desires was not wise. He didn't dare send flowers.

He would ask her to dinner away from his home. Get a gander at her cave. All done with a dash of teenage eagerness. He was unfuckingbelievably nervous. Once the jitters coincided with the first kiss, now Gene suffered post-coital anxiety. Did she have as good a time as he did? He hoped so. *How we have changed. Was this change for the better?* Morning rushed by as if he were running backward. Lunch consisted of red meat, pasta, tea with lemon, and a ten-minute nap. Not unlike an athlete in training. Back in his tower of almost-power, he saw that Karen had called. Message said no dinner tonight. She had some huge project to complete and get in front of some important clients by eight am. But tomorrow night would be great. They should meet at Stone Crab Charlie's on the beach at seven. Dress casual because the food can be sloppy. He even got a kiss and a hug over the phone. He became excited. It just didn't show because he was seated.

Afternoon was as expected. Reviewed some projects in the works. Talked to the supervisors about performance plans for expansion into a department, his review of possible prospects for their groups, and some long-range wool gathering. Home by six.

****

Hither and Yon were bouncing around like little kids who had to pee. They did. He checked the ComRoom for Mary. She has been in bed all day, exhausted from the week's activities she claimed. She was pale and seemed weak. Gene helped her out of bed to the shower. She would join him in a bit. The dogs were barking furiously.

Investigate. No squirrels. No rats, rodent or human. The back gate was open. Damned pool guy.

Dinner was simple. Mary wanted soup and toast. Her stomach was bothering her. She claimed she was well rested.

"Did you two swim well last night?" The probe was inserted.

"Yeah, I love to swim before sleep, and it's fun to have a partner."

"Did you sleep well after your swim?"

"Like a stone. Dropped off in less than ten minutes."

"You two were quiet this morning."

Busted!

"We tried not to disturb you."

"I was up most of the night. Couldn't sleep so I worked on the Net. Went back to the chatrooms."

She began to whisper. Did she learn something about the bug last night? Maybe it's just the exhaustion.

"I think I discovered something very, very disturbing. I think I can predict where the next school shooting will occur. It frightens me so much I can't get excited. That's why I'm so calm. Almost numb. Let me show you what I've found."

She was too calm. The sky before a hurricane was dead calm because it knew what was about to happen, all hell to break loose. Ferocity. Destruction. Pandemonium. She was sky calm.

"Here look at this pronouncement from BloodNourishment. Look to the FireFromGod. Now look at JonnyGetYourGun...He will free us. Last, HandsHeldHigh...Shoulders carry the load. What's so important about those three quotes is that they are all entered as the last line from TruthSeeker. Always. I believe this guy is one of the monitors of the five chatrooms. Here's the kicker: I have a sick feeling this guy is doing more than listening. He is broadcasting. And through broadcasting, he leads or, at least, guides the others."

"Mary, a week ago I would have thought that was crazy. Today I won't say that. But I will say that this is very unlikely, sort of like the theory of the depth of blackholes. How can we prove it? Can it be proven?"

"There is no litmus test. A way to see if I'm right is to sit back and let something happen. If it happens as we predicted, we will know we were right. If it does not happen, we were wrong.

If we were right and do nothing, many kids will be slaughtered. If we're wrong and do nothing, no one gets hurt. This is a conundrum. What to do? What to do?"

"Here is another thought: If we alert the authorities, I doubt they will listen to us, then they will do nothing. If nothing happens, we are branded as loonies and no one will ever listen to us. If the kids are killed after we warned the school officials, we become the prime suspects. They'll ask how we knew. Who did we tell? Who are we really? No one else would step forward and admit that they ordered the killings? Not even the killers, who are oh-so-proud of their actions. If we know there will be violence, how do we know where the violence will occur?"

"That part may be easier than we think. The fire from God could be Lucifer or Saint Ignatius. He will free us could be Lincoln. Abraham Lincoln set free the slaves. And where is the land of Lincoln? Illinois. Shoulders that carry the load is Chicago the broad shoulders of the nation. So, we have St. Ignatius High School in Chicago, Illinois. We just don't know the when?"

"Wait a minute, sis. Taking all those factoids could also give you a high school in Lincoln, Nebraska near the Broad River or at Shoulder Bend. What about Lucifer? You might even have Prometheus. Or Moses as the freer of the Jews. We would have to check all the high schools in every state, in every town, and in every District to determine if any fit all the clues. And, in which order. If these are clues, that is. Or simply incredible intellectual leaps based on the emotions of two people, who don't know to where they are jumping. Besides all this, remember that the three shooting incidents have occurred in small towns: Carter, Menthen, and Lutztown. Chicago, and even Lincoln, don't fit that part of the puzzle. The cities are too big. So, where are we?"

"We have to do something to stop the slaughter, I know it will occur. We owe Dorothy, and every other child, that much. We can't just sit back and let it happen. That would make us as guilty as the shooters and the entire evil force. Passivity is no excuse."

"Fair enough. Let's go to the net and do some deep diving. We'll start with a list of metro areas with fewer than a quarter of a million people, then we'll check the states containing appropriate metro areas looking for names that have any relationship to our keywords: shoulders, fire, and free. Then we'll cross reference the resultant lists with schools with the same commonality. The last step will be the toughest: State school systems are available, just hidden. This will take a few hours using the right websites. But it is the only way to do this that I can think of. Are you up for it?"

"We can both go online if you go to the office. I'll be fine here with my boys. I'll take states east of the Mississippi. You've got the ones west. See you in a few hours, assuming you're up for learning the truth?"

Gene left for the office. During the trip he was on the lookout for possible tails, none were visible.

****

After five hours, he had four possible targets and headed for home. Mary had five on her list. They had a baseball team of possibilities. It was three AM, too late to go to bed. Now what? It frightened him that they were pursuing a course of action based upon some very questionable assumptions. What if TruthSeeker was anything other than their bleak assumption? What if the messages were a deeper code? What if there was no significance to what was on the scroll? What if someone were baiting a trap? What if? What if? What if? Between anxiety and fear lay the great void of indecision. They had to do something. But what? Narrow the list? How? Call all nine targets? How could they warn the possible targets of unsubstantiated fear based upon a shaky hypothesis?

Later in the day, Gene would call school principals and speak to them very calmly. Mary promised, "I can help this after I get back from the doctors. A woman's voice will be a better communication vehicle than a man's. Plus, this is really my mission. Your work for now is done. So, scoot."

X

The external call came at nine. The police officer just said to come to the hospital in Tampa. Mary Thomas Benton had been in an accident. The police had gotten Gene's name and address and both telephone numbers from her wallet. Strange how using her full name objectified everything. Mary was no longer his sister. She was Mary Thomas Benton in the emergency room of County Hospital. On a good day, this trip would have taken forty-five minutes, today it took twenty-five. Gene used tricks to shorten the drive time. Lights flashing. Horns blasting. Screaming for the snails to get the fuck out of his way. Changing lanes every three hundred yards. Darting in and out of traffic. Eased through two red lights. The no-cop God watched over his trip. Screeched to a halt in a spot normally reserved for some member of administration. He yelled at the guard where he was going.

This must have been a slow morning for the ER. Or maybe they were just very efficient. That concept was encouraging, yet disturbing. How did they get to be so good at moving bodies in and out? Practice was the correct answer, but not the one Gene wanted to hear. No gurneys in the hall. No one in the admitting area. No one waiting for an injured loved one. Just the usual paging and telephone ringing. Officer Davis met him halfway down the hall. Young. About six feet tall. Solidly constructed. Kevlar vest. Dour look on his face.

"Mister Eugene Benton?"

"Yes, I am he."

"Mister Benton, your wife has been in an accident. She was brought here to County via Medivac from downtown. She was admitted about eight forty-five. We called you right away. Let me get Doctor Kenney for you, he has all the details."

"Officer, Mary is my sister. She has no family except for me. Moved here from Wyoming, is living with me until she can find a place of her own."

"Sorry for the mistake."

"An easy one to make."

"Mister Benton, this is Doctor Kenney."

Christ, she looked like she was no older than twenty-five. Gene wondered if she was good or just eager and strong enough to put up with the long hours and bullshit. Maybe a combination of all three. He hoped she was good. She was homelier than a stick, barely four feet ten inches tall, and skinnier than a beanpole.

"Mister Benton, your wife has been in a serious auto accident. She has multiple breaks in her legs and right arm, a skull fracture, and her left lung has been crushed. We're not sure the amount of internal damage. But, given what we know...what we can see, I have to believe that she suffered very extensive internal problems beyond the crushed lung. We'll have a better fix on this issue in a few moments. Doctor Lopez, our resident internist, is examining her now. Why don't we see what he has learned?"

"Doctor Kenney, just for clarification, Mary is my sister. I am the only family she has. Both her husband and daughter are dead."

"Sorry for the error."

"Not a problem."

"Doctor Lopez, this is Mister Benton, Miss Benton's brother."

"Sir, we are doing all we can to sustain your sister. The internal injuries have been extensive. Spleen, left lung, and liver are all damaged. Apparently, she has had polio at some time in her adulthood. This disease weakened her substantially. Thus, her ability to fight this massive trauma is not strong. Miss Benton is holding on.

Barely. Frankly, I'm not sure we can do more for her than just minimize the pain and help her hold on. So, we're in a bind. We can keep her alive. But, for how long before her body just quits? We don't know. No one knows. We do know that she is not suffering. And won't."

"Doctor, are you asking me to consent to pulling the plug? Because, if you are, I'm not empowered to do so. I am her brother and only living relative, but she never provided me with the authority to assist her demise. There is no DNR on record. However, if there are forms to complete by which I could legally assume that power, I will sign them. Just in case. This assumes that her life is in a true downward spiral, and you would be responsible for that determination. In court if need be. Or should we just wait and let nature take its final course?"

"I believe we should wait for at least four hours. By then we'll have a better assessment of her condition and our ability to stabilize her. If you would like to see her, you may. She can't recognize you at this time. But, if you would like, she is in room six."

Soldiers and police say that you never hear the bullet that kills you.

Gene didn't want to remember what Doctor Lopez looked or sounded like. He didn't want to remember anything specific or unique about Mary's temporary hospital residence. No matter what the process or event, a hospital room was just a functional, sterile booth in which humans were placed when they enter this world, recovered from trauma, or reposed before departure. He would remember a bandaged mass of near life with tubes and such into and out of her body. This mass was formerly known as Mary Thomas Benton, smartass sister who tormented her adoring brother every day. Bull-headed young woman who left the East Coast sanctuary of her family to start a new life with a lowlife. Mother of a now dead daughter. Re-builder of her own life. Teacher of adult youths. Seeker of truth. Lover of dogs. This fragile life was in the pre-departure repose. And all the king's horses and all the king's men couldn't put Mary Thomas Benton together again. Maybe the doctors did not display frustration and anger because they had faced similar situations many times before. They had to act detached and professional. Not Gene. He was pissed. He wanted answers. How? Why? He could do nothing but wait for the inevitable and talk to Officer Davis.

"Do you know what happened?"

"We know that the RV she was driving failed to negotiate the ramp at Exit Fourteen from the Interstate. This is one of the exits that leads to the West Side of downtown. Do you know why she was on the road at that time?"

"She had a doctor's appointment. She had been feeling weak lately and thought it was a good idea to have a check-up."

"Well, the vehicle seemed to run straight on a curved exit ramp and stove-piped on the concrete barrier about six feet from the road. Seems she was moving right along and just failed to negotiate the turn. Investigators are on the scene. I'll have a full report by tomorrow. We have impounded the RV. You can retrieve it in a few days. That's all I know now."

Gene called his office and left voicemails for the appropriate people. Then he sat in Mary's room and waited. And waited. *I thought Godot was next door.* No sound other than the whooshing of air breathing for her and the ping of the monitor. The magazines were three months old, which was fine because he never read them anyway. He felt the sap oozing from his body as he slumped forward in the uncomfortable easy chair by her bed. His head rested beside her arm. He put the magazine down and held her hand. No response. The flurry around him startled him awake. He sat up. Spittle had run down the right side of his chin. A nurse checked dials, printouts, and the screen with all the lines. The ping had become a constant ring. Trouble was evidenced by change.

"Sir, excuse me. But you'll have to step aside. This is Winters in room six. We have a Code Blue. Check monitors at station. Call Doctor Lopez. Stat."

No matter what she tried there was no change in the change. All bells and whistles indicated that Mary was in permanent stillness. *I failed to keep her alive on my watch.* Doctor Lopez confirmed Gene knew. He completed the requisite forms and went back home. Stunned. Numb. Soulless.

****

The dogs could sense something terrible had happened. They paced, whined, and moaned. Feral sadness was deeper, more powerful than human sorrow. Not as noisy and far fewer recriminations, but Gene could see the sorrow, thick like fog and dark like a thundercloud. The pacing. Constant motion. Then the dogs plopped. Stared woefully into space for twenty or thirty seconds then arose to pace. This cycle continued for hours. There was nothing the human could say or do to change their natural process of grieving. Should he start to clean up? Pack up her belongings like he did for Dorothy? Not today. Tomorrow. Now, answer telephone.

"Gene, I just heard. What happened? Are you OK? I'm on my way over. If that's all right with you?"

"Sure. I'm not sure I'll be good company with snappy patter. But I could use your presence."

The hug at the door was designed to initiate the restoration of his soul. Gene hugged her back. Thus, the rebuilding commences. With friends or family, tears were a strange comfort. Helping her was helping him. No food. Iced tea by the pool with the dogs. Karen was good for them, too. They liked her. They talked about Mary's life as they knew it. He shared bunches of I-remember-when's. Childhood. The teen years. When she left to get married. Et cetera. Et cetera. With each memory, he realized how little he knew of her adult life. With each story, the pain diminished, and the new void was being filled with fondness. The idea to continue Mary's work came from somewhere. He said it unprompted. Karen thought it was a great idea. He gave her all the details of Mary's recent digging as the apostle related the teachings of the master.

Finally, the list of nine possible targets and the complex philosophical issue of what to do with it. They were both lesser zealots. They had not lost a daughter. It was agreed to do nothing. Wait and see. There were too many ifs and what-ifs inherent in Mary's work. He needed to sleep alone. No touching. Just alone with his sadness and guilt. Karen slept alone beside him. The dogs paced and plopped and paced and plopped.

Gene had taken a few days from work. Frankly, that's no big deal. Nothing going on that his troops couldn't handle or that he couldn't change when he returned. The call from the police stirred some embers. They asked that he come down to the station. Breakfast with Karen. She will be by his side for the next few days, then they should decide where they went from there. For now, two reeds in the wind were strength for each other. Now the unpleasant trip. Police station. The morgue. The mortuary.

****

"Mister Benton, it seems that the steering and brakes on the RV simply wore out at the same time. She was not strong enough to control the vehicle when this happened. The failure coincidence happens occasionally on older vehicles. Your sister's RV had one hundred and eighty thousand miles on it and was twelve years old. So, frankly, failures to the brakes and steering are not an unexpected event. The tubes and wiring were old, and they failed. We are sorry about your loss."

What's wrong with this picture? Mary had her bus completely serviced and checked out before her trek to Florida. She even bitched about the amount of money she spent. The service center must have checked brakes and steering. Gene wanted to understand this inconsistency. He checked the papers from the glovebox. Big Bob's RV Center had replaced the brake fluid lines to the front wheels and did a six-point check on the power steering and found that no repair or replacement was necessary. Karen agreed that something was amiss and called the service center. Harold, the service manager, told her that he remembered Mary Benton. She had the RV serviced every three thousand miles. Kept real good care of her second home and was very fussy with mechanics. She had told them to give the vehicle a thorough going over, as if their kids were going to drive it to Florida. She wanted no problems. When she pulled off the lot, Harold felt that the RV was ready and enough for his mother or his kids. There was nothing wrong with the steering. The brake lines to the front wheels had been replaced because they were a tad worn. Nothing real serious. Just a precaution because of the long trip.

Now Gene was scared. There was contradictory knowledge that only Karen and he could share. Couldn't tell the local cops that they were wrong. Didn't want to stir up some a major brouhaha with investigations and media digging. Didn't want those who altered the RV to know that he and Karen knew. Best to remain silent for the time being. They had to get many more of the puzzle pieces on the board before they asked for serious help. The Scots have a saying:

'Sometimes you have to lie in the bushes and wait before you scream like a banshee.' The couple will lie in the bushes.

The morgue agreed to release the body to Mosser's Funeral Home. Mosser's will turn Mary into ashes. The RV remained at impound. No reason to reclaim it. It would be sold by the insurance company to the junkyard. They will send Mary a check. *Who will cash it?*

****

Back home, Gene and Karen started to pack Mary's belongings. Boxes upon boxes of personal stuff. The ComRoom was stet. This activity is more than he wanted. Karen suggested that she go shopping for dinner. She'll cook. He sat with the boxes, memories, and dogs. They came to him and rested on his lap. Sadness of loss had replaced pitiful woe. The next stage for the remaining humans and dogs was acceptance and moving on. What could he do with the dogs? Will he adopt them or vice versa? They must stay with him, because they are the last vestiges of a family, which was part of him. They were good company and this place might just need vicious security.

Dinner went quickly, silently. Clean-up was by rote. Sitting by the pool, he whispered real fears. Fears, which he had not taken seriously before were like daggers in his heart. Was Mary killed? Was the house bugged? Who were the guys in the pictures? Was there a connection between Senator Miller's campaign and the shootings at the schools? What was really on the websites? Who were all those characters? Could they predict future slaughters? Should they? What principal would close a school for a week on the insane supposition that mayhem might happen? What the fuck had they gotten themselves into? He had no answers. Just lots of questions, which produced even more questions, which produced even more...ad infinitum.

Karen took him by the hand and pulled him close. He could feel her breath in rhythm with his. The warmth of her embrace calmed his trembling. They turned off the lights and closed the doors, keeping one partially open to let the dogs have run of the house and backyard. The bed was comfortable and lovemaking tender. He was so self-involved that he forgot whom Karen was or why she was there. This she must never know. Four am coffee was an old pattern, which returned him to a pre-trauma state. Fed the dogs. Threw tennis balls for them to retrieve for him to throw for them to retrieve. Checked the back gate. Fetched a new lock for the latch. Remembered to call the pool service and the garden genius and left a new key hidden for their use. No duplication allowed. The dogs were the guards. They had already been introduced to the regular workers. It's the strangers they would pursue with due diligence. Their attitude now that Mary was dead would make them unpleasant with interlopers. A huge battle would commence upon intrusion, and the bad guys would die. Oh well. Oh, well.

From the ComRoom, Gene checked his office voicemail and email. Mary and Karen showed him how to do this off-site magic. Maybe he'll never go back to the office. The voicemail was soporific, except for the call from Mike Duncan. He was afraid to listen to this message over the home line for fear that others outside the house would hear it also. He would have to go to the office right now... before the throng arrives. He could be there in thirty minutes, or so, and wouldn't be noticed by anyone but security. He scribbled a note for Karen, who slept sensually in his space.

****

"Gene, this is Mike. I have learned something about your buddies. They work for the Federal Government: I think the CIA. Very strange operatives working outside their area of expertise. Their names are Brent Forbes, Roger Thompson, and Alan Campbell. All are well-educated. They seem to be assigned at the whim and fancy of the director who reports only to the President. Their histories are fuzzy. But it's safe to assume they have been all over the world. Hot spots only. Places where the national interest needs special, prejudicial attention. I know that Brent and Alan were in the Middle East for about two years. You know, the usual stuff: Organizing small groups of dissidents to work together for a common good. Overthrow some bad guy or protect someone who loves Uncle Sam. Men with no pasts bother me, because you never know where they are going.

"Now, Roger is a piece of work. The only place he has been is the Non-union of Soviet Socialist Republics. He visited most of the small, but incredibly angry, states. The ones that have all the nuclear warheads and oil, but no food and clothing. The ticking time bombs. Somehow these three were put together to protect or monitor the good Senator. Why him? Why them? Why now? None of my sources know. But the questions intrigued them enough that they wanted to dig further for me. It will cost about seventy-five hundred for them to get to the bottom of all this. Is it worth it to you? I realize this is steep and sudden, but my guys have moles all over. They could dig up dirt on the Pope. If I were you, I would consider the expense a good investment. Still no lock on any connection between the *tres banditos* with Miller and the fuzzy faces from Carter. I hope to have an answer in two days. By the way, do you ever get the feeling someone is following you? Or just watching your house? Call me with your decision."

I called Mike.

"Mike, I'll send three thousand for your associates via FedEx to your address. The balance of the requested total is payable upon receipt of real information, not just histories. The connection remains key, if any, between Miller's boys and the mugs at Carter. And, yes, I feel that I am watched. But so does a goldfish. Stay in touch."

****

Out the door and head for home. No pick-up truck or small sports car. Had they given up? Were they awake at this hour? In the front door at home. The dogs were happy to see Gene. Karen was asleep. He turned on the TV for early CNN. There it was bigger than death: the slaughter of seventeen children at a Spring Prometheus Festival sponsored by the eighth grade Classic Club. Their celebration of school completion. They were killed in the evening by the traditional bonfires, in the soccer field of John Brown School Middle School located in Ox Bow, Maryland.

The killers used two Barrett Fifty Caliber 82 A-1 Rifles. These were semiautomatic sniper rifles designed to destroy armor reinforced vehicles, turn ballistic glass to sand, and abruptly crash-land low-lying airplanes. They were deadly accurate at more than a mile. Ammunition was available in black-tipped armor piercing and silver-tipped incendiary varieties. Killers had a choice. How nice. The victims didn't. These guns were easier to buy than handguns. The buyers had to show proof that they were eighteen with no felony convictions. Handgun purchasers must be at least twenty-one. The children did not stand a chance. Chunks of small bodies were spread all over the soccer field. It looked like the aftermath of an explosion in a robotic factory except for the pools of blood.

The area and school were not on the list of nine, but the criteria matched. Gene and Mary were too narrow in their search. Too arrogant that they had deciphered the code. Too blinded by their own importance. Pride went before a fall. Unfortunately, this time seventeen middle-schoolers fell. Gene was crushed. The tears welled up in his eyes. Frustration. Anger. Fear. A promise to Mary. No more. The wasting of the innocents must stop. This was his line in the sand. Now he sobbed and sniffled. The dogs wanted to know what the hell was going on. They came into his space and gave him nuzzles and kisses. Karen slid by his side and held him, he floundered in a sea of powerful emotions.

Breakfast. Karen went back to the sites and chatrooms. She was the new GirlFromOz. Armed with knowledge and fearful respect, she read and reread the recent past with knowledge of the then future. She was looking for signs that would have given a clearer indication of place and date. She was convinced that they were on the right path. She wrote down everything that TruthSeeker said, as well as that which proceeded and followed the pronouncements. Where was BrokenArrow in all of this? Was anybody crowing over the events of the evening? Concentrating on the five chatrooms would consume her day. Gene must go to the bank for the mole money then FedEx the cash to San Diego.

Back home, the networks were reporting on the efforts of Senator Miller and President Sessler. Each was stumping for success. Miller was in Duluth, Minnesota. Sixteen thousand people at the Palli Auditorium. S.A.F.E. was alive and growing in the heartland. Same faces. Same speech. It's weird. Miller's responses were not canned, but they were eerily the same with each rally. The questions were also almost the same each time. At the very least, they lead him well. Did the questions come from audience plants? Called on to help the Senator get the complete and proper message to the people. All the while the people think they were getting the message to the Senator. House of mirrors like the ending in The *Lady from Shanghai*. Where were the real bodies? What were reflected images? The only way to find out was to shoot all the panels. The ones that shattered were not real. The one that fell were a person.

Did the people in the audience know which speaker was an image and which one was real? Miller's roadshow was working. He was getting more and more ink, as well as better and better op-ed words each week. First the small town, more conservative and traditional papers were talking about him and his crusade. Now the mid-size markets were awakening. Not all of them. And, not always positive. But the trend was there. He had the buzz. Soon the liberal press of the top ten markets will have to remove their blinders. Maybe they will dig up something of disrepute about the Senator. Maybe they will nominate him for sainthood.

President Sessler was in a vastly different position. His was a house of cards attempting to withstand a force six storm. Leslie Tremaine and Huang Tsai abruptly departed the inner circle. Miss Tremaine cited a prior movie commitment. She was replaced by Jennifer Chessman, a young actress of much lesser note, but a big favorite with the teens. How could Leslie justify her departure? No one had a prior commitment when the President asked. Master Tsai was admitted to a Dallas hospital suffering from exhaustion. He was replaced by a wannabe from the valley. The *L'Enfant* terrible was fine last weekend when he was sighted surfing off Corpus Christi. The lie was too thin. Were they deposed? By whom? For what reason?

Beyond the new weaker mix of celebrities, the changing of horses in midstream does not bode well for the Commission. The A Team was now the B+ Team. In the face of Senator Miller's onslaught, the weakening of the castle guard was dangerous. The next panel discussion was set for this Friday. It will be interesting to see how the entire mess would be handled. Worth watching to see the emergence of the powerbroker, or brokers. Gene's bet was on Elizabeth Pendleton and John Wenger. They appeared to be the cleanest, and therefore, the ones to be trusted the least. If they emerged as the king and queen of the hill, the results of this Public Relations exercise would be predictable.

Plus, there were reports that the President was lobbying Congress for a change in Constitutional Amendment Twenty-Two. It seemed the good President would like to serve for at least a third term. How could he abridge this amendment or place it in abeyance for his pleasure? For what reason was a third term in the best interest of the people? He and his party were obviously afraid of Senator Miller and his believers. The tradition of running the Vice President was guaranteed to fail. Harrison Paul was a blob of tapioca. Big on brains, small on personality, and zero on experience. He had served in the shadow of a very charismatic, often erratic, world leader. Vice President Paul had lived through a six-year bull market of astonishing economic growth, and peace in the industrial world was now the norm.

Both were the sole responsibility of President Sessler. Or at least that's what he says. The Veep just carried the bag and showed up at minor state functions. Rarely went outside the country, except for a wedding. It was his daddy's oil money that financed the first election. Then daddy died and Sessler took control. Now Paul was just a Vice President, never to be President. Never to even run. In this environment and given the fact that Sessler is a megalomaniac, a change in the Constitution was the logical step, in Sessler's mind, to retain the power. Why should little things like Constitutional Law and Due Process stand in the way of President Sessler?

****

Karen worked in the ComRoom. She was noticeably quiet. Gene was not sure she lived here, although she was here every day so far. If she lived here, when did she move in? The blur of time was fogged by the sorrow of loss. The dogs liked her, and they listened to her. He did as well. She was good for all three males. Gene felt her presence throughout the house, and it calmed him. She was in the door to the den motioning him to follow her poolside. They sat and dangled their feet.

"Gene, look what I've found: Something we missed. These are the three lines from TruthSeeker that led to the list of nine possible targets. We were on the right track. We just overlooked the input from BrokenArrow because it did not appear near the keylines. Quotes did, however, appear on all three scrolls. The first two quotes are number clues. See, BrokenArrow tells us: 'Extensive Filly Faves' and 'In thirty-nine houses liberty has been lost.' The third quote is a date clue: 'Classic Comic Books are for the masses.' These are nonsense lines at the end of his ramblings. Clue seekers would know to look for the words, their importance relative to those of TruthSeeker, and would know how to decipher them.

"If we check the atlas, we find that Ox Bow, Maryland is roughly at longitude seventy-six and latitude thirty-nine. The Philadelphia basketball team is the Seventy-Sixers. Extensive could be considered a synonym for longitude. So, we have longitude seventy-six. Following that same path, liberty is synonymous for latitude. This gives us latitude thirty-nine. And Classic is a reference to the Classic's Club which puts on the Prometheus festival. There you have it. A complete guide to what, where, and when the killings are going to occur. If all this is accurate, we must watch the chatrooms each day, so we can predict the next where and when. And, make no mistake about it, there will be a next."

"Karen, this is more than I can deal with now. I think we need to call in some professional help. Someone who can act with authority. The authority we don't have. We should also check the dates of the massacres. Is there any rhyme or pattern there?"

"I've done that already. Carter, Menthen, Lutztown, and Ox Bow occurred no less than three weeks and no more than four weeks apart. This is definitely a serial killing effort. There does not appear to be shortening or lengthening of that schedule. If the timing holds, whatever will happen will do so in three weeks to four weeks from the last slaughter. What we don't know is when the clues will be posted. But I suspect the clues will start to appear soon. This will give the killers time to prepare, assuming they are not part of an already armed and poised militia. We don't know if the clues will be posted by BrokenArrow and TruthSeeker. Or, which of the two will give the right clues. We don't know if the two *cluemeisters* will provide the same type of clues in the same order. We don't know a lot. So, we must be ever vigilant.

"I'll take some time from work. The three big proposals are complete, and my assistant can mop up any details. I haven't had a vacation for nearly two years, and I am due. My boss took his time before we began the big crunch. It'll be a sudden request, but they'll get over it. What about you?"

"I'm still on family emergency leave and can extend that for a few more days. Then, I'll go on vacation. The problem is that I'll need to get to my office for communication with Mike Duncan. I told him that was our only contact point. But I can do that at night. I'll sneak in and out under the cover of darkness."

"We can call Mister Duncan on my cellphone if you're concerned about using the landline. We can call from the lanai or standing in the pool, as crazy as it sounds. That way we'll be safe. It's just that he can't call us here. We can even access your email by using a complex trail from here to my office to your office and back again. We can read it then trash it. Wipe it clean. If someone is watching and listening, they will note our activity but not what we see."

"Will you be moving in?"

This was a big question. Suppose she had already moved in. Was Gene inviting her? Yes.

"Temporarily."

"That's a good thing. Your presence here on a full-time basis is desired by the three males. If we are to live in the bunker, I best go grocery shopping. And you will want to retrieve clothes and your girl stuff. I'll get you a key to the front door and the back gate while I'm out. I'll be back from my chores by three. See you then. Thank you for your care."

Their kiss was brief and non-sexual. Husband-and-wife buss. Off to the grocery store, cleaners, and hardware store. Home again, naturally.

****

Karen followed in about thirty minutes. She unloaded her car alone. Wanted no help. She moved her clothes into Mary's room, clearly establishing the social acceptability of her abiding in the house. She would sleep with Gene, but not live with him, strange but acceptable. The dogs were happy to see her. The pair changed for a swim. The beginning of a new relationship.

XI

Midnight, right after the guard change. Night was black with the sparkle of stars like a dancehall ceiling. BOOM!!! Sergeant William Darny was disintegrated by the explosion and its heat. Pieces of the small truck, which carried the mass of explosives, were found two hundred yards away...shreds of one tire, a piston, shards of the side mirror, and a twisted ignition switch. The blast lifted the side wall of the embassy compound about six inches from the foundation, bowed it in toward the buildings, and turned the reinforced concrete into lace. The lattice fell into the courtyard. No one saw the men carrying the rocket launchers. They were kneeling in the compound wall's maw before the dust settled. Their three blasts thrust one highly explosive armor piercing shell and two incendiary shells into the wall of the building that housed the soldiers and the embassy personnel. The collapsing walls and fire claimed thirty-six American soldiers who were proud to serve. They knew there would be some tense times and a reasonable amount of danger. No one, top to bottom, could have predicted this event, although they should have been wary.

Approximately two minutes later, a small pick-up truck stopped at the gate of the United States Embassy in Takrit. Takrit was a strategic city because it was the home of two Sunni tribes. Friend and foe depending on the time of day or day of the month. One gate guard left his booth for a coffee break while the other stayed in air-conditioned comfort and called the Officer of the Watch. Before the guard reached the OW, the smoke belching small truck appeared. The driver had abandoned his vehicle and was running into the night. BOOM!!! The explosion targeted the guardhouse, and the guard disappeared in the fireball. The gate and the surrounding walls disappeared in the fireball. Alarms sounded and pandemonium reigned. From the back of a lorry rushed five black clad bodies. They knelt beside their lorry and fired rocket launchers.

All projectiles struck the first-floor front. The wall, weakened by the shock wave of the first blast, slid to the ground like mud down a hill. The entire face of the six-story building disappeared. Everything was on fire. Smoke enveloped the building. The five combatants scurried like rats back into the lorry as it pulled away and headed south. The alarms blared and orders were barked from top to bottom. The perimeter was secured. Full battle alert. Just ninety seconds too late. The digging would commence shortly. Forty dead.

****

In another time zone to the east, over uninhabitable wasteland, a third small pick-up truck bumped and wove its way through the undersized streets of Nesset. Nesset controlled the oil within a two-hundred-mile radius. Food, clothing, medicines, and all manner of necessities for this land-locked center of wealth came through Takrit's airport. The relationship between the two governments was cordial on the surface but acrimonious underneath the visual niceties. Nesset was the home of a large Shia tribe. The faith of both governments in Allah and hatred for the Western World seemed to be their only commonalties.

The truck stopped on the avenue that led directly to the American Embassy and military barracks. Two men exited the truck and wired the bomb in the bed of the truck. One moved to the front and activated the detonator. He left, and the driver reentered the cab. The wheel was lashed right and left to keep the truck on target. A carefully crafted piece of metal was wedged under the accelerator to keep the engine roaring. The horror was about to begin. The truck hurtled on its appointed path. BOOM!!! The crash at the gate and blast were simultaneous. The fireball could be seen for miles in the pitch-black sky. This was no oil storage tank explosion. The conflagration and confusion were cover for the second vehicle. The old army truck ground its way to the much-enlarged gate opening and the truck paused. The tarpaulin on the building side of the truck was raised and six bodies became visible.

Their firepower was unleashed on the interior building. Four small mortars and two rocket launchers. Three rounds each. What was a wall was now rubble. What was behind the wall was now more rubble. In less than three minutes the men reentered the truck, the tarp was lowered, and the truck waddled off into the flame lit night. The total lives lost in the three-pronged attack left many bodies which are just lots of components.

The Pentagon was saying nothing. The White House had scheduled a briefing for eight am, Washington time. The visuals replayed and the voiceovers were repeated. After an hour, the shock had worn off and the pain ever so slightly diminished. How many times can Gene hear about and see the butchery before he just didn't give a shit? The body count rose with the sun. The rescue squads scampered about in the background directing heavy equipment and lifting pieces of the structures from the bodies. They were calling for the medics whose futile attempts to save lives long since lost were sad. The outcome was predetermined, but the medics must try, nonetheless.

****

CNN reported that this was the beginning of Shia' Feast of Great Joy. For three days, there would be parades, dancing, and great feasts. The local non-combatants were delicately controlled by a group of multinationals cobbled together and given sanctuary in this land. Hitler's iron fist of control would be more like a debutante's white gloved handshake relative to the absolute power exercised by the jihadists. If they smiled, one may or may not smile depending on whether he meant the smile as happy and only he knew that. Just about any day could be your last if you didn't curry favor like a toady each and every moment.

About every six months the jihadist group changed its make-up because most of them died. No one retired. Some who have spoken against the leaders become targets for his weapons testers after being tortured for a few weeks. His marksmen were not particularly good. It took several of them several rounds to kill one dissident. Those who were truly evil became unfortunate subjects for the chemical and biological warfare labs. This was exceptionally excruciating because death took up to six weeks. The gestapo was just an angry teacher next to these jihadists. The populace was poor, suffered from regular inquisitions, and had little or no western life amenities. All the basics were reserved for The Battalions of Allah. There was a never-ending supply of new recruits. Facing death on the battlefield was more desirable than starving at home. Many of the young men sent their rations back to their families. The war machine efficiently ground on.

The Sunnis and Shiites had been waging war with one or another for more than six hundred years. The wars had been minor border disputes for the most part. Necessary honing steps for a much larger conflict. A struggle to lead the faithful out of the dark ages and to their rightful position as leaders of the world. Beginning in the last century, the sides had progressed, or regressed, from soldiers, some with rifles from before World War One, to well-trained killing forces that command tanks, artillery, and sophisticated communications. In the last big conflict, biological and chemical clouds were used to eliminate helpless, noninvolved villagers. The message was read loud and clear: 'Don't fuck with us.' The sides received financial and weaponry support from just about every nation that hates the US. Loans in the form of credits used to purchase equipment and technology. They used big and they owed big. Oil sold on the black market could not pay for all the support. They were mortgaging their futures. This debt was a drug. The more they wanted, the more they got. The givers accommodated because they knew when this internal strife ended, they would get land and oil. The only way the fighters could pay was to control more land and more oil. But when did the dog become bigger and meaner than the master? When will the borrower tell the lender to eat shit?

The war machines are run and staffed by groups from all over the world, but mostly the desert region. These were troublemakers, who had been banished from their own countries. Revolutionaries. These were the men and women who tried to depose the old monarchies but failed. Sometimes the US gave them aid and sometimes our global nemesis gave them weapons and training. Just enough so that they could cause trouble, but not enough for an immediate and complete overthrow of power. Both superpowers used these militants to foment unrest, so each could come in and help rebuild the land of those who could win. Both would shore up defenses, provide basic needs, buy the country's export, and build our own airbases.

Now the exiled militants served and trained in several countries, in the hope that one day, very soon, they would be able to return and take back their own from the international bullies. This suited the leaders. Most of the countries were, at one time, friendly to the US. Or, at least, The US thought so because that's what they told Uncle Sam. Now, they received more support each year from the US to keep the bad guys contained. The US had become their drug dealer, tightened the noose around necks. Restricted their trading ability by devaluing their export: oil. If the US could keep the price of oil at an artificially depressed level for another five years, the jihadists would implode. They had no way to kick the massive drug of debt. At least, that's what the government told the people. This was the tension that kept the Middle East hot. The dealers had their own problems and could apply the screws to their fragile economies to heighten their woes. If they had to pay more for basics, they would have less and less to feed the junkie. If the junkie got less and less, he became more and more anxious to expand. We were working both sides of the street. A very dicey situation. But the wall around them was resolute. We hoped.

This was the arcane nature of international politics.

****

The Feast of Great Joy started with a two-hour parade and a ninety-minute diatribe from several leaders. The latest tanks and artillery, as well as the elite guard battalions paraded before the people. The people stood on the hot concrete beneath the sweltering sun, while their fearless leaders sat in an air-conditioned, bulletproof viewing stand. The stand came complete with delicacies and cold drinks. Visible on the boulevard was the best hardware the people's money and blood can secure. Tanks from Russia, mobile artillery from China, and missile launchers with appropriate warheads from Sweden. Nothing from the US. The elite guards goose-stepped to a beat that was part native and part Wagnerian. The battalions are segmented by the type of weapons they carried. The variety was wide—assault rifle, sniper rifle, and anti-tank. The banners and flags represented the various battles and wars in which the men had fought. Several of the banners were fictitious and two of the battle flags had been dropped in defeat. After years of rhetoric and misinformation, thousands of deaths, including the historians, few could remember the truth. The Boulevard of the Revolution can carry sixty men across. The marching music stopped as the supreme leader approached the microphone.

"Today is truly a day of Great Joy. The dog has been taught a lesson, and he flees with his tail tucked between his hindlegs. For years, the forces of oppression have attempted to thwart our manifest destiny. All we ever wished was to live in prosperity and peace with our neighbors and the world. For years we have held forth the olive branch of love and understanding. For years we have been treated as less than human by those who would take our land and our precious resources. We have been held prisoner in our own land. We have been cheated in international commerce. Our women have been raped. Our children slaughtered. Our farms and cities pillaged. Our factories sabotaged. Our borders moved at the will of those who hate.

"I say to you, my brothers and sisters, that today this evil ends. Today we stand alone against the forces of tyranny. We stand tall that others may follow. Today is the dawn of a better tomorrow. Last night, while the dog slept, the people he has enslaved rose against him and struck a blow for the freedom of all. We will continue the grand and glorious revolution. We will rout the devil. Let us dedicate this day to our fallen. Let us dedicate this day to our strong warriors. Let us dedicate this day to the death of the oppressor. Let us dedicate this day to a safe and secure tomorrow for our children and our children's children."

****

Gene's mind and soul were spinning out of control. He couldn't make sense of anything. Well, they've done it. Sent saboteurs into the countries with whom they have been fighting. The guys slinked around and did the dirty deeds. The countries took the heat from the US. Why couldn't the allies keep their houses in order? They claim the sibling nations were acting in the best interest of the region and needed help. Troops were sent to complete the job. They took over the country. Installed the former rebels, who had been practicing for this day.

The land was annexed. More oil. More food. More debt repayment. More credit. *The US was on the horns of a dilemma. Did we fight to preserve nations about which we don't care? Did we retaliate against the accused or the real culprit? How did we save face? What did we have to do to save the world? How could we not lose? What about the other lender? Would he join the battle?* The geography was small but strategic.

The massacres. The phony pageantry. The twisted truth. The lies. The hatred. The set-up for revenge. Who was the biggest liar? Who was behind the killings? Were there many forces competing in a great killing tournament? The one that got the most deaths wins. There must be more deaths to come. Were Gene's niece and sister just insignificant bugs under the jackboots of the power mongers? His sister was watched. The people in the chatrooms were watched. Was Gene being watched? Who was this woman in his house? What did she want? Was she here to help him find Mary's killers? Was she here to kill him? Would she lead him off the path of truth? Could she be trusted? He couldn't trust the police. He couldn't trust anyone in government. Certainly not Sessler or Miller.

He dared not move. He could not move. The images and noise from the television seemed to move away. The sound was so distant it was almost not there. Sort of barrel hollow, but no echo. The picture on the screen jumped as if it were skip framed. The motions were herky-jerky. Then they were in slow motion. The timber of the voices vacillated with the changing picture. Black and white became color, which became black and white. This ebb and flow of sight, sound, and motion was almost soothing. Hypnotic. The pendulum swing of the gold watch. Was he trapped? Was he stuck in this chair? Why was he crying? He could not hear sobs, but he could feel the shudder. Pants were wet. Seat was wet. Did he spill his coffee? He never got a second cup. What was the wet mess? Arms were locked at his side.

Who was this woman? Why was she standing before him? Was she yelling? He could barely hear her. Her hands were on his shoulders. She was holding him. Rocking him like a baby. Looking into his eyes, trying to get a response. Nothing. Her voice was far away. Telling him to move his arms and his legs. He cannot. He really didn't want to and didn't care to try. Had he stopped living? Was this death? Darkness surrounded them. There was no light from the TV and no lights in the room. Just deep dark gray. She shrank and grew with the light. Now she was shrinking. Her voice disappeared. She tugged his arms to pull him up. He stood but did not move. He turned around to look at the chair and noticed big dark stain on the seat. His? Too big for tears. His shirt was wet. She unbuckled his belt and removed his trousers and underpants. Walked him to the bedroom and helped me onto the bed. Not the right time for that now. When was the right time? Helped him on with new pants. Led him to the door and into the garage.

****

The light in his eye hurt. The doctor was exploring to be sure of something. Did anyone really know what the doctor saw? His hands were gentle and his grip firm. His voice was soothing. Gene couldn't understand what the doctor was saying. His nurse took notes. That woman was not here. Did she deposit her trouble on the doorstep of another? Two pills and a small cup of tepid water. Why not a big glass of ice-cold mountain spring water? The ceiling was incredibly low. The ceiling lights were flickering. That made him nauseous.

The two men helped him down the chilly dank hall to his room. Not his room where his wet pants were. His new room. Green and gray walls and ceiling. Incredibly soft lighting. A bed and a bed pan. A window in front of Gene and the door behind him. There was a heavy metal grate on the window to keep him in or to keep them out? The door had a small window in it. Would they watch? What would they see? Was he to stay here for a long time? Forever? Would they feed him, clothe him, and bathe him? He was sure he couldn't do all of that. And didn't really care. He was tired. The bed linen was fresh. There was something special about freshly cleaned and lightly starched bed linen. It was comforting to the skin. Cool, but not cold. He rested. He did not sleep. Head on pillow, he could see the window in the door. He would watch them, think about where he was and why.

The square route of pi was 1.7724531. Pi squared was

9.86958772. He was better with his times than his "gazintas". The rule of seventy-two predicted the doubling rate of the value of money. One divided the interest or growth rate into the number seventy-two. The resultant number approximated the time, expressed in number of years it would take the value to double. The sum of the squared values of the horizontal and vertical legs of an isosceles right triangle equaled the squared value of the hypotenuse. That was the three-four-five rule. Why were there only three hundred sixty degrees in a complete circle? Why were there three hundred sixty-five and one-quarter days in a year? Who says?

Time and distance were arbitrary measurements applied by mankind and womankind? Would humans really age faster in space? Did Sherpas age faster than people who lived below sea level? The tree falling in the forest did make a sound. We just didn't hear it if we were not there. How strong was a mother's love? Being rich was nice. But there is always someone who was richer. The same couldn't be said about happiness because happiness was subjective. What constituted a good parent? What was the proper balance between the impact of heredity and environment? When were choices programmed? 9.869587728 plus 1.7724531 equal 11.63833038. That's wrong.

The light in the room came from outside. This room was his. Where was it? The doctor. The pills. The nurse woke Gene up to give him pills to help him sleep. How stupid was that? Why not wait until he awakens and needed the pills? Are all these pills good for him or just a way to control him? He needed to shower and shave. Get cleaned up. His crotch itched from peeing incident. He was tired, but jittery. Where were the men who brought him to this room? Where exactly was he? Two female nurses lead him to the shower. Hope it was not a communal event. They were toads. They took his hospital pajamas. The towel was so fucking small it barely covered his genitalia, and he was not that big. They handed him a new pair of hospital pajamas, a robe, and paper slippers to take him to the end of the hall. Three examining rooms. Gene was deposited in number two to wait. And wait. And wait.

****

"Good morning Mister Benton. How do you feel?"

"A little groggy from all the downers you guys dumped in me last night. What am I doing here and when can I get out? By the way, where are my real clothes? Look, I'm over twenty-one, and I can come and go as I please. And I please to leave. So, give me the forms to sign, and I'll be on my way."

"Mister Benton, you were brought here to Saint Joseph's Hospital for observation. Miss Leach brought you. She was genuinely concerned. You had become catatonic. You were not responding to light, motion, or sound. She claimed to have found you in this state yesterday morning at your home. You urinated on yourself and were sitting stock-still in front of the television set. She was worried because she could not reach you. She wanted professional advice. You have undergone the recommended twenty-four-hour observation. We must now decide if it is in your best interest to keep you here for more tests and treatment or to release you."

"I recommend letting me go home. I may not be healthy in its purest form, but I'm not violent. I haven't hurt anyone, not even myself. So, I don't need or want to be here. I will endure out-patient counseling and take whatever meds you script, but I will not stay here."

"Sir, that is not your decision to make. It is the decision of Miss Leach and me."

His pronouncement rang like the gong in a Road Runner cartoon. The solid sound and the vibrations of the impact. Gene was stopped cold. Someone outside of his immediate and trusted family was asserting control over his life. His coming and going were controlled by a doctor he didn't know and a woman about whom he was not sure. He was the mouse in the maze. They had the corn and the keys to the doors. Better to be pliant and win than to be stubborn and stay here.

"Listen to me doc. If I am to be held under the Baker Act, you had better get a judge's order or a signed consent form from my next of kin. Who, by the way, lives a thousand miles from here. I make my own adult decisions and I decide that I like me, I trust me, and I want me to go home. OK? What forms must I sign? What promises must I make and keep? Tell me. Beware that I am not prone to violence or rage, but I can get very pissed if lied to or contained."

There was panic and power in Gene's voice, and the doctor sensed it. What he didn't know was why it was critical that the patient get out of the rest ranch. One, he had been here before and was not crazy about a repeat performance. Gene assumed the doctor was aware of his emotional coming out party of years ago. He could read the hospital records. It was a brief run at the palace and the shrink who saw him gave the patient a clean bill of health. Two, Gene had some life or death information to extract from some chatrooms. This was not the good doctor's concern.

"Miss Leach is here. I'd like to talk to her before I make my decision."

****

The pompous arrogant prick. He wanted Gene to be sure not to miss the fact that the good doctor was holding the patient's balls in his iron grip. He left the examining room: the sterile, bright, and very unpleasant examining room. Three shades of the most bilious green. Gene says to himself, "Hold on there, big fella. Don't get buried in all the details of everything. That was how you got here in the first place. Holding minutia under a microscope. Examining a nit on a gnat's ass. Looking for termite feces in black pepper. Too fucking much detail and not enough perspective." Gene couldn't tell anyone what Karen and he knew. Or what they were doing. Shit, both of them would be locked in this hellhole. No one would believe the details of the conspiracy. Conspiracies were only good and fashionable among the fringe. He must take the meds, see the doc. Tell the doc only what he wants to hear from someone who was susceptible to depression.

Just like the last time. Pressure built until the black cloud engulfed him. Then his self-preservation system shut off all contact with the outside. Only temporarily. Just enough time for the psyche and soul to regroup and begin working in concert. Kept still and do as he was told. Rely on Karen. She was his only true friend. He hoped.

Enter the angel of mercy and Doctor Putz: "Gene, the doctor has decided that you can come home with me. You don't need to stay here any longer. We'll stop at the drugstore and get these prescriptions filled. You're going to be alright, but you need lots of rest. You've been going too fast and too hard."

"Mister Benton, you have experienced a serious episode of depression. So serious that it took over your mind and body. I stress episode, because it is my belief that this event, just as the previous one years ago, was triggered by something outside of you and, just as the previous event, this episode is not a long-term, clinical situation. With rest, the proper medications, and therapy, you'll be able to get to the cause of the event. Through therapy, we can deal with the underlying issues. It's a process, Mister Benton. So, the faster we work at it the faster we can resolve the issues. Do you understand what I am saying?"

"Shit, doc, I'm not deaf or stupid. Just depressed. Yes, I know I need help. I don't wish this event to recur. So, I'll do what is required."

"Good, you may get dressed, check out, and leave with Miss Leach. With her consent, we have designated her as the responsible adult. We assumed that would be suitable for both of you."

On the ride home, the two stopped at the local drugstore. Gene realized that his pants didn't fit. They were baggy. The waist was at least an inch too large. They hung on his hips like some latest teen fashion. He had lost substantial weight over the past two or three weeks. How was that possible? He ate regularly and slept well. That was not enough to fend off the black cloud. He received three prescriptions: one for mood enhancement, one for energy, and one to help him sleep. These were his happy pills. A pill for every mood and a mood for every occasion. Synthetic body elements. Ain't, modern technology grand?

The dogs were happy to see Gene. He was happy to see animals that loved unconditionally. They didn't give a damn what kind of day or night he had; they were just happy he was home with them. They would be a big part of his therapy. The pee stain was visible. The local newspaper warned of war. In the President's news briefing, and later in his speech to the nation, he spoke of planned, coordinated response to the attempted, destabilization of the Middle East, the protection of our sovereign rights, the revenge for the slaughter of Americans, and a joint global effort to combat the criminal acts of the marauders.

Sessler confirmed that he'd had dialogues with all the major powers and the countries of the Security Council. He could not divulge details of his conversations but assured Americans that the world would not stand by and permit this form of aggression. The peace-loving people of the region and the world were seeking a swift and definitive resolution to this affront to sovereignty. He asked the appropriate cabinet members, advisors, and military leaders of the United States to develop a plan with various scenarios, which would be reviewed with international allies. In the meantime, the embassies and military barracks throughout the region were being fortified and bolstered with men and materials. The people of the United States must stand tall. We must stand together. The sooner this conflict is resolved, the better. Film at eleven.

****

The U.S. Navy could steam into the seas and gulfs, surrounding the warzone. Destroyers. Aircraft carriers. Three heavy cruisers, that could lob shells from infinity. No one called it a war. But a state of war preparedness existed. So, the country must be about to be at war. The Air Force would speckle the sky like starlings over the three sheikdoms. F-15s, 16s, and 25s would soon deposit their shitstorm of death and destruction. Stealth fighters and bombers, and all types of single purpose aircraft were ready. The troop mobilization was fierce. Men, tanks and artillery were assembled, loaded onto the jumbo aircraft, and flown somewhere. Lots of pictures of wives and children kissing their heroes goodbye. Was this real or a show for the enemy?

Most of the news editorials, electronic and printed, were calling for an international program, not one comprised solely of the US military. Then there were the usual *vox populi* on the left and the right. A few publications called for cooler heads. They made the case for an international dialogue, including certain objective third parties, a stand down of the massive air and sea armada and the withdrawal of US troops. At the other end of the spectrum, some pundits wanted us to take full responsibility for a war. The military should bomb the enemy back to the Stone Age, free all the people, and rid the Middle East of revolutionaries. This was countered by the reminder that this approach worked so well in Vietnam. The neocon hawks wanted the military to start at the east shore of the Mediterranean Sea and carpet bomb up to the border of India.

Amid all this saber rattling and clamoring, normal everyday stuff like death and taxes were relegated to the sixth page of the second section or as brief filler in the soft news half hour before the real blood and guts, doom and gloom hour.

Senator Miller and his S.A.F.E. campaign were sucking hind teat. His constituent base was in the small towns and rural areas of the country. Most of the members of the military, top to bottom, came from the small towns across the nation. The mothers and fathers were still there. These voters, who had expressed unrest and a lack of confidence in the federal government, were now shoulder to shoulder with the President. Yes, the safety and security of children and grandchildren were important. The country will get back to that after it rained vengeful havoc on the Butcher of Basjar. A big international threat came before the domestic slaughter of children.

Shit, Gene, doing it to myself. Diving into the turmoil, details, and hypotheses that just recently drove him to the brink. Fewer that twenty-four hours ago, the black cloud of depression had engulfed his mind and soul. He became catatonic. *I peed myself.* A loving stranger got him help or, at least, a medical observation. Now he was home, safe and secure. She was here to protect him. He had meds. He must rest and not think about Dorothy, Mary, the school kids or dirty politics in any arena. Not even think about his job. He must concentrate on only those things, which will help him return to normal. What was normal? Who are the norms? GI Joe, George Lincoln Rockwell, and Norman Bates? Episodic depression could be controlled. He would do that. Where was Karen? Could he kiss her? Would her kiss lift this veil of confusion? He remembered an adage from his sons: 'It's not over 'till I win.' He was a Scot and had just begun to play. What could he do while he was recovering? How far could he push himself while digging into the morass that caused his depression? That's what the happy pills and Karen were for. Make sure he didn't fall back under the black cloud.

XII

"We are now on ready-hold."

"Roger that."

All these commands were predicated on the successful launch of four birds of prey. Now approaching their designated targets. When the jobs of the launch teams were completed, they casually awaited the successful conclusion of the missions by the KITs and the return of the birds of prey.

In four isolated gatherings of tents and small buildings, guards and dogs patrolled the perimeter of the camps while men, women, and children went about their everyday activities. There was no desert breeze to cool the noon sun. The families enjoyed the peace of a meal together. Later, the children would return to the makeshift school to continue to learn a warped version of the Koran. Women would study bomb making. They were also responsible for maintaining their households. The men learned battle strategy and logistics, as well as training with automatic weapons and RPGs. A select few were learning the intricacies of heavier weapons and artillery, while others were responsible for upkeep of the transportation: trucks, cars, and acquired military vehicles. All adults and children over the age of 14 were expected to know how to kill and why they had to kill:

eliminate Westerners from the tribal homeland by any means necessary to attain the goal of freedom.

****

"Raptor One, you have a green light."
"Raptor Two, you have a green light."
"Raptor Three, you have a green light."
"Raptor Four, you have a green light."
Four sets of eyes locked onto targets displayed on four screens. Four very expensive hand-held devices were moved ever-so-slightly to bring the cross hairs of each drone into the center of the targets. This was the delicate part of the mission because a drone did not fly with the stability of a jet fighter. It could bob and weave or swoop and yaw almost at its own choosing. Control from so far away, with no knowledge of wind currents, was difficult. But that was what the KITs train for.
"Raptor One away."
"Raptor Two away."
"Raptor Three away."
"Raptor Four away."
Four red buttons pressed. With the simple message, four firebombs were let loose on an unseen enemy. Within three heartbeats, the bombs found their targets and four monitors flashed white as they showed the clouds in the sky above the camps as the four drones headed back to

their bases. These bombs had been developed for precisely this type of mission. Each bomb contained clusters of canisters that, in turn, contained a recently developed and extremely vicious version of thermite. Each internal canister had its own detonator. When the bomb hit, it did not explode. It broke apart and the canisters scattered for up to one hundred yards in all directions. Only when the canisters hit the ground on their own were they able to work their malevolent magic...independently. The resultant four explosives covered an area the size of two football fields. Each fireball burned so hot that it turned sand into glass. Because of the chemical composition of the new and improved thermite component, the fire could not be extinguished by traditional methods. The fire must burn itself out. These fires burned so brightly and comprehensively that they made the conflagration of Dresden look like an outdoor cookout. The flames would last for at least two hours. The damage forever. Each massive fire could be seen by nomads and people in other camps many kilometers away. The four explosions completely erased the camps of el Jahdiq in Chadar, near Riatta in Qratri, near Basjar, and Najret.

There was jubulation in the Pentagon and DOD. They had done the job requested by the president. They bluffed the enemy with the massive build-up of traditional weaponry and hit them from behind with technology. This pincer tactic saved many U.S. military lives, and it warned the rest of the world. From the White House, President Sessler smiled as he pronunced that the response to the previous attacks demonstrated the US strength on the international stage. It was a planned, coordinated response, to the attempted destabilization of the Middle East. It protected US sovereign rights and avenged the slaughter of Americans via the criminal acts of the marauders. He whispered to his innercircle that just as important as the raids letting the enemy of America know we were serious about control of the Middle East, they would also divert the attention of the voters from the Miller campaign which has become a real threat. Pay back was not a bitch when you are the one paying back.

****

"Gene, I've got some interesting and disturbing information for you. Give me a call before eleven am your time."

Gene got the message at eight. Mike Duncan sounded nervous.

"Mike, good morning. What have you learned?"

"Gene, thanks for the call back. I gave you another number, a secure number, on your email. Hang up, check your email, and call me back at that number in thirty minutes. I'll tell you why then."

Karen helped Gene with the elaborate procedure of bouncing emails from the ComRoom to her office to his office. It took fifteen minutes. They read and trashed all the mail, the vast majority of which was business related. A message each from Gene's boys about their aunt. Both have to beg out of Gene's proposed trip to Grand Cayman. Children and work. The curses of the married and ambitious. He would get back to them later today. There was a cryptic message from Mike. A second emergency telephone number and a box number at the main San Diego post office. It looked like he was going off the grid. Back to the pool and the cell phone. Karen and Gene agreed that soon the bad guys, if they were watching, would access the company cellphone records and determine who and when they called, just not what was said.

"Mike, what the hell is going on? Why this second telephone and the post office box?"

"Gene, remember when I asked you if you ever felt watched? Well, I'm sure that someone, or ones, are watching me. I think they may even have my apartment bugged. And somehow, they may be monitoring my computer travels. Whatever you got me into is bigger and more sinister than I could have imagined. I started to dig a little deeper about the three guys in the pictures. You know, Forbes, Thompson, and Campbell. And everywhere I dug, I hit a granite sarcophagus. I mean the history, and even the present, of these guys is buried deep and secure. My moles came up with little bits of unconnected info. I was able to piece together a very bizarre picture, like a jigsaw puzzle comprised of pieces from several puzzles. Nothing seemed to make sense, and I was about to give up. Quit and return some of your money. However, since all the funds had been allocated to necessities for my moles and me, returning the money was out of the question. So, I, or we, had to go on. Ethics you know. Besides, I really don't like to lose any game.

"So, back to work I went. Concentrating more closely on the details. You know when you concentrate awfully hard on something, you can see something new out of the comer of your eye. Well,

I did. I noticed a sports car and a pick-up truck. And I felt that some things were different in my apartment. Very eerie. Like I was being watched and listened to. I got the same bad feeling that Gene Hackman had at the end of the movie, *Conversation*. They had been here. I'm just not sure who they are. So, I conduct special business like ours from this phone and through a new post office box. What the fuck are we into?"

"Mike, calm down and tell me what you've learned."

"Well, the Three Musketeers are definitely not good guys. It seems as if Forbes, Thompson, and Campbell are working at least two sides of the street. And I'll bet if there are more sides than two, these guys would be working them too. All three guys work for *Grande tio Sucre* in the National Security Agency. Hell, they may even work for more than one government agency. Your suspicions were spot on. The three of them are visible at both Senator Miller's rallies and the Carter, Wyoming massacre. We had to do some significant computer enhancement and jiggling, but we found their faces at Carter. Hairline, profile, noses, and earlobes are matches. So, we know that they are both places, we just don't know why.

"Given the interest that someone has taken in my activities, I suspect the why is deep and very nefarious. Here is what I think: I think that the three guys are in both places to do more than just keep an eye on the events. I think they are in both places to facilitate and control the events. I think they somehow fuel the rallies then manage an event like Carter. Take that one step further. Let's say they start events like Carter. You know, like the forest rangers, who start a fire for a planned purpose. Here is the real scary scenario. Just like the rangers, My Three Sons extinguish their fires when the blazes have accomplished their objectives."

They both held their breath. The silence was audible. With no noise over the line, the pool water noise in Gene's other ear sounded like an ocean during a storm.

"What in Christ's name are you saying? Are you saying that Forbes, Thompson, and Campbell started the shooting, then killed the kids? That's impossible. The kids did the shooting. No one is sure who shot the kids."

"What I'm saying is that maybe, just maybe, the kids, the outlaw gunslingers, are given permission or encouragement to commit the atrocities by the three gentlemen in question. Then these gentlemen either waste the innocent pawns or give the go ahead for the locals to snuff them."

"If they give permission to snuff them, certain local and state police have to be involved. This could be a huge evil network."

"The locals will step aside for feds. Let the feds take the heat for anything that goes wrong but claim credit for a successful completion of a mission. The feds will hit and run. Disappear into the shadows or the night. They are trained to do this in their international efforts. They can then apply this training to domestic issues that need the same type of invisible death squads."

"OK. This is not yet beyond my ken. Let's take this to the extreme. We are saying that these guys are responsible for the shootings in Carter and perhaps, Menthen, Lutztown, and Ox Bow. They foment the killings by children, then kill the children to silence them. The silencing is done to keep the fomentation or permission a secret. Loose lips sink ships, and all that. How about loose lips sink Presidential candidates? Isn't slaughter of innocent children a little extreme to set up a candidacy? It's hard for me to accept that Miller would commit the crime to do the time at Sixteen Hundred Pennsylvania Avenue. There has got to be something we're missing. I mean I can follow your path. I just can't arrive at your destination."

"Gene, at this point, our guesses and speculations are just that. But, if I'm being watched, it's more than for my good looks or to learn my habits. Someone is worried that I am on to something. And this has to be it. My moles and I have more digging to do. We must find out to whom Forbes, Thompson, and Campbell report. That's the critical piece of the puzzle. It will help confirm or refute our present position. I should have that information back to you by tomorrow, five pm my time. I'll call you and then you can call me on this line at the time I specify. OK? Talk to you then."

****

The dial tone echoed in Gene's ear for about fifteen seconds until disconnect. He must tell Karen. Must not hold any of this information inside. That was one of the biggest causes of the breakdown issue. Too much too fast and all held inside. This new stuff must be shared. Share the paranoia. Share the burden of knowledge.

Karen summarized what he told her as being preposterous enough to be true. Then she told him to take his meds. Then, take the dogs for a romp. Not to think about anything, but the fresh air and sunshine. He obeyed. Back, he changed for a swim. He noticed the pool boy left the gate ajar again. Must talk to him. Leave a message on his voicemail.

Hither and Yon loved the game of fetch. It took two tennis balls. The repetitive nature of the exercise reminded Gene of insanity, repetition of an act anticipating different results. Except the dogs didn't expect different results. Man threw. They chased after the yellow orb and returned it to his feet. No struggling with them for the balls. They must have played this game a lot with Mary, because every so often one of the dogs wouldn't just drop the ball on the ground, he would drop it in Gene's lap. To add variety, he had to think of different areas into which he could throw the balls. Just straight ahead won't do. So, maybe it's not the same act over and over again.

Every third or fourth toss went in the pool. They loved to splash and retrieve. He noticed that they chase only their own ball. This was territorial to the extreme. If Gene threw both balls at the same time, the dogs would bring back only their own. And he knew which was which by the black mark on Hither's. Trying to trick them with feints was useless. It's their game and the thrower was just a player. After twenty or so tosses, each dog brought a ball back to the area where he was sitting. They dropped each soggy, masticated sphere and put a paw on it. Game. Set. Match. Hot and tired, they stretched out under the table.

****

Gene headed for the pool. Now was his time to focus on himself and not issues. Swimming, like running, allowed for introspection, wool gathering or fantasizing. Today he would concentrate on sexual adventures. He could select anyone he pleased. They would do anything. As often as his mind wanted. No physical limitations. His mind was clear and free from angst. The time and distance went quickly. He knew when to quit;

when his muscles were warm, and his mind returned to the task at hand. Time for lunch. Sandwiches, fruit, and iced tea. Karen joined him on the lanai. The dogs napped. *Lucky bastards.* Karen leaned forward and whispered: "I think I've found the next set of clues. TruthSeeker and BrokenArrow are at it again. Copied their entire conversation off the screen. Here, look at these. The bulk of TruthSeeker's message is posturing. The last sentence reads: 'there is a banner on the edge of Santa's table.' This sentence is repeated in one other chatroom within the body of a different text. BrokenArrow responds in one room, as well as the room in which TruthSeeker did not go: Woolworth is open for business. I think these are the clues. Let me show you. What is a banner? A flag. What is an edge? A rim. A coast? A border. Who is Santa? Saint Nick? What is a table? A platform? A mesa? Who or what is Woolworth? A retailer? A five-and-dime store started in Lancaster, Pennsylvania? From all of this, I have extrapolated. Area Code five ten. That's in Northern California. Coastal Mesa is a town in the area. It's a small town. Like all the others. There is a high school in the town named San Nichols. And, the upcoming holiday is Flag Day, June fourteenth. Four days from now. If this is accurate, we have precious little time remaining."

"But, what if it's off by only a little a bit? We guess wrong and alert the wrong place, while kids get butchered in another part of the country. Are you willing to risk that? Shouldn't we do more digging? Cross matching to be sure we have the right place and time?"

"Well, if we do nothing kids are going to die. If we are right, we save lives. The key is going to be to stop the carnage and catch Forbes, Thompson, and Campbell at the same time. We must not tip our hands, or the three bad guys will cancel their event. We must let them think the event will occur and stop it, and them, on the scene. We must be able to apprehend them immediately before the carnage. I know only one person who might be able to help. Someone who is clean. My contact at the FBI, Bodrim Bogatta. He said I could contact him any time. Day or night. I'll call and set up a meeting. Away from this house and not at his office. Some place obscure. Some place whoever is watching us can't find."

She went about setting up the meeting. Gene stretched out for a nap. The happy pills facilitated napping without bad dreams. He looked forward to this pleasant change. No more mountain hikes and drowning holes. The dogs slept with him on the master bed. They knew he was troubled and needed their attention. They were balms without smothering. Their eyes were not sad, but serious. They needed and gave contact. Touching. Leaning. Petting. Rubbing. Kisses. Basic love.

****

The kiss on his lips was human. Karen wanted him to go to the meeting with her. At seven thirty. It's six. He showered and had a cup of Cuban coffee. Dusk was beginning by the time they left the house. A normal twenty-minute drive took forty-five minutes. A circuitous route to avoid being followed to the mall. The massive fountain in the middle. Running water precludes telescopic eavesdropping.

"Hello, Karen. How are you? I assume this is Mister Benton. How can I help you both?"

"Bodrim, Gene and I think we have unearthed something incredibly sinister. We think we know where and when the next school shooting will occur."

"Initially, I must tell you that I find this to be highly unlikely. But please go on."

Karen relayed all the information about Carter through Ox Bow, Mary, Forbes, Thompson, Campbell, Senator Miller, Mike Duncan, et cetera, et cetera. Finally, Coastal Mesa and how she determined the place of the next slaughter. Then she told him that she wanted the FBI to go to Costa Mesa. And she and Gene wanted to go with them when they created a non-event. He listened but did not agree to the travel plans. She said that the two of them would go there whether he liked it or not. She was firm, arguing that he owed her that, at the very least. He had to think about it. First, he would check into the evil triumvirate. Most important, he needed to determine if anyone at Menthen, Lutztown, and Ox Bow remembered the three men. Do a deep check on Miller. Talk to Mike Duncan. All of this could take a week. They didn't have a week. He was aware of her urgency. But allocation of such a large amount of his limited resources based on a maybe would be difficult to hide from his superiors. And, if this was to happen, he wanted to keep everybody out of the loop until the last second, thereby avoiding the possibility of a leak to other branches and departments of the government. He promised to do some immediate investigating. It would be cursory. He would get back to Karen by noon the day after tomorrow. Fair enough? Fair enough.

****

Headed for home, the dogs and the news. Maybe something from the Classic Movie Channel, a drink, and an early bed. Single malt scotch whiskey was not only the water of life, but it is also the water of rest. Pour two healthy big boy strength drinks. Karen accepts with a sneaky smile, "We need to discuss us."

The threat in those words. The hidden meaning. The portent of conflict. When cornered, take the offense, "Yes, we do. What's on your mind? You show me yours and I'll show you mine."

"I have been avoiding you. Not because I don't care, but because I do care. I was terrified by your episode. So, I shied away. Second, I have been focused on understanding this confusing mess we are in. I feel I have an obligation to Mary, and to you, to get to the bottom of all this. Most particularly, Mary's death. So, I just want to tell you that I have missed you as much as I hope you have missed me. And I'm sorry for my reaction and diversion."

"That's enough. My episode is nothing more than just that-an episode. I had one of them before but divorced the cause, and now she lives in Wisconsin. I'm on happy pills, better ones than before. I have my physical health, two dogs that worry about me, and the love of a wonderful woman, I hope. I know I will get through this. I will do more than survive. I will be better than before. All I need is time and some personality adjustment, though I was beginning to think that I had had no long-term effect on you. My virility level had sunk to a new low. I'm glad I was mistaken. Now that that is over, what's next?"

"Make room for my clothes in my new closet which is located in the master bedroom. Move my personal stuff into the master bath. And help me, tomorrow afternoon, retrieve more of my belongings from my house."

Gene's heart swelled with joy.

****

He rearranged his clothes to accommodate the third floor of Banana Republic, Macy's, and Bloomingdales. What, in God's name, did anyone need with twenty pairs of shoes? Six pairs of sneaks, four pairs of slip-ons, and ten pairs of business heels. Skirts, blouses, slacks, jeans, shorts, T-shirts, eighteen dresses. For gawd's sake, this is Florida, home of casual attire. How much more of her stuff would be revealed by the trip tomorrow? Gene would lose two-thirds of the three-panel medicine cabinet over the double sinks. He moved some of his occasionally used items to the small towel closet near the shower. If she wanted to take a bath, she would have to use the other bathroom. He was so happy he was bitchy.

As they passed from one room to the next. They brushed against one another. The sexual tension created by physical contact was nearly overwhelming. It was time to retire. He commenced undressing in the bathroom. She left. She turned out the houselights, re-entered the bathroom, and lit a candle on the vanity. The light, reflected off the corner mirrors, seemed to come from six or eight candles. It illuminated the entire area in a sultry, flickering warm orange light. She slipped out of her skirt, pulled her halter over her head, and pulled off her thong. He re-entered the master bath and approached the shower stall. She was behind him. In one fluid motion they embraced. Too long away. Too long lonely. Tender kisses evolve into mouths trying to engulf the other. Tongues are on archaeological digs, probing areas recently considered to be dead.

They parted and slid the glass door to the shower stall. Eight feet by eight feet square. Nearly a separate room. They coat each other's body with lather. Rubbing deeply and slowly as the water from multiple showerheads cascaded over them. Her back was smooth with form muscles, not overly developed. Her glutes were pliable. Thighs covered by delicate baby hair. Calves strong. She turned so he could retrace his path up the front of the emotional mountain. Shins. Thighs. Hips and small round tummy. Rib cage. Breasts. Arms and shoulders. They kiss. He is aroused from the inside out. From the depth of his soul. His heart yells for continuation and completion. She reciprocated his lathering as the temperature in the stall climbed and steam-coated the glass. She was pulling him onto her. She turned to face the wall, leaned into it with her hips raised, inviting entry. If Gene wanted to, she was his. He paid attention to the signal. Loving her was easy because she wanted it that way. She was on fire. Gene matched her passion. Rubbed her shoulders and arms. Kissed her neck. The back of her head. Nibbled her ears. Lathered her scalp and rubbed it vigorously as they were joined. Her quivering became trembling became shaking. He was thrusting as slowly as he could. His mind said, 'go slow,' but the senses of his body said 'go fast.' He can no longer be the master of his own fate. He pulsed within her. Her moan was deep and long. She turned. Their kiss lasted forever. Soap and fluids going down the drain.

Toweling off was almost as much fun. They got to explore areas which had been hidden by soap and water. The flame flickered with their activity. Curves were accentuated. Skin color was a warm sensual tan.

The wax flame was extinguished. Saved for another time. Remaining nude, they slid beneath the sheets. She settled her head on his chest. His arm under her shoulders. It was natural. It was good. He missed this closeness. Had his heart been that hard?

****

The mental alarm sounded at five am. It's coffee time. Padding to the kitchen, the dogs eyed Gene's arrival into their night world. They had been guarding the fort. Now it was time for them to search the grounds for any barbarians who might have scaled the walls in the blackness. They scampered out the sliding door. Man, the servant, must put water and food in separate bowls for their return from the search and destroy mission. They could rest outside this morning until it got too hot for man or beast. Breakfast coffee was a wonderful experience. Truly a good drug and Gene was needy. The first long draft calmed his spirit and lifted him. Every day the same activity. Every day the same result. Gawd, life was good.

The electronic media was frantically dissecting the president's

Rose Garden Chat of last evening. He used phrases such as: 'partners in peace,' 'one nation indivisible,' 'cancerous growth,' 'put aside differences,' 'common enemy,' 'safe, secure, and armed.' He confirmed that the evil had been isolated from the rest of the world. The trading partners of both the Sunnis and the Shiites had been briefed. The Security Council of the United Nations was meeting. One last envoy of peace would be sent before final action. All the right hot buttons for both the domestic and international audiences. His smile was wide, but about as deep as the Pecos River in August. His voice was mellifluous, but the words were pointed. His eyes glowed with a sincerity every mother would believe. In the background, his wife and three children sat politely. The clothes of the entire group delivered the message that this family was what every American family could and should be. Light brown hair. Neatly trimmed and combed. Scrubbed freckled faces. Red, white, and blue shirts and blouses. Freshly starched khaki slacks and skirts. Only the president wore a tie and blazer.

To Gene, the message was clear: *We were God's chosen. We were the leaders of this millennium. Barring a miracle of contrition by the evilest human on the face of the earth, the president would have to order complete war. He meant war to crush this evil man for peace in the world, an increase in his international stature, and reinforcement of his political party's domestic constituency.*

The president was making political hay. The price would be thousands of shattered lives and billions of dollars' worth of buildings, roads, and infrastructure in an unstable region of the world. Our economy would benefit greatly in the rebuilding. The reopening of the region. What the fuck did he care if the process involved massive amounts of death and destruction, so long as his party was able to continue in power? The question was no longer if we would go to war. The question was how soon after the envoy's return would total war commence. There was no counterpoint news conference by the other party. The outs just had to go along. When this would blow over, in about six weeks, if the knife was swift and sure, the other party would have its chance to second-guess and criticize. They would urge us to get back to the most pressing business at hand: A Secure America For Everyone. It would behoove the outs to use this time wisely. Consolidate their power base. Strategize for various scenarios. Focus sharply on the national election next year. Long after this international bump in the road.

Karen was more beautiful in dawn's light than in the candlelight of the shower. Maybe because of the shower. Gene poured for her. She liked morning coffee black. Not unlike her mood, she joked. Dressed in shorts and a New York Giants football jersey, number fifty-six, she's sexy in a dangerous teenage way. Her hair had not yet been brushed. Skin glowed. They headed for the lanai to sit at the table beneath the fan. No words. He extended his hand to hers and traced the fingers. Smiles all around. The dogs wanted in on the attention. Hither came to Gene's side and plopped his head on Gene's lap. Yon did the same to Karen. God, how saccharine, it's the Nelsons with Ricky and David. The peace of the early day was broken by a ring on her cellphone. She had to go back to the master bedroom to retrieve the culprit. Karen was not happy that the modern convenience disturbed her reverie.

She moved from the lanai to the edge of the pool and commenced rapt listening. They had agreed, the less spoken the better. She pressed the off button and motioned Gene to the pool.

"That was Bodrim Bogatta. He wants to help. Did a lot of digging after he left us. Apparently found out more than he had anticipated. Most of which was troubling, no... disconcerting. Each question raised six more. Paths crisscrossed each other until he lost sight of the starting point. He promised not to go to up the chain of command until we get closer to the next event. Did you hear what I said? I said event. An objective, non-descript portrayal of a brutal loss of life. Have I become so inured to the horror, that I describe it that way? Or do I find the slaughter so abhorrent that I can't deal with it on its own terms? It's a planned killing. Whew, that was rough. Sorry. I think I better understand what you have been dealing with. Anyway, Bogatta will call us again later today. We will meet either late tonight or early tomorrow. In the meantime, we are to just monitor the chatrooms, like we always do. Do not post. Make no waves. I told him we would just hang."

The truth had sunk in. *We could be in serious trouble. Like Mary. And all we can do was wait. Act normal. Act as if we didn't know that they know so they wouldn't know that we know that they know. We had become isolated. Just what the bad guys would want.* This new pressure called for a happy pill. *We wait. Read. Watch the magic eye. Movies all day. Australian Football. Old championship basketball games. Bad talk shows. The world according to schlock.*

****

The telephone rang.

"Yes. Are you sure? OK. Ready in twenty minutes. Thanks."

"Gene, we must pack and leave. Now!"

"What about the dogs?"

"We will take them with us. Pack only what you deem essential to your existence for three days. The rest can be retrieved later. Two bags. All this will be explained by Bodrim. Now, let's go."

Gene could pack in less time than most people, because he valued little except his life, his children, and now Karen and the dogs. None of them fit into his suitcases. Two ties and a blazer were his concession to being well-dressed. Slacks, sport shirts, shorts. Florida clothes plus a sweater and a windbreaker for the outdoors. The doorbell rang. He was expecting no one. Karen was. She nodded for him to answer. He moved quickly and peered through the window to the right of the door. Time was waning.

Frank's Water Service, but not Frank. The nametag said Bodie.

"Hello, Mister Benton. It's nice to see you again. I understand your water filtration system in on the blink. If you open the garage door, I'll pull my van in and check out the pump and system."

He turned and headed to the truck. Gene went to the door leading from the laundry room to the garage and pressed the garage door opener. The van pulled inside. The van's side doors opened, and a hand motioned for Gene to get Karen and the bags. The van contained no plumbing equipment or tools of any kind. Just a padded bench seat. Bags were stuffed behind the bench. The dogs jumped into the space between the bench and front seats. Gene slid the door closed. It closed with a solid thud.

Bulletproof? Okay, now the driver had Gene's undivided attention.

He would do whatever was required. Bodrim was talking in a loud voice to no one. Except those who might be listening. He backed the van out of the garage. Gene pressed his clicker to close it and the van drove off with the driver waving at the now empty house.

"Will somebody tell me what's going on?"

"Mister Benton. All I can tell you is that you are now safe. We are moving you to someplace out of harm's way. You will have a guard with you at all times. Tonight, I can tell you more. Just not right now. Damn it! They're trailing us. I'll just have to make a stop at the mall. Bear with me."

They headed for the East Shore Mall. Bogatta called someone on his cellphone. In a few minutes he pulled the van into the narrow loading dock. A big delivery truck slid in front of the dock for about thirty seconds. The dogs, Karen, and Gene hurriedly exited. The van doors closed. Two men heft the luggage and ushered the couple into the shipping department of a hardware outlet. The semi pulled away as the store door closed. The van stayed. Everyone waited. In about ten minutes, a Bogatta look-alike entered the van and backed it out of the dock.

As Frank's Water Service drove off, Gene noted that the small pickup truck, which had followed them, was now on a phony trail.

The small group walked to the front of the store. The dogs and luggage remained behind. A clerk came up, Karen and Gene are turned over to her. She walked them to a side entrance at the other end of the roofed retail world. Going from climate control to bright light and oppressive heat was a shock. The limo doors opened. All of us, save the dogs, entered. The doors slammed. Casually the black boat glided through the parking lot and headed toward the airport. The woman in the passenger seat handed us our tickets. Destination: San Francisco. Two stops and two plane changes.

****

"Ladies and gentlemen. Before I board any plane, I want to know what the fuck is going on! I mean I am whisked out of my house in a bulletproof van by someone I don't know. The van is seemingly followed by someone I don't know. Our mode of transportation is changed because of the unknown trackers. I am now being driven to the airport and escorted by two people I don't know so that I can be shipped to a city where I know no one. What's wrong with this video?"

"Mister Benton, please relax. Everything will be explained to you in due time."

"Well, the time to do the explaining is due now. If I don't get the answers I like before we get to the airport, I won't get on the plane. I'll raise such a ruckus that the local police will have to intervene. Then, you can explain the kidnapping to them. That's the deal. Talk or I walk."

"Gene, I know these people. They helped me out of my jam a few years ago. When I needed friends, they were the only ones. Trust them."

"Trust them. Hell, I'm not sure I trust you. You brought them into my world. I have had to go a long way on faith. And that precious commodity is running thin. So, somebody better tell me everything. Now!"

"OK. I'll tell you what I know. Then Jenny will tell you the rest. Bodrim determined we were in danger. The house was being monitored. We were being monitored. All because of our snooping. They were closing in on us. Maybe to do us real harm. He is convinced Mary was murdered. The accident was no accident. Bodrim learned that Mike Duncan died yesterday under strange circumstances. His car caught fire while he was pulling out of his spot in the underground parking garage. Before he could be rescued, Mike, his car, and six other cars had become a charred mass of metal and glass. The Fire Marshall believes flame accelerant was used in the mishap. It all happened at three am. Bodrim was convinced that we were next on the list. We were getting too close to the truth. He decided it would be best that we disappeared, before we were really disappeared. So, we're going to San Francisco. Just remember the pretty flowers in your hair. Yes, I'm scared. But I've had experience with Bodrim's rapid clandestine departures, and I recognize a few of the other players, like Jenny here and Robert at the store. I think I've seen this driver. Jenny, it's your turn."

"Mister Bogatta is my boss. Here is my ID. Yes, we are incredibly concerned for your lives. Our initial investigation has indicated that you may be right in many of your assumptions. There may be another school slaughter in two or three days, the three men you identified are rogues. We're not sure who is paying them. We are not sure if it's Senator Miller. We are taking you to a safe house in San Francisco. Your dogs and luggage will be there when you arrive. From there, at the appropriate time, we will go to Coastal Mesa. That's all I can tell you now. Mister Bogatta will have more details when you meet him in California."

"One last item. The stops and plane changes are for security, I assume."

"We are dealing with too many unknowns and some enormously powerful people. Your safety is our single concern for now."

"Karen, I feel slightly better about what I am doing."

Gene and Karen hold hands. Fear and fondness are great motivators.

XIII

Hither and Yon are their solace in this new place. Nothing soothed a frightened traveler more than friendly, happy faces. As they unpack, Gene surveys the accommodations: One bedroom, one bath, sitting room, kitchen, dining area. Very singular. Spartan, but practical. Their official protector is Robert. He's black. About six-feet-three-inches tall and approximately two hundred and forty pounds. Handsome. His smile friendly, but not warm. Eyes constantly darting, searching for something, anything. Ear plug and lapel mike let him communicate with home-base, wherever that is. Wearing a jacket to conceal twin Glocks. Wearing a Kevlar vest for protection. Gene and Karen would wear him. They can't leave the apartment without him unlocking the door. He let people in only after knocking. Will he walk the dogs? Maybe he should have one or both with him. They growled at him when he entered. He stared back. Did not growl back. The three protectors respected one another. Gene must introduce the guard to the dogs the next time his watch is over. But he must go through the same ritual Gene did in Wyoming. What a fun way to humble a fed. The knock announced Bogatta's arrival. Now, some answers.

****

"Mister Benton. Karen. How are you both feeling? How are the dogs?"

"Their suspicious glare is an indication of my deep feelings. Mister Bogatta, I need to know what the hell is going on. Why are we here? Where is here? Is there a here after here? What do you know? Tell us everything."

"Mister Benton, as you know, you are in San Francisco. Actually, in a suburb of little importance. We are here to stop what you have indicated, and we agree, will be the next school massacre. The bloodshed is planned for San Nichols High School in Coastal Mesa sometime during the Flag Day parade and picnic. It is now three thirty in the afternoon local time. We have approximately thirty-six hours to set the trap for the shooters and to catch the three men identified as Forbes, Thompson, and Campbell. Now, let me tell you what we know about these men. They are rogues. Supposedly, they work for the

National Security Agency. Except I was unable find a record of them ever, I stress ever, having been in the employ of the NSA. They do not presently work for the CIA, although they once did. They have varied and checkered pasts. Not suburb cocktail conversation, but their pasts were necessary for the safety and security of our country. They had been out of the country until they flew beneath the radar and re-entered. They dropped out of sight. Then resurfaced at Carter. Maybe before. But Carter for sure."

"We think they were spotted at Menthen, Lutztown and Ox Bow. We're not completely sure, but sure enough. They come into the killing zones slightly before or just as the shooting begins, but well before the local or state authorities arrive. The three, along with a few underlings, establish a command center beyond the anticipated sphere of influence of the locals. From there Forbes, Thompson, and Campbell can direct the locals. When the time is propitious, our three enter the fray, most likely from behind, and execute the executioners. To do this, they must have detailed knowledge about the shoot: Who. When. Where. How.

And they scout the killing zone in detail so that they know the entrances and exits. The first line killers are recruited from the vast sea of loonies. Emotional trash that floats beneath the surface of society. These are people ready to kill anyone and everyone. Rage is so deep, so severe that these people will explode spontaneously. All they need is the proper venue and good handling.

"That's what the three men in question do. They determine the desired place and time. Then they recruit from the area. They let the misguided know the details via the chatrooms. After the planned butchery, they eliminate the eliminators. Then they leave the scene. The locals, who have taken orders from the bogey feds, are all too pleased to take credit for cleaning up the mess. And afterward the locals know only what they have been told by these three.

"We are sure that's how all this happens. We are not sure why. And we are not positive about the connection between Senator Miller and the three. Our suspicion is that they are handling him as the three handle the killers. If they are functioning as bodyguards and as controllers, they have a master other than Miller. The question then is: Who is the real master? Is Miller involved in the killings to further his campaign? Is he setting up the slaughters to prove the need for S.A.F.E.? The key is to learn for whom the three rogues really work.

"You two are honored guests of the service. I am giving you the opportunity to watch the event and my promotion unfold. Yes, that's my plan. You'll be close enough to see, just not close enough to be hurt. You will know almost as much as I know so that you can be witness to the heroic efforts of my team. We have alerted no one. Except for a few locals. Not the state authorities. And certainly, none of the federal agencies. About an hour before the planned event, I will talk to my office and let the information filter down and out of the agency. Now as for Costal Mesa, we have strategically planted personnel so that all venues are secure. We have taken over the sanitation department and will be responsible for establishing the parade route. Buildings are now being scoured. The picnic area is blanketed. We have even taken the precaution to stakeout the area around the grounds. We have a vague idea who and how many are the planned killers. If our suspicions are accurate, we know their weapons. Nothing long range.

"These boys and girls, yes girls, most likely plan to rush the revelers. Their weapons of choice are Tec Nines and Mac Tens. Big sprayers. But they'll never get a chance to use any of them. Will they? You know that was the biggest question we dealt with. Do we stop them before they start? Or do we let them start, then engage them in a firefight and capture the ones not killed? Or slaughter all of them just as they would have been slaughtered by the three? Do we want to be John Wayne style heroes? Or do we want to be the heroes who prevented disaster? We opted for the latter. It gives our investigative prowess more play. I mean, we saw the train wreck coming and we diverted the runaway engine. We will be idolized. Now why don't you two rest? We'll dine in the backyard at seven. Then early to bed. Tomorrow is a long day. Leave here at noon and go to Camp One. From there we will commence Operation Unsafe."

What an ice cube in Gene's shorts. *Carpe Deim*, Bodrim Bogatta. He had the area secured. Shit, he knew the where, when, and maybe the who all along. It's our beloved protector, who was the instigator.

Where do the bad guys fit? Between the two government forces. Who was doing what to whom? If he was successful, he could leave the service and command a huge salary in the private sector of law enforcement. Maybe he would become a rogue like the three bad guys. Maybe just an independent contractor. Gene can't fault the goal of stopping the crime before it started, and Bogatta should get credit for that. He could stop it now before anybody gets killed. That would not serve his purpose. He was going to use Gene and Karen to validate his valor. *Whoopdeefuckingdo.*

****

Dinner was cordial. Not joyous. What was Gene expecting? This afternoon was illuminating, but unsettling. The dogs were not introduced to anyone. In fact, Gene made sure they stayed remarkably close to Karen and him. They are to be their protection against the protectors. This entire mess had become too convoluted for him. Will the couple die in the midst of the firefight? Oh, it was a terrible accident. That would be their story. These distant relatives from Florida just happened to be in the way. *Boofuckinghoo.* Gene was frightened. Hither and Yon didn't care for the handlers. They adored Karen. Gene was their pal. To them that's everything. Hither sat at his feet and Yon sat at Karen's. They were not fed from the table. They ate from bowls thoughtfully provided by the hosts. No one tried to pet them.

As a stranger approached, the dogs froze and stared. They did not growl or bark. When a dog silently stared, he or she was about to attack. That's why they feel threatened when a human stares at them. The men and women who surround the grill and table were kept from the couple by the dogs. Each of the hounds positioned himself next to Karen or Gene and between the person with whom they were talking. The canines sensed all was not right. Their protective instincts, honed by Mary, were super sharp now. That's good. Very good. His feeling is that they would give up their lives to save the two humans. The agents would kill the dogs without a second thought. Gene didn't like where this was going.

Sleep was fitful. The sense of dread was now based on his understanding of facts. So much was going to happen tomorrow that the chance of something going wrong was great. He didn't dream about anything specific. Just the visceral, feral premonition of death. There were stories of dogs whining and moaning before a master died. Hither and Yon knew, without knowing, that Mary had died. Maybe he should ask them what was going to happen. His eyes popped open just as he was falling asleep. *It's time to rise and shine.* Karen was wrapped in the arms of Morpheus. The coffee was foul. The dogs needed walking. Robert had the day shift and was not yet on duty. Jenny volunteered to walk the dogs. About forty minutes. They loaded a van. People, dogs, and hardware. The second bigger van, agents only, was about two lengths behind for the entire two-hour trip. A mini convoy. Camp One was a storefront with whitewash on the windows. On the main drag and accessible to everywhere. The school was less than two miles away. The marshal's stand was about three hundred yards in the other direction. The picnic grounds were just beyond the school.

****

The place was fully operational when they arrived. Communications had been established with men in the field. Twenty-two armed and alert agents. The shirts and coveralls of the people at Camp One had logos that match those on the vans and pickup trucks parked in the back...Event Exposition International and Coastal Mesa Department of Sanitation. The agents would blend in, hidden in plain sight. At the rear of the space, Gene noticed partially opened crates of guns, flak jackets, and grenades. One could never have too much firepower. The pace was orderly but driven. No anger. No loud voices. Just questions, orders, and commands. Bogatta was in total control of this military operation. The next two in the chain of command were Jenny, our guide to the airport, and an excessively muscular Mediterranean looking hulk named Joe. The others were worker bees. Completing small tasks as required by the thinkers. Each of the small tasks fit into a slightly larger combination, which, with others, forms a complex procedure or action. Coffee was gulped, and sandwiches inhaled on the fly. No time for a white tablecloth, candles, and silverware sit-down.

"Well, Mister Benton, what do you think? Have you ever been in a Command Center before? This is where we try to eliminate any possibility of mistakes. This is where we pretest our planning. This is where the adrenaline rush starts. Impressive, right?"

"Mister Bogatta, there is nothing in my experience to which I can make a comparison. My only assessment would be possible after completion of the mission. Before that time, I just sit in awe."

"Bodrim, is all this firepower necessary? I mean it looks like you're outfitting a third world country. If you must use this, a lot of people will get hurt or dead. How can you justify fighting fire with fire when civilians are the losers no matter what?" Karen had taken a less than completely supportive posture. Strange. She seemed to be questioning God.

"Karen, these guns are not to be used unless absolutely necessary. Remember that the killer kids will be armed and dangerous. They will gather at this place to kill. We must prevent this action. We must show a greater amount of resolve. That resolve will be manifested in our weaponry. The strategy to achieve our primary objective is to freeze them, show them our force, and back them down. Bluff and bully with a show of superior firepower and tactics. Hopefully, no shots will be fired. But we must be ready. If they get ballsy or stupid, we will have to kick them real hard. The three men behind all this pose a different problem because of their training and discipline. I believe they will offer resistance because they think their total team can win a firefight. They don't know the depth of our firepower. And they are accustomed to winning firefights. Our superior numbers should influence them otherwise. But we must be ready to eliminate with extreme prejudice. Now, if there are no other questions, I ask you both to sit on the couch in the comer and be still for a few more hours. There is plenty to read on the table."

****

The afternoon throbbed into the evening. Alternating between slow motion and jet speed. The sudden flurry of activity told Gene something important had or was about to happen. One foot soldier brought a TV from the other room, while another readied a place for the set on the long table.

"Ladies and gentlemen, the President of the United States."

"Please be seated. Today, at one thirty Eastern Daylight-Saving Time, the combined armies of the Peace Alliance initiated a pre-emptive strike against the aggressive jihadist forces. This strike involved the armies of Egypt, Saudi Arabia, Israel, France, Great Britain, United Germany, Spain, Poland, and the United States. Combined navy and air corps struck offensive installations in Basjar with great dispatch. Missile sites, troop assemblies, and artillery emplacements suffered the concerted might of the Peace Alliance. The preemptive strike continues as we speak. Ground troops are standing ready to mop up. Before I turn this briefing over to the Allied Commander, General Warren, I want to assure the people of the region, and the world, that our strike is not intended to cause any nation or its people permanent harm. Rather, we wish to rid the region of the war mongering that began thirty years ago and has escalated recently.

"The attacks on our embassies and the death of hundreds of innocent civilians cannot go unanswered. The peace-loving people of the Middle East, and of the world, cannot and will not tolerate the jihadists' abhorrent behavior any longer. Their actions have threatened to destabilize the region and drive the world into a conflagration of apocalyptic proportions. We ask that all people pray for a swift and complete resolution to this conflict. Now, General Warren."

The agents were ecstatic. High fives. Big smiles. Prancing. A lot of noise.

"People. People. People. Listen up. Calm down. I share your enthusiasm, but remember, we can't let anything deter us from our appointed tasks. The children of San Nicholas High School in Coastal Mesa must be protected. The children of this country must be kept safe and secure. The perps must be apprehended. This is our responsibility. Let's conduct ourselves in the most professional manner. Our mission is not yet completed. Now back to your duties. There will be time for R and R after tomorrow."

****

Back to work with no grumbling. These were professionals. They did their jobs so that a bigger job could be done. Gene took his pills. Time to check on the dogs. They're in the rear. Walked past the unisex restroom, past the packing cases that carried the electronic and communications gadgets, past a heap of scrap paper which would be shredded and burned before liftoff: Memos. Letters. Hand-written notes. Out of the corner of his right eye, he noticed the name: Alan Campbell. He dipped and scooped up the paper on which that name was written. Casually, stuffed the paper into his pocket. Outside with Hither and Yon, he bent down to nuzzle them and filled their bowls with water. He retrieved the paper and smoothed it so he could read whatever was on the page "...the subject, Alan Campbell, has been sighted at various shooting sites. He, Brent Forbes, and Roger Thompson are believed to be responsible for the incidents at Carter, Wyoming, Menthen, New Hampshire, and Lutztown Pennsylvania... "

The memo, addressed to someone Gene assumed was Bogatta's superior, was dated six weeks ago. Well before Karen and he went to

Bogatta with their suspicions. What the fuck was wrong with this picture? Did the agency send the memo up the line? Was it bogus? If they sent it, what were they doing here? Was it a cover your ass or some post facto blame missive? Was the couple window dressing? Were they part of the 'good guy' group? Part of the 'to be exterminated' group? Were they here to validate? His best bet was that he and Karen would be here after all this is over. They will be a dead, not living, testimony of the great efforts of Bogatta and his men. The couple will be unfortunate innocent bystanders in the war on crime. Karen must know. Hide the message. Fold the paper into a small square. Insert the square into the plastic identification box on Hither's collar. Mary used this box to carry the dog's latest vet information, her name, address, and telephone number. A duplicate of the census information on the collar tag. If the dogs strayed or were injured, a Good Samaritan would know whom to contact. Hither carried the safety deposit box of truth. Passed by paper heap and reenter Camp One.

"Hey, Agent Bogatta, would you mind if Karen and I went outside and spent some quality time with the dogs.

It's getting hot and sweaty in here. And that may do a lot for Karen, but it does nothing for me. Besides the dogs could use some TLC. They have been yanked from home, placed on an airplane, shipped to San Francisco, then driven here in a van. A little schmoozing will go a long way. We want to play fetch with them."

"Mister Benton, that will be fine. One of my men will accompany you and Miss Leach. Just don't get lost in the big parking lot."

They exited the building. The dogs were ecstatic to see Karen. Obviously, Gene was insufficient entertainment. The two tennis balls went into play. First Hither, then Yon. After a few reps of this activity, the human watchdog sat on a garbage can and lit a smoke. He was distracted. Gene retrieved the memo from Hither's collar box and palmed it to Karen. As she read it, her eyes grew, and her skin became pale. She was afraid, very afraid. Returned the note and Gene replaced it two throws later. They were sitting cross-legged and side by side on the Macadam. The sky was clear, and the breeze kept the feels-like temperature in the sixties. This should be a great day. But it's not. It may be the last day of the rest of their lives.

Karen wrapped her arm around his shoulder and drew his mouth to hers. She was trembling and not sexually. As they separated yet continued the embrace, she began to sniffle, "What does all this mean? Who are these guys? What are they going to do? What do they want? What's to become of us?"

"I don't have any answers. Only suspicions. I think we are in *mucho caca*. These agents are not what they purport. They may be FBI. They're probably rogues. They may be the real bad guys. If that's true, then the three men we have uncovered may be good guys or just other bad guys. There definitely will be some heavy shooting tomorrow. And I am afraid that we are to be targets to one of three or all three groups. This is not good. But, if Bogatta's Boys and Girls Club doesn't know that we know, we can prepare to avoid what they think is the inevitable."

"You're no comfort. I'm so scared, I may just pee myself."

"Play with the dogs for as long as possible and let me think."

Fetch was a game that could be played while thinking about anything else. Fetch did not require concentration or mental agility. And these dogs had their own way to play the game. They had trained Gene well. He did as Mary had taught them the way a human should play the dogs' game. The ball was thrown. The dog stayed at the human's side until he was told to fetch. The dog absolutely will not move until the command was given. The dog fetched only his ball. Retrieved the ball and placed it in the lap or at the feet of the human. Sat by the human's side until the next throw and command. This was a very regimented game. More like an aerobic workout. Between the time of throw and retrieval was blank mental space for planning.

They couldn't stop Bogatta's operation. But they must stop the slaughter, while they keep from becoming the slaughtered. How do they intervene and take control of a situation over which they have no control? Neat trick. If all the players knew each other, an outsider was needed. Someone objective, who could sort out The Good, The Bad, and The Ugly, and save our asses at the same time. The only choice was the local police. Gene knew no one. Also, Karen and Gene needed to be armed. Handguns. Maybe the element of surprise would make the odds less formidable. Hell, Bogatta's team had the firepower, training, and discipline. What was he thinking? At least they could take out a few of them. The last act of the truly desperate. Where the hell did he get these thoughts? How could he know what to do? No military training. Some gun training. No combat weapon training. He didn't know what to do. But fear was the great motivator. The father of all lifesaving activity. If he thought of everything through carefully and acted with authority, the couple might survive. Slim hope. He leaned into her and whispered, "Karen, sweetie, we need you to go to the bathroom, inside. Scout out the handguns and grenades and return. OK?'

She turns to the keeper, "I have to go to the restroom. Do you mind? I'll be right back."

The keeper's grunt is an affirmative. He was enjoying his rest. Four throws for each hound before Karen returned. She smiled at the agent and hugged Gene again, "There are pistols and ammunition racked in an open box to the left of the restroom. Grenades in the open crate to the left of that box. Have no idea what kind of grenades they are. Now what? How do we get our hands on the weapons? What do we do once we have them?"

"First things first. I'll let the dogs into the building. They will no doubt continue romping and go to the front room. We will pursue them in a feeble effort to corral them. However, we must continue to stir up the dogs' activity before we actually catch them. I'll lift two guns and a few grenades during the diversion. We will stand, and they'll come to us. As we turn to head inside, we'll have to shoo them into action. Ready. Let's go."

The melee of two large dogs and their supposed handlers bounding around the electronic equipment in Camp One created near panic among Bogatta and his people. The fear of destroying or disabling this lifeline with the field was strong. Finally, Karen grabbed Yon, and Gene held Hither's collar. It's almost as if they came to the two after they had completed their hidden agenda. Did they know their role in the charade?

"Get those fucking dogs out of here now. They are only alive because we must control all factors. So, take care of your children, before we must. Men, make sure no damage was done. Re-check all connections and reconfirm with the field."

The four of us were panting with exhilaration. It was time to re-leash the dogs, double-check their bowls and return to the couch. One last hug.

"Gene, were you successful?"

"Yes, were you?"

"I got a bunch of ammunition clips. But no guns. What did you get?"

"Three automatics and some clips. Everything is stuffed in my pants and under my sweater. I notice that you look a little chunky yourself. We need to plan the second step."

The couch was not for sleeping. Sitting bunched up their clothes so that the stolen loot was not obvious. Next question. How to alert the police at the appropriate time? Bogatta would hear from his field force once they found the shooter's nest, with or without shooters. Then he would go to the general area to direct operations from nearby. A position where he could capture both enemies. He must take Gene and Karen with him, hopefully. Yes, that's where all four of them were to be caught in the crossfire. They had come from Florida after discovering the evil deed and the evildoers. They were just not professional law enforcement. They got dead.

The trip to the school, to the outside world, would be their only chance to contact the locals. But how? Yon. A detailed note inside his collar box. Will he be found in time? Who will find him? Will they understand? Will the police be called? Gawd, this was like Gramps and Lassie with Timmy in the well. We had to be incredibly lucky and Yon had to understand. Gene was betting their lives on this combination multi-bank long shot. What else did they have? Now to write the note, surreptitiously. Paper and pen were easily found. He reread his message, in a whisper, to Karen. It sounded utterly preposterous. Karen agreed. What civilian or cop, in his right mind, would believe this cry for help?

****

The heavy foot and auto traffic outside the windows were the going home variety. The shadows of dusk were beginning to stretch across the street. The call from Camper Six was one of discovery. The vipers' nest had been found. To the north of the picnic ground was a mound of rock and earth on which sat a stand of pine trees. In front of the trees was a trench, recently dug. Looked like a hunter's dig. The road behind the mound would provide easy exit if exit were to happen. The road also provided easy access by Forbes, Thompson, and Campbell. Bogatta ordered his people to box all the communications equipment and go mobile with the system. Shredded all paper and burned it. Poured the ashes in the dumpster. Loaded the vans with the weapons. Made it look as if no one was ever there. Cleaned of debris, Camp One must not look as if it were recently swept. The entire process took about thirty minutes. Very efficient. Obviously, they'd done this before. All saddled up and headed for the hill. The fire keepers had to stay behind to dump the remains. They would morph into sanitation workers.

The trip was orderly, but not in a convoy format. Did not want to arouse suspicion. Forty-five minutes and all were at Camp Two. The entire field force around the site. Alerted to not leave footprints or crush the grass on the mound. The troops were dispersed to a control perimeter. The van moved to the other side of the picnic area. It seemed normal that the event crew would be at the festival site the day before. No one would suspect the military deployment. Bogatta advised us to get some rest: "Wake up is at 0400. Oh, by the way, Mister Benton, sorry about your sister. She was getting to be a nuisance to our work. Nothing personal mind you. Just business. For the greater good and my success."

Gene had just been kicked in the solar plexus. Stabbed in the heart. His sister's killer is now his keeper. This entire event had now become very personal to him. He fought to not go numb. Stay sharp for Karen. She, the two dogs, and Gene were ushered into the school. Down the hall, beyond the gym to the library. The door is locked behind the four. Immediately visible were the couches, the tables and chairs, and the door to the bathroom. No computers and four windows with bars to prevent entry or escape. There was also a small, levered window in the bathroom. It could be opened to a horizontal plane. Too small for Karen or me. Dog size. He double checked the note. Told Yon to get the ball. Get the ball. *Please get the ball.* Picked him up and squeezed him out to safety. He meandered around beneath the window. Not sure what to do. What did the human want? Told him again to get the ball. The game of fetch had a much bigger meaning than ever before. He loped into the evening. This was it: Do or die. He was not wild about their chances. Weapons spread on the couch. Three Glocks and nine magazines.

****

Gene started to show Karen how the loaded handgun was to be used. After firing...How to remove the empty magazine. Reload and reactivate. Firing...Point, not aim. Quarters would be too close for the time required to accurately aim. The discharge pulled up the gun and the hand holding it. The noise would scare her and nearly deafen her temporarily. Hold the gun tightly. Start to shoot as the gun comes up from the side. Continue to shoot until the target drops, whether that required two or eight shots. Move quickly to the next target. Keep moving while shooting. Hide as much as possible. This was a killing activity. Either she killed, or they killed. One was good. The other not. She hid the fact that she was insulted by Gene's chauvinism. He was preaching to the choir. She had a previous working knowledge of handguns. Her father had many on the farm. Target practice was a regular monthly event. She was not the best shot, but her father felt comfortable she could stop a wild pig or an intruder of unknown origin at close range. Guns in the front of belts beneath sweaters. This was not the original use for the garments, but it was the primary use now.

They agreed that they should disarm the guard when he came to awaken them for the morning's activities. Not shoot. Just disarm, tie up, and stash in the bathroom. Liberate his communication link. Then they'll have to figure out how to get out of dodge. Had Yon been found? Was the message read by the police? What have they done? What can they do? Their only job now was to get out of here alive. Rest before they acted. Who can rest? Their naptime passed in a heartbeat. The noise of heavy footsteps is an ominous series of thuds. Gene went into the bathroom and turned on the water. Returned to the couch. Karen stood to the right of the door. When the agent stepped through the doorway, she clobbered him with the first volume of the Encyclopedia Britannica, A-B. He staggered. She hit again. Again. Again. He dropped to the floor. Blood flowed from his nose. She hit again. Again.

Again. Again. Blood was splattered on her sweater, the floor and the nearby walls. He was out cold. Maybe dead. His life curve was just shortened. Pulled him to the couch. Stripped him of his clothes. A sign of their anger. Stashed his clothes in the bathroom. Lashed his wrists and legs. Taped his mouth and eyes. Clear packing tape in lieu of duct tape. So, lots of it. Two full rolls of extra wide. Hither was quiet through the entire ordeal. He knew. Gene peered down the hall. Empty and dark.

They moved as quietly as possible. The dog's nails created a rhythmic click on the tile floor. Outside was only slightly lighter than the hall. The couple sensed activity and saw a dim light emanating from the van. Must get to the road and then literally run for their lives. Wending through the picnic ground to the mound and the road was easy. Once on the road, they loped toward safety. Suddenly, they see two sets of headlights moving cautiously toward them. They became off-road travelers, to avoid contact with anyone who was not a friendly. And everyone they had met, so far, was not a friendly. Then they heard a male voice.

****

"Camp Two. This is Scout Baker. Do you copy?"

"Baker. This is Camp Two. We copy."

"Camp Two. Two vehicles approaching. About six clicks. Speed is slow. Unknown occupants. Advise."

"Baker. We are deploying to Perimeter Two. Hold your position. Determine occupants. Advise. Do you copy?"

"Camp Two. Baker copies. Will advise, and then join you at Perimeter Two. Further information in about ten minutes."

Gene and Karen must give the scout and the vehicles a wide berth. Headed to the hill on the left. The adrenaline pumping. The run started. It's difficult to run in a stooped posture, but they must stay below the vision line or horizon. Running uphill in a stoop was something professional athletes don't attempt, but the pair had no choice. Failure meant death, and death was not a viable option. Despite the handguns and magazines, Gene ran with authority. His years of swimming helped his stamina. Karen almost kept pace. She was as tough and as frightened as he was. Hither was by their side. He knew. No sound other than feet pounding on the tall grass. It's almost as if they were holding their collective breath. Definitely no conversation. Prone on the crest of the hill, they could see a farm, replete with two barns, a tractor shed, and three-story house. Hither bolted down the hill to the next stop.

XIV

No time for niceties. Gene banged on the front door. Lights appeared in upstairs windows. He continued the banging. Finally, he heard someone and saw lights on the first floor.

"What's all the ruckus about? Who are you? What do you want?"

The farmer looked to be about thirty-five. Dressed in pajamas. Right hand by his side held a revolver. His hand was so huge it nearly hid the gun.

"Sir, we mean no harm. We would like to use your telephone to call the police. There is some big trouble about to happen and they need to be told so they can stop it. Can we please use your phone?"

"What kind of trouble?"

"Without meaning to be crass, one hell of a firefight. Kids shooting picnickers. National Security Agency shooting the shooters. And FBI shooting everybody. It's too complex to explain in detail. You must trust me. Call the police yourself. Then let me talk to them. You can be on another phone. Listen in to be sure we are telling the truth. I see you have a gun.

315

You won't need it. We just want to use the phone. Then we'll wait until the police show up."

Gene heard a familiar whine. Yon. Hither whined back. No barking. Both dogs were outside the house. Yon chained to a clothesline on the side. Hither rushed to him. They nuzzled. Tails wagged furiously.

"Mister, what's your name?"

"Sir, I'm Gene Benton and this is Karen Leach. We're from Florida. And you have one of my dogs, Yon. He probably showed up last night. His playmate, Hither, is here with us. Did you check Yon's collar? Did you find his identification and a small box on the collar? If you opened the box, then you know about the planned slaughter. If you haven't opened the collar box, do it now. Read the note and warn the authorities, we have precious little time. Please?"

"The dog showed up last night, just like you said. He is really friendly. The kids love him, and he is particularly good with them. Couldn't understand how he got here from Wyoming. You say you're from Florida. I saw his name, Yon. But I didn't open the collar box. Stay where you are, and I'll open it now."

He came through the door with his right hand slightly raised. Walked to the clothesline. Unhooked the snap from the leash to the collar. He took Yon's collar gently and opened the box. Hither sat patiently. The night watchman returned to the door, passed us, and turned on a table lamp to read the note. He turned and looked at the door with disbelief.

"I guess it's safe for you two to come in. Remember, I'm armed."

It was best not to reveal their arsenal. He turned and headed toward the kitchen. All four of the crew followed.

"I don't know what's going on here. Maybe the police can sort out this mess. I'll dial and listen while you talk."

"Hey, Alex. This is Barry Welch. I got a guy and his lady friend and their two dogs here. The guy wants to talk to you. You better tape this. It's too weird for anyone to just take your word for it."

"Hello, Officer. My name is Eugene Benton..."

Twelve minutes and myriad questions later, Deputy Sheriff Alex Blagojevich agreed not to alert the state authorities or anyone in the federal government. He would call the sheriff and the entire force, including the traffic squad. They would be at Barry's farm in thirty minutes. Fully operational. Ready to deal with any potential danger. Sheriff Camera would be in charge. Mister Welch offered the couple coffee and they tried to explain to him what they knew. Gene could see the confusion and disbelief in the farmer's expression. He had to work hard to prevent his jaw from dropping. His wife, Leia, joined the three. They had to leave the kitchen, so the Welch children could be fed. No chores today, because of the picnic. They tell her nothing. The squad cars and two vans arrive. It's time.

****

To the sheriff, Gene and Karen explained everything he needed to know in minute detail. He decided to set up a perimeter outside of Camp Two and slowly tighten the noose. An ever-shrinking circle like a wild hog hunt. Until the game was closely surrounded with no place to go. The regular sheriff helicopter and the one borrowed from the farm bureau would swoop in at the last minute and land on the grounds. Each chopper would hold five fully armed deputies in complete body armor. The head of the sanitation department, Alex's uncle, had been called. He explained the feds had warned him not to talk to anyone. The feds were on a secret mission. They took over his department and were working alongside his men. Blended in, so to-speak. He was aware of the event trucks but thought nothing was unusual. Camera tells him to contact his people and tell them not to report to work today. That way the only ones on the job will be the bogeys. He would explain it all to the sanitation force later.

They were ready to go back over the hill. The police cruisers and vans were loaded with men and weapons and scattered to appropriate drop-off points. Some men were sent back to keep an eye on the parade and the sanitation department. Gene and Karen turned over two Glocks and a handful of magazines to Camera. Just not all their weapons. They were now officially observers. Mister and Missus Welch were asked to stay at home. Karen thanked them profusely. Fear in their eyes. The kids were focused on inhaling their breakfast.

Alex, the sheriff, Karen, the two dogs, and Gene headed to the crest of the hill. Bogatta must now know that they were not in his fort. The agent who was responsible for guarding them had been severely chastised. No doubt. Would Bogatta alter his plan? Gene suspected the professional had numerous 'what if' scenarios in his bag. There seemed to be a normal amount of non-activity at the school. Camera looked through the night scope of his rifle and spotted four bodies in the trench on the mound beneath the pines. They were making ready. This explained Bogatta's inactivity. The sentry had alerted the forces in time for them to go to Perimeter Two. From there, they would move back to the grounds. Not in a wave, but individually to avoid suspicion. The van would drive up at the proper moment.

Bogatta would take command. The shooters and their three executioners would be executed, and the world would be a better place. Where were the three executioners? Where was their black van? When would that arrive? All of this must be choreographed to the tenth of a second, and all this planning was done by three different forces, who don't really know what was on each other's minds. On top of all that, they hated each other. Add to this unholy trinity, the local sheriff, and there was a smorgasbord of testosterone and guns where anything could go wrong. The sun was painting shadows and shapes into real life.

The parade should arrive in full force in two hours. Then the games and finally the food. The kid killers, most likely, would try to rain their destruction around mealtime when everybody was seated, or at least in a concentrated area. The arrival of the threesome would foretell the slaughter. It was at that time that Bogatta's men would move in. Upon this cue, Camera's men and choppers would become visible. The plan was for it to be over before it began. Nobody shot...nobody dead. That was the plan. A plan with so damn many moving parts and twisted egos. For now, they just sat and waited. The sheriff kept everyone off the radio until the last second. All men and machines must hang tough. No small talk. Karen and Gene had been without sleep but were so jacked that pacing was relaxing. They waited. And waited. And waited.

****

"Well, it's a fine mess you got us into. A while ago you called me sweetie. What did you mean by that? Am I your sweetheart?"

"Yes. And more, I hope. But let's save this romantic banter for Florida. We have something important to think about now. I kept one of the Glocks and three magazines. I trust no one except you, me, and the two dogs until this whole thing is over. When the shooting starts, and it will, I want you to stay in the police van where it's safe."

"You chauvinist pig. I can take care of myself. I'm not some shrinking violet, some dainty flower who needs to be protected by the big strong man. I've been through more than you'll ever know. My ex and his playmates were pond scum. I could deal with them. I could protect myself then. Yes, I was scared. But I never sought the safety and security of anyone other than my own wits. I will go where you go. This is as much my fight as it is yours. Mary was my friend and we know her killer. You are my lover. The dogs are my children. I put us in with the FBI, the rotten fucks. Therefore, the damage they cause is my responsibility. Besides what do you think became of the poor guard's Colt forty five. You remember the guard I knocked some sense into."

She lifted her sweater and blouse to reveal the steel blue American made weapon. Resting sensually against her soft tanned stomach. Her naval was stretched from round to cat's eye. The baby hairs on her belly were aroused by the motion of the fabric, the chill in the air, the metal of the gun, the excitement of the moment, or the internal engine of someone who is about to go to war. Gene suspected the last reason. For a moment she was so sexy, he started to get aroused. Not the right time or place. He would just have to hold that thought for Florida. The sweater was pulled down over her belt. She smiled and winked. What could he say to someone who gleefully kicked the shit out of an agent, removed his pants, and stole his weapon?

"OK, then just stay beside me. I'll need protection. We better hide the dogs. Keep them back here. They wouldn't get in the way, but they could get shot. We'll make sure they have bowls and are properly leashed so that they don't follow us as we move into the picnic grounds. Yes, I said we because they are just as much my children as they are yours."

****

Gene and Karen could hear the first part of the parade. The Drum and Bugle Corps of the local fire and police auxiliaries followed by members of the VFW, the American Legion, Am Vets, three high school bands. Lots of patriotic themed floats, including the usual Miss Liberty, The Flag Day Queen and Her Court, the Raising of the Flag on Iwo Jima, The Drummer, Flag Bearer, a Space Rocket, et cetera, et cetera.

The throng, which had viewed the parade in town, was walking alongside the last of the marchers. The parade was now a parade within a parade. The men and women who were to feed the throng had arrived ahead of the human wave.

Trucks were unloaded. Fires for the hotdogs and hamburgers were beginning to smoke. Picnic baskets. No card tables, just blankets. Lots of blankets. Picnic baskets. Long makeshift tables for the pie eating contest. Horseshoe pegs had been pounded into the ground. Sacks laid out for the three-legged race. Six long heavy ropes for the tug of war pulls. All of this was done with military precision. They had been doing this for years. No need to do all the work the night before. Like ants, each with his or her own chore, the tasks were completed, and they fit into the larger entity called the day. Food, non-alcoholic beverages, and a ton of good, old-fashioned fun. From sunup to sundown, then home to collapse. What a perfect small-town event. A picture of Americana to be destroyed by the haters, by the forces everyone hoped were there to protect citizens. But who wanted to control the masses, to oppress them for their own benefit. For power. National and international power. Power was the ultimate aphrodisiac, and the bad guys drank it daily. Today, they were drunk.

Camera started to stir. He went live as the first of the parade unraveled into the grounds. The choppers were called: ETA five minutes. Told to stay over the Welch farm until called. The black van appeared. The FBI began to move. The noose tightened. Sheriff's men, who had infiltrated the crowd, closed in on the trench on the mound beneath the pines. Gene's heart was now pumping. The timing was everything. Camera called Alex to apprehend Bogatta. "Cut their communications, now." The commands were barked like an angry quarterback. He was directing men he couldn't see to people he hoped would be there. Alex answered that Bogey One was secure and the radio was dead. Local Two reported to Local Leader. The black van was in sight. What should they do? Camera ordered to secure the van and its contents. Cut all communication. Then they hear the first pop. About twelve or fifteen shots. The screaming from the crowd blankets the radio communication.

The choppers were called to the LZ. Set down in the middle of the picnic area. The dust, flying blankets, cups, and plates made the landing zone look like the path of a hurricane. The police exited with weapons at the ready. Lumbering, they fanned out. The full body armor made them look a little robotic. They searched for their targets. People began running about in a frenzy of unknowing. The crowd moved in a wave, away from the van and the gunfire and away from the helicopters. The bad guys were left standing alone. Their camouflage of bodies had dissipated. Local Three and Four report that the trench was secure. The four occupants in custody were terribly angry. Local Two reports that the van was secure, but two of the occupants were dead. The third was wounded, did not appear critical.

The sheriff moved his men. Closed the noose completely. Arrested all event staff. Left no one behind, as clean and surgical as possible. The sheriff's van and two cruisers headed to the grounds. Without much explanation, the bad guys were swept up, placed into trucks and taken downtown. The sheriff had notified the State Police and the news media. The only way to get all the answers was to expose all the rats at once. The couple went back to the school to find their guard. Still naked, bound, and gagged, he looked like he was sleeping. Except for the large pool of blood behind his head and the quarter size hole in the middle of his forehead. The reward for failure was death. Bogatta's law. If he knew about the pair's departure, his ego must have tricked him into thinking they were of no consequence. The reward for arrogance is failure. Benton's law.

The local jail was not large enough to hold all the detainees. They'd be squeezed in until they were removed to state facilities. A California version of the Black Hole of Calcutta. The media was swarming like flies around a broken jar of jelly in the hot sun. The press conference was set-up at the parade stand. All the big guys were there: The four major networks, cable, and broadcast. The sheriff was flanked by his deputies and a State Police Colonel. The elated officials were standing on the porch reserved for the parade judges. Red, white, and blue bunting festooned the superstructure. Roses and emblems of eagles were on every corner. All the trappings of a political rally.

****

"Today, we prevented a massacre of innocent people in this community. Today, we stopped the serial killings that started in Carter, Wyoming and went through Menthen, New Hampshire, Lutztown, Pennsylvania and Ox Bow, Maryland. Your sheriff's department single-handedly took a huge bite out of crime. We are not at liberty to give you all the details, as of now. The perpetrators are being questioned. When we have all the facts, all the who, what, when, where, and how, we will issue a report. As we speak, the captured are being moved to the state correctional facility in Lancaster. Now, if you'll all bear with me, I'll answer as many questions as I can.

"There are three groups. First, there are three young men and a young woman who were preparing to fire into the crowd of picnickers. These four were heavily armed but were subdued by squads led by Officers Molina and Whyte. We can't release the names of the four until we have more details as to why they were there and the reason behind their planned action. The next group we secured is comprised of three alleged members of a government agency. We have reason to believe that these three have been sighted at the previously noted school slaughters. We are not sure who they really are or if they do, in fact, work for our government. We believe their names are Brent Forbes, Roger Thompson, and Alan Campbell. Unfortunately, Mister Forbes and Mister Thompson attempted to resist arrest and were subsequently dispatched by our officers. Mister Campbell was wounded and is presently receiving medical care. He will be questioned at length as soon as the doctor says he is strong enough.

"The third group is comprised of alleged FBI agents headed by Senior Agent Bodrim Bogatta. He and his force purportedly came here to stop the shooting by the first group and the supposed subsequent shooting by the three other men. Let me clarify that: We believe that the three men we mentioned previously, Forbes, Thompson, and Campbell had fore-knowledge that the four youths were going to commit the heinous butchery. How they got the knowledge, we are not sure. We further believe that the three men just mentioned were going to kill the youths after the youths had killed the picnickers. This is consistent with the pattern established in the four previous shootings. We don't know why they wanted to kill the killers, but we feel confident that was their plan.

"The FBI agents were here to kill the killers of the killers. How they knew the agents knew to be here is yet to be determined. There are some very strange and evil connections among all three groups. Once we ascertain that connection, we will know how far up the quasi-governmental ladder this entire mess goes. For now, we are confident that the cycle of death and destruction has been broken. We have taken a giant step to make this country safe and secure. Please forgive me, but we must get about the business of getting more information."

The reporters clamored for more information. They thrusted cameras and microphones into faces of the sheriff and his deputy. Politely rebuffed, the crowd of newshounds did not dissipate. They made their assumptions and final pronouncements to the millions of people on the other sides of the lenses.

****

Gene and Karen exited stage left with dogs by their sides. Headed for the sheriff's van and Motel Six where they stashed the dogs and their guns. Immediately they were driven to the California State Prison at Lancaster for debriefing. Their day was far from over. The prison was an imposing sight: Four stories of gray walls ringed with razor wire and highlighted by gun turrets every one hundred feet along the second outside wall. The huge front doors swung open to permit the van and its precious cargo to enter the inner sanctum. A short drive to the inner wall and another door. This one slid open. The yard appeared vast now that it was empty. The recently acquired bad guys were being housed in one wing. Triple security. The former residents of this particular wing, the physically impaired, had been dispersed, for the time being, to facilities in three counties. For now, Wing D was the wing of activity. All other wings were in lockdown and would stay that way until the temporary residents left.

They were escorted to a very sterile, brightly lit room. This was where they would be questioned. Those in attendance included the sheriff, someone from the state police, and two very important people, one man and one woman from the FBI. They had the right badges and credentials. Gene had a low level of concern that these new faces might be part of a coverup for Bogatta. They assured the couple that their only objective was to get to the bottom of all this. They were upset at the behavior of the rogue Bogatta. They had orders from the very top to rid the agency of this cancer. The questioning was excruciatingly thorough: Dates, times, activities, places, people, thoughts, suspicions. Karen and Gene were questioned at separate times to ensure their stories matched. Even the second time, with questions derived from the answers to the previous questions. They told the inquisitors that Bogatta was responsible for Mary's death. They are satisfied that the two have given enough to move forward with the questioning of Bogatta and his people.

****

The evening news carried the story with great regalia. No action shots. Only the news conference. Lots of interviews with those who were at the picnic. No one found the Welch's. Their anonymity was safe. Overshadowing this story was the success of the Peace Alliance. Whose decision was it to put the nation's success on foreign soil in front of or above domestic dirty laundry? Who wanted this story as quiet as could be without outright censorship?

Between the carpet-bombing, the long-range missiles, and the artillery barrages, the forces of el Jahdiq did not stand a chance. The rain of death endured for thirty hours straight. There was no meal break. Enemy missile batteries disappeared into the sand to be stalked by a return of the drones. Tanks, planes, and long-range artillery were in gnarled heaps. The men inside the bunkers were buried alive or burned to cinders. The commanders of the sea and air raiders were jubilant. The smiles and the tenor of their voices a dead giveaway. The boys from the 'hood beat up the bully from across the sea.

The briefing by the Commander in Chief, General Fraser Warren, was nothing short of a party. His normal conservative countenance had given way to the heady glee of one who had led the crushing of an enemy. The high-tech warrior did not talk of quarter or peace. This would be a discussion for the diplomats. The goal of the Mastiff of the West was to rip the throat from the Beast of the East. That was the reason he was in the desert. The troops under his command had executed his plan with surgical precision. Over three hundred missiles had been fired from carriers and land-based batteries. The combined air force had flown over two hundred high and low-level bombing sorties. The armies had successfully utilized new long-range artillery technology. With this, the batteries were able to pinpoint targets over fifty miles away. Pinpoint meant to hit the ground within twenty feet of the X. The payloads of this artillery varied. Some exploded upon impact. Some burrowed up to one hundred feet before they exploded. The army had the capability to blow away the surface protection then deliver these moles. The result was a crater hundreds of feet deep and over a half mile wide.

The enemy had lost most of its communications network. The elite fighting battalions were in flight. Their tank capacity had been reduced to less than thirty percent. There was little, if any, artillery. No enemy planes in the sky. The invaders avoided large population centers, despite the fact that el Jahdiq used his population as a shield for his military forces. Yes, some civilians had been killed. This was an unfortunate aspect of the war el Jahdiq started. The armies of the contributing countries performed with excellence. A true international team. Coordination and cooperation were the keywords. He couldn't reveal when the invasion would move to the next phase, that being the intervention of ground troops. The British and Jordanian Colonels handled the film clips.

****

Sleep was absolutely necessary. Gene's eyes were wide open. He couldn't sleep. There were too many unanswered questions. He wanted to go back to Lancaster at the Wing D of the State Prison and question the interrogators. He wanted answers. The people wanted answers. Karen collapsed upon entry to their room. He arose and walked the dogs. The guard went with him, a likable young man. Wanted to make a career of the service. He couldn't understand why Bogatta and his people would do what they had been accused of. Wanted to know all about Alan Campbell, so did Gene. The dogs and the walker headed for the room. They curled up on Karen's side, but not on the bed. They loved her, him they tolerated. He couldn't fault their attitude. She's beautiful, kind, intelligent and trustworthy...a fucking Girl Scout. He suffered episodic depression, was not handsome, and didn't care for strangers. He was the dirty guy that the den mother warned the Girl Scouts about. Dawn arrived in about six seconds. Got coffee for the three of them. The new guard was a young woman, not unattractive. Her body properly disguised by the government issued hardware and vest. The dogs got a walk. Karen was nuzzled awake and offered the legal drug. They showered separately. Gene shaved for the first time in three days. Deodorant was a refreshing addition. Dressed in clean clothes, they headed back to Lancaster.

The debriefing was brief. Gene get the distinct feeling they were told about one tenth of what the others knew. Bogatta was operating outside of his jurisdiction. He had no authority to lead his people into this environment. Acting without supervision was a bad thing. Campbell was not an independent contractor. He and the other two were operatives within the National Security Agency. Why the NSA was involved in this was unclear. Their jurisdiction was international, not domestic. The FBI agents and Campbell were being shipped to Camp Chaffee in Arkansas. Very safe and secure. They would be questioned further by other members of the agency, the interrogation experts. Everyone was satisfied they had accomplished their objectives. Gene was not.

"Wait a minute. These guys had planned to be killers of killers of killers of killers, ad infinitum. Surely, you can give us more information than

that slim gibberish. I know you know
more than you are telling us. What is
the connection between the two
forces? Which one is the killer of
killers and which one is the killer of
the killers' killers? This all sounds like
an R.D. Lang poem."

"There is much we don't know
yet. What I've just told you is
confirmation that we are on the right
track and that we must continue
moving on this track to get resolution.
There are too many loose ends, which
need to be tied before we can go
public. And you are the public. We ask
that you relax and let us do our job."

"Hell, that's how Karen and I got
here in the first place. We were letting
Bogatta do his job. We simply didn't
know what his job was or how we were
not going to fit into his plans.
Therefore, we want more facts before
we go home. Like whom are
BrokenArrow and TruthSeeker. You
owe us that."

"This we can tell you. All that
you saw is not what you think you
saw."

"More bullshit. Who are the real
bad guys behind the real curtains?
The second these guys are stashed
away at Camp Chaffee, the tighter the
lid will be screwed down on the entire

operation. So, tell me now. Talk to me, or there will be consequences." He had to be careful to not lean too hard on the threat. They are not sure what he'll do. Will he go public? Will he just skulk into the shadows?

"As soon as we know more and confirm its validity, we will tell you. We hope this will be very soon. The true identities of all the people involved in this plan will be ferreted out. People, from those in the chatrooms to the agents and the killers at the schools. We know there are many connections and perhaps one main thread. But right now, we are not sure. We, your country, ask that you be patient and quiet for a little while longer. You are safe. That's all I can say. So, let us take you back to the motel. Then you and the dogs can return to Florida. Thank you, Mister Benton and Miss Leach. Your service to your country will not go unnoticed or unrewarded once we have all the facts and the bad guys are in custody."

With that, the couple was dismissed like small children from the dinner table when adults wanted to have adult conversations. As they packed at the motel. Karen held up a mini-cassette recorder and winked.

XV

Home again, home again, jiggity jog. The air in the house smelled and felt like Gene imagined the air in a crypt. Stale. Damp. Dank. Even if he had set the thermostat at eighty, the air would smell the same after four or five days. Fortunately, they could open the windows and doors, turn on the ceiling fans and crank up the AC. So, they unpacked in the stale air after making sure the dogs had bowls of food and water. Dirty clothes from their brief other life were dumped in the hamper. Toilette articles returned to the bathroom. Candle wax still on the counter. A fond memory rekindled. Bags were dumped in the back of the closet. The mail and newspaper accumulation hadn't been too severe. Now he wanted a real break. Into the pool with his children. They frolicked, splashed, and cooled off. Afterward, with a long list from Karen, he shopped for larder replenishment. For dinner, chicken breasts in a mustard, wine, and tarragon baste, wild rice and sliced tomatoes, and an exceptionally good bottle of Chardonnay. Dinner was on the lanai, lit by pool lights and a few large candles. Karen's idea. Was she hinting at something? A cigar and a stiff Balvenie completed the evening.

"I am uneasy, Gene. We have to do everything we can to protect our asses, and I feel we haven't done that yet. I want to make a few copies of the tapes I acquired in California, then we should take a set to an attorney and make a sworn statement with other details. Charge him with holding the evidence, which would be released if anything untoward happens to us. I know a guy. He was a judge. He is so honest, he is revered. And he is feisty. He'd love to get involved. I'll call him tomorrow."

"What I can't get away from is the relationship between Campbell, et. al. and Bogatta? Who was the puppet and who was the puppeteer? There must be a link. Is it at the hip? Or above them both? The lawyer idea is good. Maybe we should go public. Should we include Sheriff Camera in our outing? I don't know. But I do know that I can't solve this issue tonight. I'll take care of clean up."

"I'm exhausted. I'm going to bed, so you can tend to your kitchen chores without being bothered."

While he scraped, loaded, washed, rinsed, and stacked, he

turned on the ten o'clock news. A familiar voice to keep him company:

"Today on Capitol Hill, the Senate initiated an investigation into the allegations concerning Senator Baldwin Miller of Pennsylvania, his S.A.F.E. campaign, and the recent school shootings. This investigation was hurriedly called based upon evidence provided by the FBI. This evidence dealt with the agency's investigation of the aborted shooting at Coastal Mesa, California. An unidentified source indicated to us that there may be evidence to prove that the Senator knew of the shootings before they occurred. There is even speculation that the shootings were choreographed to be precursors of Senator Miller's S.A.F.E. rallies. The Senator's aides deny all the allegations and innuendoes, stating that this is a smear campaign initiated and driven by President Sessler and his party. The campaign to discredit the Senator is preposterous and is the act of an obviously desperate politician. The battle lines have been drawn. The ad hoc committee hearing starts tomorrow. We will be live from the Senate chambers all day. This is Wendy Mynard reporting for CNN.

"On the international front, the armies of the Peace Alliance continue to hammer the beleaguered jihadists. At a briefing earlier today, the Allied Command issued the statement that, and we quote, 'The enemy appears to be without resolve, troops are scattering, communications are nonexistent, missile and artillery batteries are nonfunctional. Our ground troops and tanks may go into Basjar only as a mop up force after the surrender and peace terms have been reached.' Obviously, the Allied Commanders are pleased with the progress of the campaign."

Due to a near blackout of news coverage, the Western world heard what the Allied Commander wanted them to hear. The Eastern world saw and heard only what the jihadists wanted them to hear: the civilian suffering, the resolve of the jihadists to fight until death, and how little damage the invasion has done to the military machine. There had to be some truth in the symbiotic mixture.

Did Sessler use the war to divert attention from his domestic problems? His inability to run again excludes that. The party's obvious lack of a viable candidate was a handicap. How the hell did he get the other countries to go along with his domestic policy? If this was true, the attack on the three embassies was very convenient. Too convenient. Could these have been staged by Sessler? Did Sessler have balls big enough to sacrifice the lives of hundreds of men and women in the Foreign Service for his own historical grandeur? Did Roosevelt sacrifice the troops and ships at Pearl Harbor to justify the Pacific Theater of World War Two? How many young men and women had been sacrificed, by how many governments, for the sake of national pride and expansion? This was too deep and emotionally destructive for tonight.

Karen was in a deep sleep when he finally slipped quietly into the master bedroom. The dogs were beside the bed next to her. Now, all was well with his world.

****

Before dawn, the morning liquid fix was ingested. Dawn brought the end of tranquility. He took a cup of joe to his lover and bedmate. The dogs were free to roam and relieve. Karen showered and they had breakfast together. Her preoccupation could be interpreted as aloofness, but her smile and tender touching of his arm ruled out that possibility. They were due at the lawyer's office at eleven to make statements. She had to dupe the tapes for the lawyer's files. He called the office. No one knew where he had been. Gene told his administrative assistant that he would be in the day after tomorrow, rested and ready to kick ass. To coin James Brown, he felt good. He was back at it. The morning paper repeated the news heard last night. A small item on page eight in National News: The Coastal Mesa town council had decided to cancel next year's Flag Day parade and picnic.

The trip to the lawyer was uneventful. On the return home, Gene got the feeling they were being observed. A sedan, noticeable on the way downtown, was again behind them as they turned off the interstate. Coincidence? Not likely. He told Karen and she attempted to identify the driver and passenger via the vanity mirror on her sun visor. Nope. Who sent the eyes? Agency, service, or some other group, which had a burning interest in their activities.

Gene and Karen chose not to hunker in the bunker. They would take steps to keep everything in the open. They didn't care about loose ends. They didn't have to follow protocol. They had to protect their own interests, and these interests were based on living. Time to go to the chatrooms. Tell all to anyone who would read. The risk of retaliation was real, but there was a big upside with the spread of knowledge...protection by the masses. They told everyone about BrokenArrow and TruthSeeker. Told the chatters about the system of clues. Told them about Bogatta and Campbell. About Mary. Told them all and let the chips fall. The rush of danger brought him to life. He was daring death. The Light Brigade dared death with an incredibly stupid move. Look what happened to them. Was he repeating the stupidity? What would happen to him? To them? Neither wanted to die. He feared its inactivity. So, if he could roll over and kick once in a while, he could deal with death. He was concerned about Karen. A clear sign of caring. Love. Just a basic need-based emotion. Going public was something they must do. The best defense is a great offense.

She wrote the manifesto. Together, they reviewed it. Complete. She then downloaded it into as many chatrooms as she could find. Even the ones for the news networks. The die was cast.

****

The Senate hearings hit the ground running. When they wanted to move with great dispatch, they could. Questions were designed to ensnare liars, not to elicit facts. Like when your father questioned you about the dent in the car, he already knew the facts. He just wanted you to admit the truth. All else in Washington and the rest of the country seemed to be on hold as if freeze-framed. Two volumes of information had been provided the Senators. The word processors and copiers throughout the Washington metro area must have been exclusively devoted to this desktop publishing. It was time for the committee to ask questions about the reports. The accused government agents were the first to testify. Public gallows were built in this fashion. After Sheriff Camera, Bogatta, and Campbell, the committee promised that Senator Miller would testify tomorrow.

Sessler did not gloat...publicly. Vice President Harrison issued a statement that the administration's first priority was to supervise the successful completion of the war in the Middle East and the subsequent peace agreement. His hopes were that no additional ground troops would be necessary. The administration would not interfere with the duly appointed Senate Committee. Harrison pledged the administration's full support of the committee and its endeavors. He wished swift and clean closure to this domestic blight. Behind closed doors, he must have been giggling like a fifth grader at the paddling of a classmate.

Camera confirmed all the details in the report. Added little. Kept Karen and Gene's names out of the events. Step-by-step, the prosecutor, judge, and jury hydra-nailed another plank to the platform. The prima facie case was now part of the public domain. Lunch. Reconvened at two. Gene was now bored. What to do for two hours? Swim so that he could indulge in eating too much fat.

Karen joined Gene for laps. As they exited the pool, she wrapped her towel around them both in an embrace. Their kisses lingered. Stimulated. Revitalized. A promise of the evening. Got the mail while she prepared two small steaks, green beans, and pasta. An athlete's meal. Dinner for lunch. So, the evening meal would be light. They and the committee reconvened in the den. Bogatta first.

He testified that he had been ordered to feed clues and information to young dissidents via the chatrooms. He could direct them to do his bidding. Lead the angry youth, the youth committed the heinous crimes. Since Bogatta knew where the crimes were to be committed, he could send agents to help with the mop up. No, he and his men were not ordered to kill the killers. No, he and his men did not kill the killers. They were there to assist in the mop up only. No, he would not divulge the name of the individual who gave him the orders. Yes, he realized he would be held in contempt. Yes, he realized he would go to jail. He explained how he got his orders. Unmarked email. His payment for service. Electronic deposits. How he recruited his agents. Yes, he had violated the code of the agency. He never killed anyone but criminals. He and his men were too far away to stop the events. Bogatta was removed from the room by officers, who would take him back to his cell.

Jesus H. Christ, this sounded like the testimony of the Japanese and Nazi war criminals. The absence of guilt, culpability, and responsibility enjoyed by this type of mind is incomprehensible to mere humans. The thugs were just following orders. But, whose?

Campbell was helped to the witness table. He related that he, Forbes, and Thompson were private contractors. They had been in the employ of the federal government. He received orders from one of Sessler's supporters in the Department of Defense.

"We broke the code used by Bogatta's group before the incident at Carter. The government has been monitoring the chatrooms for years. We followed the path each time. Our job was to observe, but not to interfere with the events or the subsequent cleanup. We had hoped to learn how all this started, who did the killing and who was killing the killers. We were placed at the service of Senator Baldwin Miller. We were positioned as federal agents. We were part of the security team at his rallies. We were there to keep an eye on him. I figured out quickly that we were working for Senator Miller and going to the shootings because somebody thought there was a connection to him. I assumed that the administration thought there was connection, and that Miller was setting up the killings to promote S.A.F.E. Getting elected must have been especially important to him. Politics is a crappy business. Too many hidden agendas.

"We were never able to prove Senator Miller's connection. We were never able to stop the shootings. That was not our job. We did not know what to do except what we were told. What we did know was what we saw. And, we saw the bogeys, Bogatta and his men, step in before the local and state authorities could arrive and kill the shooters. They did this at every shooting, except Coastal Mesa. We were there to stop them. Capture them and turn them over to the locals. But the locals beat us to the arrest. All hell broke loose. Two good men died, but that's the risk soldiers run. Before the Coastal Mesa event, Bogatta and his men killed a freelance photographer, Mike Duncan. He was trying to dig up information on our operation. Bogatta's men were moles for Duncan. He was getting too close to us. Too close to the whole truth. He would learn that we were not dirty. He would learn that Bogatta was dirty. So, Duncan had to disappear. Hell, we could have disappeared in the firefight at Coastal Mesa. Bogatta had a ton of firepower. They just got out-smarted by the locals."

The arrogance in his voice was unmistakable. The captured lion feels contempt for the lucky hunter. He was returned to a hospital jailcell. The stage set for Senator Miller.

Vice President Harrison issued a statement that the administration had no knowledge of the illegal activities of the aforementioned member of the Department of Defense. The White House abhorred any use of power without responsibility. That was abuse. The manipulation of the truth. It seemed right for the administration to conduct a thorough investigation of the various Cabinet Departments, from top to bottom. This would require independent counsel and, to be done properly and thoroughly, would take about one year. But, for the American people and the honor of the federal government, this investigation had to commence immediately. Let no stone remain unturned. President Sessler had flown to the Middle East to meet with the Military Commanders and the political leaders of the Alliance. He was attempting to bring about an end to the retaliation, expedite the peace process, and initiate rebuilding of the region.

****

The day was over. Gene turned the to the Wall-2-Wall Movie channel and ordered a chick flick for Karen. She had endured one of his 'nothing but news' days. His display of male appreciation was appreciated. He even prepared the cheese, crackers, and fruit. Uncorked another bottle of wine. Gawd, he's good.

Six tissues later the wife died, and the husband faced the future with two small, adorable children. Catharsis. Switched to CNN.

"This late breaking news from Washington: Senator Baldwin Miller has apparently taken his life. The facts are sketchy. We go to Wendy Mynard."

In hushed very somber tones.

"This evening, at approximately eight thirty, the body of Senator Baldwin Miller was found in his automobile, which was parked with motor running near the Lincoln Memorial. Apparently, Senator Miller had committed suicide by means of a single large caliber bullet. We have been told he placed the gun barrel in his mouth. The explosion and impact removed the back of Senator Miller's head and shattered the rear window of the sedan. As of now, there are no other details. Speculation is that Senator Miller took his own life rather than face the Senate Committee, which was investigating his involvement in the recent rash of school shootings. Police have cordoned off the area and are combing it for clues. Neither Senator Miller's family nor his office is available for comment or elaboration. We anticipate a statement from his office shortly. This is Wendy Mynard, CNN, from Washington."

Gene's stomach churned. Miller just admitted his guilt and took the cowardly way out. The young thug's credo... 'If you can't do the time, don't do the crime.' There was a sense of relief on Karen's face. Her muscles relaxed, and tears returned to her eyes. Lachrymose relief.

"He was the culprit behind it all. He led the wolves to the sheep and then shot the wolves after they had done his bidding. He was evil. His family will suffer the stigma for about three generations. Maybe they'll change their names and move to a distant planet. Yes, I am angry that he won't stand before the people, admit his crimes and take the appropriate punishment. Yes, I'm relieved this is all over. I want a drink."

Gene poured two big boy belts. She took hers. They toasted. Breathed a huge sigh of relief and went to bed.

****

Her profile was illuminated by the full moon. Exquisite. Gene moved to kiss her, and she moved to kiss him. Tenderness gave way to passion. Kisses on her neck and shoulders. Kisses on his throat. A sudden shove rolled him over onto his back. Her legs straddled his hips. She commenced a gradual grind. Arousal. She was not yet ready. He pulled her nightgown off her shoulders. Her breasts felt soft yet firm. She lowered her torso and dragged her nipples across his lips. She liked to be nipped. He obliged. Reaching behind her and removing her panties. Off the hips, down to the knees. Right leg out, then left. Synthetic fabric discarded into the corner. Passion was now rampaging. Mouth to mouth resembles resuscitation rather than kissing. She rose to insert him. The telephone rang. Gene was sliding in. Three more rings.

He withdrew. Fifth ring. She was upset.

"Hello."

"Is this Mister Eugene Benton?"

"Yes, it is."

"Mister Benton, this is Special Agent Weaver of the FBI. We met in Lancaster, California."

"Yes, I remember the voice. Could you give me your badge number for purposes of verification?"

"11347963-W."

Gene confirmed this by checking the card Special Agent Weaver gave him in California.

"Special Agent Weaver, how may I help you?"

"Mister Benton, I am sorry to bother you this late at night. But I thought you should know that Agent Bogatta escaped from his detention cell and is reported missing as of seven thirty this evening."

"Do you think he would come to Florida?"

"Sir, we know that Agent Bogatta is desperate. We believe he knows how Senator Miller died. In fact, we have reason to believe that he shot the Senator. We feel confident he will attempt to flee the country. We have a tight surveillance on exit points. But he could come to Florida as a way out of the country into the Caribbean. Therefore, we have taken the precaution to place you and Miss Leach under observation. We presently have men watching your house. We are fairly certain that he will not bother you. Were I he, I'd run to a foreign country far away. One with no extradition treaty with the US. But Agent Bogatta is not thinking clearly. We believe he is deranged. We just want you to know the status of the situation and that you are being protected. Sir, do you have any questions?"

"Will you call again in the morning and give me an update? Miss Leach and I may want to go to the mountains for a few days if he is not apprehended immediately."

"Yes, sir, I'll call you at seven am. Thank you for your cooperation. Have a good night."

Gene told Karen. They were both uneasy, but not frightened. It must have been Agent Weaver's men who followed them.

"Now, where were we?"

"You were on top. I was in the process of getting remarkably close. I think it started this way." He leaned forward, and the kissing started anew. This time his tongue followed the contour of her body from ear to ribcage. His kissing continued. Her breathing was more like four-four time than a waltz. Her hands found his head and guided it to her zone. This joyous interaction reached a crescendo. Release after the relief. Sleep followed rapidly thereafter.

****

Gene was awakened by incredibly primeval growls. A deep, barely audible rumble of impending disaster. Centuries ago, wolves slept around the camp of the hunters and gatherers and growled as a warning of the intrusion of a Saber Tooth Tiger or a Mastodon. They warned man then, and Hither and Yon instinctively did the same. They couldn't see the danger, but they knew it was there. They didn't move. No reason to let the intruder know the whereabouts of the defenders this soon in the conflict. The sentries were letting the pack of two humans know. The alpha males.

Gene slid from the bed and slithered on his stomach across the floor to the walk-in closet. Found the Glock and a magazine. Inserted and made the piece ready to fire. Where the hell were his shorts? Why was being clothed important now? Crawled very cautiously down the hall to the great room, den, and kitchen. During the day, this distance was covered in about four seconds. Tonight, given the circumstances, travel time was well over a minute. Each move measured for life and death. The sliding door was open. The dogs were free to run, but they stayed beside him. Then a deeper growl. The singular ominous growl that rolled from their throats as it did from time before man's arrival.

It had reverberated from the Black Forest primeval and the caves in the Balkans. This rumble alerted the pack and warned whelps. The dogs would not move, just growl. It was like sonar. It became louder as the sentinels homed in on the threat. They were stock-still. They would not move until they were thoroughly convinced that they could spring and kill the intruder. They were staring into the backyard. Eyes and snouts focused on the pool. While they were stationary, Gene slid along the wall to the doorway. What did this red light mean? It's on his head. Rolled to the right, away from the light. He never heard the report or saw the flash. But he felt the pain and the searing heat.

The impact on the left side of his chest was beyond his wildest experience. He slumped on the floor, about three feet from the door opening. Stunned and gasping for breath. Not sure if the bullet hit or the fall to the floor hurt more. The pain coursed throughout his entire body. It's like a huge weight had been dumped on him and was pressing him through the floor. The protectors responded to the gunfire by charging through the open door. They had committed to an offensive defense. Their growls became barking snarls. Incredible ferocity. Ears pinned back, neck hair bristled in a natural defense, and all their teeth visible. An eight legged, lightening quick, very pissed bodyguard rushed toward the pool.

The pool lights popped on, having been triggered by the ferocious mass as it exited the house. There was a dark figure in the blue green, very bright liquid environment. The figure appeared frozen upon being lit up. Both arms were raised and joined at the gun in front of the face. The red light ran across Gene's eyes and held above Gene's head as he tried to get beneath the floor. The blasts from behind the prone target were loud and rapid. Three. Four. Five. Six. The Loch

Benton monster spasmed. Arms went everywhere. Body jerked back and under. The gun plopped in the pool. The monster's head looked like a platter of spaghetti and meatballs. Momentary silence.

The dogs leapt in the pool and attacked the bobbing torso. Fulminating in *basso profundo*, they ripped the clothing to get to the flesh. Parts of what remained after the gun's fusillade were beginning to rise to the top of the red brown water. The intruder was a roiling stew of bone fragments, flesh, and fabric. Blood and chlorinated water were the medium. A canine Waring Blender rendered the intruder unrecognizable.

"Can you move? Are you OK? Does it hurt?"

"Yes. Yes. And, what the fuck do you think. Let's go outside and see what damage the boys did."

Karen pulled Gene up and helped him to walk. He was dizzy to the point of collapse. But he must be the big brave man. Macho bullshit.

"Hither. Yon. It's okay, boys. Hither. Yon. Settle down. It's over. Hither Yon. Come here now."

She whistled loudly. Gene never knew she could whistle like a New

Yorker hailing a cab. He guessed there's a lot he would have to learn.

Karen's whistle got their attention and her calls calmed their instincts. Women had that power over boys at play or men fighting, regardless of age or species. As her boys rose from the pool, bits and pieces of their quarry are visible in their muzzles and mouths. They shook dry and the pieces flew away with the water. They paced between the pool and the couple. One more measure of protection.

It's their old buddy. Even though most of his face and one shoulder were shredded, the intruder is none other than the recent escapee, Bodrim Bogatta. Now just a blob in the water. The main and last ingredient in the stew: A heaping dose of galactic justice.

"Stay right where you are. Nobody move."

"Gentlemen, we're safe. Everything is under control. Karen, catch me. Hurry."

All was black before he hit the ground. He felt nothing.

The light in the room was brighter than he liked. The doctor was peering into Gene's eyes. Fuzzy look to everything in the room. A warm hand, *familiar*, took Gene's.

"Mister Benton, you'll be fine. A few stitches, isolation of the arm, and bedrest. Miss Leach has decided to take you home as soon as the forms are completed and signed. We agree it would be in your best interest."

"Gene, I have Agent Weaver of the FBI on the phone."

"Mister Benton. It seems your country owes you and Miss Leach another vote of gratitude. I understand Miss Leach took care of business before our men could intervene. Hope you mend quickly."

Home again, home again, jiggity-jog. The dogs were happy. They never got tired of protecting, their expression of love. Karen had moved the TV into the bedroom, so he could watch news all day every day. The news, the History Channel, and two nature channels. Knowledge is good: it makes him feel alive.

"Your office called and wanted to know if they should reschedule the meetings. They wanted to know when you would be back to work. I told them in two weeks or never, whichever you decided. They understand. Call them when you get a chance."

"We interrupt our regularly scheduled programming to bring you this bulletin."

"Ladies and gentlemen the Vice President of the United States."

"We are sad to announce that President Paul Sessler' plane, Air Force One, has crashed in the Atlantic Ocean. At this time, there is no word on the cause of the accident. We do know there are no survivors. President Sessler had just completed a successful Peace Mission to the Middle East. We stand united in grief and extend our condolences to President Sessler's family. Personally, I have lost a good friend, the country has lost an unparalleled leader, and the world has lost a peace-loving statesman. As we learn more, we will advise the nation."

How strangely serendipitous. Gene peers over the pool. The gate has been left open. Damned pool boy.